3 WOMEN WALK INTO A BAR

ALSO BY LINDA SANDS

Simple Intent
Not Waving, Drowning

LINDA SANDS

3 WOMEN WALK INTO A BAR

First Print Edition: July 2015

Down & Out Books
3959 Van Dyke Rd, Ste. 265
Lutz, FL 33558
www.DownAndOutBooks.com

Cover design by Aaron Wood

ISBN: 1937495973
ISBN-13: 978-1-937495-97-8

For those who will never be
satisfied living just one life.

JULIE ANDREWS SAID TO START AT THE VERY BEGINNING, BUT DO YOU?

Chapter 1

The smell that drifted out the propped-open door to Flannigan's was sweet coppery blood with an undertone of fish and chips.

On the sidewalk, a pigeon pecked at a lipstick-stained cigarette butt. A gust of warm wind ruffled his feathers, sent paper trash skittering into the gutter. He cocked his head as black rubber-soled shoes passed by, pushing a gurney.

At the entrance to the bar, cops milled about in various stages of procrastination. Some were putting off returning to the station out of dread of the paperwork that lay ahead, another thought that although there was no investigation to speak of, he'd rather be standing around an empty bar than go home to a wife who was still pissed about that thing last week. The two rookies leaning against the brick front, drinking coffee and sharing photos on their cell phones, knew there was no hurry. They'd be the last to leave—after the detectives and investigators, after the reporters, the extra cops, the coroner and the guys rolling out the corpses, after the technicians and the photographers. They were the tail end of a grisly parade on this Monday morning.

Inside, a well-dressed detective removed his latex gloves, tucked them into his pocket, and nodded at the crew to indicate they should continue collecting evidence.

It seemed like an open-and-shut case. No sign of struggle, three dead girls shot at close range. The murder weapon, a .45 caliber Glock looking more like plastic kid toy than real, on the floor near the killer. A man who'd taken the easy way out, offing himself with a shot to the head after the murders. The front door was locked from the inside, and a quick glance showed three surveillance cameras that would probably provide the rest of the answers. Murder. Suicide. Open-and-shut. It wasn't a bad way to start a morning—for the detective, anyway.

A shadow passed over the bodies as a broad-shouldered man in a ball cap stepped through the door. He pointed to the camera hanging from his neck, flashed a lanyard holding credentials to the rookies.

"Hey Sam," the detective said without turning around. "Took you long enough."

"I was going to stop for donuts too, but . . . you know," Sam said, adjusting the flash on the camera.

"Yeah. I know."

Sam approached the four bodies, careful to stay out of the way of the forensics team. He raised his camera and fired off a burst of flashes, finishing with a chopped-beef looking shot—the close-up of the killer's face.

"Looks like someone got seriously overserved," he said, focusing on the three girls. They'd fallen side by side and were still holding hands. If it hadn't been for the blood or broken glass or splintered wood, they might be sunbathing, napping at the shore, waiting for low tide.

The detective made a grunting sound.

Sam clicked away as happily as if he were the lead photographer at a wedding. "Pretty," he said.

"What's that?" the detective asked.

"I said, they're pretty. All three of them. Unusual, don't you think?"

Sam stepped back and reviewed the digital pictures on his camera's screen.

The detective peered over his shoulder. "Yeah, unusual. Like their names."

"How's that?"

The detective pointed at the display on the camera. "That one is Roxanne Dupont."

"Was . . ." Sam said.

"Right. And that one." the detective said, pointing to the palest girl. "Crescent Moon."

Sam chuckled then clicked the display again.

The detective leaned in. "The last one is Chamonix Leonard. She tried to cross the Leonard off her driver's license though. Must have preferred just Chamonix."

"Like Cher?" Sam said.

"Or Madonna."

"And the shooter?" Sam asked, tipping his chin to the faceless dead man.

"No ID. I'm betting on the owner, currently MIA. Guy named James John Smith."

"Is that right?" Sam turned off the camera and tucked it back into his jacket. "I went to school with a J. J. Smith."

"I think everybody knows a James or John Smith, don't we?"

"You mean like we all have an Aunt Rose?"

The detective laughed as he walked Sam to the door. He said, "That last photo, of the three of them? You can have it. We'll need the rest."

"Just one? That's all you're giving me to run?"

"That's all for now."

Sam looked over his shoulder into the dim bar. Black body bags were being unfolded. "Reminds me of a joke," he said. "Three women walk into a bar. A blonde, a brunette, and a redhead . . ."

TEDESCO. I'M THE PI.

Chapter 2

When the real estate agent showed me the Mercer Building last year, I thought no one in their right mind would want to rent space there. The brick exterior had been painted with a Pepto-Bismol wash, the halls smelled like cat piss, and all of the interior doors hung askew—as if a giant had lifted the building, shook it, then placed it down on a hillock. But when she told me the price, I surprised us both by saying, "I'll take it."

Six months later, the place had been transformed under the careful eye of my HGTV-watching, wannabe-designer wife, Michelle, and an artist client, Jean Claude.

They sandblasted the exterior to reveal a maroon-and-cream brick facade accented with decorative inlays. According to Michelle, the black iron railings and window grates added a certain *je ne sais quoi* to the whole place. While I felt the interior paint choices of "Seafoam Surprise" and "Linens on Holiday" were a bit too froufrou, Jean Claude assured me it was perfect and would provide an air of calm and serenity for my clients.

I told him as long as it didn't cost more than three hundred bucks—the exact amount he owed me for following his boy toy home one night and taking the photos that broke up their relationship—I didn't care about the color of my walls. And if the color palette produced a soothing ambience that meant an irate client might feel a little less compelled to jump across the desk and strangle me . . . well, I was all for it.

I put "Bill Tedesco, PI" on the door and the mailbox, added some furniture, some cheap art. The office really wasn't half-bad, which was good because it had also become home since Michelle had recently found out an old grudge wasn't the only thing I'd been holding against my secretary, Lindsay.

I understood Michelle's anger but still thought there was a chance she'd take me back. In the meantime I made do with the living arrangements: showering in a two-by-two mildewed shower, shitting in a community bathroom, and waking up in pain every morning on a mattress that might have come from the set of *The Princess and the Pea.*

If you had asked me, I would have admitted that I missed my wife. I also missed conjugal sex, Turkish linens, and the NASA-approved king-size memory foam mattress we had shipped in from Ottawa. But there was a decent parking spot in back for the Lincoln and I hadn't nailed the landlady yet—meaning she still liked me, or at least the idea of me—a handsome, fortysomething, former exotic dancer and karaoke star also known as "Free Willy."

I tried to not think about my size-zero wife as I downed the third pastry of the morning and finished my extra-large coffee. Michelle had never been one for breakfast—or any meal for that matter—something about food taking too much energy to chew.

The ding on my phone reminded me of the morning's appointment, a new client.

According to the note Lindsay had left before she quit, the new client had been reluctant to leave her full name. She'd said that she'd found me through a friend of a friend and that the issue was urgent. Apparently urgent enough to earn three exclamation marks.

From my experience, I knew women could be vague like that. Not willing to give up anything more than they had to but usually asking for a hell of a lot in return.

But this was different. This was business. Though, I may have read something between the lines that touched me. I'm not ashamed to say I have a soft spot—or two.

I dropped some bills near my plate and left the coffee shop, cutting through the back alley and making it up to the second floor in plenty of time to shove a week's worth of newspapers off the couch, restack the folders on my desk, and reach into the bottom drawer for a blue bottle.

As I swished a slug of mouthwash for that minty fresh feeling, I thought about how Lindsay had left me high and dry on three counts. First she had given up her luxury condo to which I had a key, next she had stolen the power of the grudge match by saying "You win," and last, by taking that talent-management job she'd always wanted with a Caribbean cruise line.

She had some advice for me before she left. "You know, Tedesco," she said, "Women get married so they don't have to play games anymore. They like having the same predictable sex with the same predictable man in the same predictable bed twice a week. They want to cash the paycheck, pick up the kids from daycare, and pay the sitter on Saturdays. They don't want marriage to be like dating. They don't want to wonder, guess, or pretend. There's nothing that a wife hates more than a lying husband. I heard it on Dr. Phil."

I spit into my trash can. Lindsay was right. I saw it every day. Red-eyed women came to me with a wad of cash and a tinge of suspicion. They said, and I believed most of them, that the *cheating* was something they could forgive, work out even—if only the guy hadn't lied.

Because once you lied about a thing like boffing some broad in the back room of a strip joint when you were supposed to be driving your cousin Andy home, well then, wasn't it easy to lie about the *little* things—like where you got those scratches on your back, how much you lost at the casino, or why you logged in as Russell Indaleeves on a sex addicts' website.

Lies hide secrets. Secrets destroy trust. Women are big on trust and the only secrets they like are their own, the ones they'll spill to their girlfriends over a few glasses of white wine and a Cobb salad.

I checked the clock, thinking about the broad coming to see me. I'd recognized her last name, Leonard, as also belonging to one of the girls who'd been murdered in a local Irish bar a few days ago. I was all ready to give her my "I'm sorry for your loss" spiel and wondered what she expected me to do since the case seemed pretty cut and dry. Witnesses heard gunshots. Dead bodies. Bad guy—now dead guy—with loaded gun and key to the front door captured on surveillance equipment. Cops on scene. Film at eleven.

The *Syracuse Times* had run two pictures under the article, a black-and-white from the crime scene, and an older one in color, right under the headline DEATH SERVED UP COLD AT FLANNIGAN'S. In it, three sexy girls—a blonde, a brunette, and a redhead—were braced against the bar, eyes forward, backs arched in a Mae West bordello pose. They were beautiful in three different ways, but each was giving a genuine smile, the kind that crinkles your eyes and shortens your neck. Cold wasn't close to what the photograph made me feel.

It was only later that I noticed the reflection of the guy taking the picture. Turned sideways to capture the girls from an advantageous angle, he'd caught himself in the mirror behind the bar. The camera covered his face, but I could see the top of his head and one hand. The palm was facing out, like he was saying, "Perfect. Stop right there. Hold it . . ." As if he could freeze the moment. That part of the picture made me uncomfortable. It made me think of unsaid things and had me wondering about these girls who were working together, talking, and sharing secrets over Cobb salad. It was intriguing, and if I'm going to be honest, stimulating in a slightly twisted way.

My client was right on time, her knock more of a rap. Two sudden thumps. I imagined this was the kind of woman who wouldn't wait if you were running late, a list maker who would add things she'd already done just so she could cross them off. She'd spend a whole day precooking meals to save thirty minutes a night in the kitchen. She'd be the kind of woman who set a timer for sex, tossing her spouse a towel and telling him to finish it himself if he took too long. As a trained PI, I knew these things.

But as a warm-blooded male, I'll admit, her entrance suggested something else altogether. After years playing Free Willy on the stripping circuit, I'd become a pretty good judge of character. A quick scan of the crowd could save your pecker. I wouldn't hang it out there on stage if there might be a psycho in the crowd with a knife under her skirt. You had to know when to approach and when to dance behind the bigger, dumber guy.

The trick was to find the money. To figure out which women were there for more than a one-hour show. The ones who'd slip crisp twenties—tagged with their phone numbers in Sharpie—into your T-strap while running their tongue over an expensively enhanced lip.

When Mrs. Leonard stepped in, jewelry jangling, boobs bouncing, all blonde and tall and pink with one delicate hand extended, I came around my desk to meet her.

I was totally unprepared for the left hook.

When I came to she was leaning over me, her blouse hanging away from her chest, giving me the full view of a rack that was oddly familiar.

"Oh, God. Bill. I'm sorry. I never—I mean, are you all right?"

Mrs. Leonard helped me up. I took advantage of my weakened state to lean into that bosom, using it as a soft pillow for my aching jaw—a soft, peach-scented pillow attached to a fortyish body that could easily pass for thirtyish.

We made it to the couch. She looked around.

"Do you have any—"

"Cold pack in there." I pointed to a small refrigerator in the corner while massaging my jaw. Son of a bitch hurt. It would bruise, in rainbow colors. I knew from experience.

"Here." Mrs. Leonard handed me a small pad of fake ice. I snuck a look at her, thinking more than the rack was familiar. That mole under her left eye . . .

Being a man who speaks his mind I said, "What the hell was that for?"

"I said I was sorry. And you can't say you didn't have it coming, Bill."

"Yes. I can," I said, but even as I did, I knew she had a point. The breasts, the mole, the way she said *Bi-ill* in two syllables . . . this woman had a right to be angry with me. Mrs. Leonard was none other than my high-school sweetheart, Buffy Schenk.

She leaned back on the couch and crossed her long legs, Buffy-style.

"C'mon. After how you treated me? You're lucky I only punched you." She clenched and unclenched her fist of doom, then smiled. "Geez, Bill, the way you passed out like that, I could've done a lot worse. To you, or your . . ."

Her gaze drifted to my crotch and I felt my testicles draw up. I dropped a hand, felt around.

She scoffed. "Don't worry. Little Willy's fine."

But I left my hand there, like a flesh shield against thoughts of Lorena Bobbitt and the girl who'd superglued her boyfriend's erect, cheating penis to his abdomen. What might Mrs. Leonard's method have been, I wondered?

I took a longer look at my ex-sweetie. Buffy Schenk had done well for herself. She wore an expensive-looking, tailored pink suit with a Chanel scarf tied at the neck. Her legs were still firm and muscular. It looked like she'd learned to avoid the sun—the result was an unlined face with just enough creases in the right places. No, Buffy wasn't lifted or Botoxed, and I knew the tits were her own. I like my women natural. And this one was, 100 percent.

"How you been, Buffy?"

"It's Barbara now. *Mrs.* Barbara Leonard." She held out her left hand, twisting the large diamond ring on her finger. "Mick finally popped the question. Three months after you left."

"Congratulations."

"Thanks."

She looked at me, and our eyes caught in that awkward way where you know there's something happening, something that shouldn't be happening for all the conventional reasons, but also because you want it so bad it must be wrong. We both squirmed a little, then found another place to rest our gazes.

"When you called," I said, trying hard to not think of Buffy as the kind of woman who'd use a dead kid as an excuse to punch out an ex-lover. "You told me you had a case that you wanted me to look into." I rubbed my sore jaw. "*This* wasn't why you wanted to see me, was it?"

She shook her head. "No." Her face went soft. "I don't know if I can do this." Her eyes welled with tears and she turned away, talking to a spot across the room. "She was all we had. Mick and I tried for years to have more kids. Maybe that was wrong. We should have been happy—lots of people have just one child. We should have stopped trying, stopped talking about it. But for a while it consumed us. It affected us all more than anyone realized at the time."

She looked at her hands gripped in her lap, opened them, and smoothed her skirt. "Chamonix—that's my daughter—*was* my daughter. She went into therapy once, as an adult, when she was 'artistically blocked.' I don't know what it was all about, but we had to join her in a session. The shrink told us that by being so vocal about trying to have more children we had devalued Chamonix in her formative years, made her feel like she wasn't special, as if she wasn't enough for us. And that was why she relied on her art so much. It was what fed her, where she felt her honor, her pride, and her worth. But, my God, Bill, she was *so* special. You should have known her. Everyone should have known her. She was amazing, she—"

Barbara swallowed hard and shook her head, then reached into her purse for a flowered handkerchief and a photo. She handed me a picture as she blotted her eyes.

I was a little surprised. I didn't know people still used handkerchiefs.

Buffy-now-Barbara had come a long way since serving watered-down cocktails and dodging ass-grabbers at The Frisky Biscuit.

The picture was of Barbara standing beside a girl in a cap and gown. The proud mom couldn't shine brighter than the knockout redhead with the ice-blue eyes, though. Chamonix. Christ, I would have done her. I mean, if I was ten years younger—and she was still alive.

After Barbara left I sat down with the files. She'd managed to get copies of everything. I didn't want to know how. There were coroner's reports, newspaper accounts, background and logged reports, a copy of the surveillance DVD from the night of the incident, even pages from the detective's notebook.

With all the information in front of me, and as much as seemed obvious—their boss killed them—it was still only a start. The *why* question pointed in a general direction, but I'd have to reach out and open the real gate. Usually, I'd have to ram it with my hip because it would stick, and more times than not, it would squeak when I opened it, alerting the guard dogs before it slammed hard behind me.

FLANNIGAN'S

Chapter 3

The cozy bar on the corner. There's one in every city. A hole-in-the-wall that does more business than any big hotel bar. It also has more character, hides more stories, and even though most nights the biggest tip will only be a crumpled ten-spot tucked into the waitress's cleavage, the place will cash out stronger than the big guys. Add an honest owner, and it could be around for years—like Cheers, minus the high-paid actors and cheesy laugh track.

I felt it as soon as I walked in. That I-wish-it-was raining-so-I-could-have-an-excuse-to-hunker-down-in-the-corner-booth-with-a-smoky-Scotch-and-a-beer-chaser feeling. The idea hit me next that some people would do exactly that even if the sun was shining and the boss was waiting. Then another feeling began to sink in—kind of sick and wormy—that some people, even if they couldn't afford the Scotch part of the fantasy, would spend their days in that corner booth drinking away their future, trading their life for temporary liquid happiness.

It was this feeling that kept me away from imbibing in quantity. Maybe it was a control thing with me. I'd never had a problem with beer, been known to tip a few cold ones at the ballpark, but I stopped when I got buzzed and didn't drink real booze anymore. I'd learned over the years that me plus hard alcohol adds up to asshole.

Anytime I thought I might want to try the latest flavored vodka, all I had to do was come to a place like this and take note of the loner at the bar, the one trying to look like he had it under control, though you could smell the loser on him, or the guys slamming shots at a back booth, killing precious brain cells, getting louder and more idiotic by the minute. I'd be quickly reminded of the jackass nature of the drunken male and would order a soda, drink it, and leave.

Today, I was planning on spending time alone in a bar strictly for the case. I'd called in a favor at the police department with a sexy little bombshell named Sasha. We used to play racquetball together, among other things. She told me "on the down low" that the triple homicide/suicide wasn't receiving much attention at the moment, given the morning's bomb threat at The Dome. It only takes one suspicious package to divert the station's dicks. I mean that in the most professional way. Truly.

Sasha told me that the homicide location was being released at noon to the cleanup crew, which meant they'd arrive at Flannigan's around two o'clock. She slipped me the key, then whispered something in my ear that made me blush. Before I could return the favor, she waved me off, warning me to not forget while tapping her watch.

I'd figured I would drive to Flannigan's and do a quick once-over, then return and slip the key—and maybe a little something else—to Sasha in her apartment, where we'd agreed to meet for an extended lunch.

Flannigan's didn't need the flipped-over sign on the door to tell people it was closed. The bright yellow police tape across the door would have dissuaded customers well enough. And if anyone *had* been able to push through the doors, they would have first noticed crushed paper coffee cups and donut boxes by the front door and white traces of fingerprint powder on every flat surface. Cop debris. Then surely they'd notice the blood, dried in pooled ovals, in splatters on the mirrored walls, on the keys of the cash register, reflected in the broken glass everywhere. And then, they would smell what I smelled.

Something the cleanup crew must be used to. They didn't toss their cookies mopping human fluids or scooping up organ bits or brain matter. I wondered if they'd become numb to the terrible things people do. What do you think about when you're vacuuming up bone fragments or removing bloodstains from walls, stools, and floorboards? How do you not dream about that?

I took out a photo from the homicide file to study one of the dead bodies on the floor, matching it up to the stains. I could see how it would have gone down. I slipped the photo into my back pocket and made my way through the bar to the back stairs.

I imagined it would take a few months for the regulars to find their way back. Maybe longer, if the ghosts of the murdered girls kept the place from reopening.

But it would reopen. This place had always been a bar, as far back in Syracuse history as I could remember. The location was perfect and the recent renovations to the building and the block were just the sort of thing to attract a buyer. Flannigan's could even be the next Coyote Ugly.

Standing in the small office overlooking the service area, I could imagine our guy, James Smith, looking down on his bar and feeling lordly. There was a sense of omnipotence at this angle. The one-way glass wall would have served two purposes. Below, the waitresses and servers could use the mirror to keep an eye on the room, while upstairs behind the glass, their boss could keep an eye on them.

It was sort of creepy in that bad-guy-dreams-up-evil-plot way, and made me think of an ex-girlfriend who refused to ever use dressing rooms. She thought all mirrors were two-way—except apparently the one over my bed, or maybe even that one too, judging by the way she always came to bed wearing makeup and dimming the lights just so.

I stepped away from the glass and sat behind the desk. Ergonomic leather chair, high-quality paper in the printer, Mont Blanc pen in the drawer, plus various cords leading to sleek, unidentifiable electronics. Mr. Smith was no slug.

According to the file Buffy had given me, James John Smith had been born in Ann Arbor, Michigan, on April 19, 1965, and was single with no children, parents deceased. He had won the property and entire contents of the bar in an online poker game and taken possession shortly thereafter. The cops knew all that and probably more, now that they had his laptop. I ran my gloved hand over the suspiciously empty space on the dusty desk.

I figured they'd also gone through his drawers, but I was here and had time to kill, so I opened the file cabinet and went to work.

Stashed between the previous owner's folders labeled, "Recipes that work," and "Things that need doing," I found a receipt, less than a year old, signed by J. Smith for the wiring of an exhaust fan and the installation of both an industrial double fryer and a freezer. It looked like Mr. Smith had some experience in the restaurant business, or some educated help.

Thirty minutes and bupkes later, I figured Mr. Smith wasn't much of a filer. He probably had one of those machines that you feed your paper receipts into, wirelessly sending them to a magic accounting program, and then have a bonfire. He was a probably antinewspaper, an e-book lover. I shook my head and moved back to the desk, pulling open the bottom drawer. Even if Smith was technologically advanced, he was still a man, and that meant this was where he'd keep his personnel files. And if he was that predictable, I knew I'd also find his car keys and at least one intimate detail about him in his underwear drawer at his apartment.

Bingo. The files still had new hire sheets attached to their covers. Looked like Smith stole his chef and fry cook from The Dubliner and hired a college student from Syracuse University as his bookkeeper, which I saw as a good move.

Students tend to buy into the whole work-smarter-not-harder thing, and usually do the job cheap. It's a great deal on both sides—as long as they show up for work when scheduled. It's much better than hiring some thirtysomething who is so lost or screwed up by his family, girlfriend, or the last two jobs that you spend all your time fixing his shit. And, if you hire a woman you gotta worry about *that* time of the month, and even then she'll probably go get pregnant, leaving you in the lurch for fifteen months, with you paying to have her at home lying on the couch watching soaps with a kid on her tit.

Nah. Forget equal employment. Get a young, impressionable kid, preferably attractive, nonsmoking, and gay, then shape them into the perfect employee.

That was my theory anyway, and although I didn't own a restaurant, I'd had great results when I went that route and hired Tommy Bane. I had no problem with him being a student or liking the color periwinkle.

I opened the folder on top and started reading. The fry cook and chef had two pages of background that would all check out. I felt nothing squirrelly there, and I'm big on following my instincts.

The next files were for the girls: Roxanne Dupont, Crescent Moon, and Chamonix Leonard.

ROXIE ONLY SOUNDS LIKE A STRIPPER NAME

Chapter 4

Roxanne Dupont had that certain something that made people look twice, that certain aura—if you thought in those terms—that attracted attention.

She wasn't a great beauty, nor did she possess extraordinary charm. It was something inside her, something no one could explain, something that radiated outward.

Relatives and family friends of her parents, Robert, an entomologist, and Nell, a second-grade teacher, had tried to find an explanation. They ignored Robert's Roman nose and told stories of royal English ancestors—a Duke of three generations, once removed. They claimed her maternal grandmother was a famous Spanish gypsy, though Nell had been adopted in New Jersey.

Roxie might have romanticized her legacy, broadened the tales to include herself, but she chose not to. It wasn't important what her family looked like or where they came from. It wasn't important how twisted the roots of her family tree, only that they appeared to be happy, that they loved one another as families do. It was important to her that they appeared normal, that her family blended in perfectly with the dozen others on her block, the hundreds of people at their church, the thousand middle-class families on their side of town.

Robert and Nell Dupont had raised five boys when families were large, when good Catholics followed the Pope's decree on birth control.

They were already mini-men when Roxie had been born, sticking around just long enough to name her like a family pet, then zipping off to boarding school, college, and the Navy. Now the boys were grown with families of their own.

Roxie had been the "oops baby," the baby that almost never was. The baby that Nell thought she'd been too old to carry, too tired to raise. The baby that survived the saltwater abortion attempts that left Nell sobbing on a bloodstained tile floor in the boys' old bathroom on the third floor.

Nell made a few prenatal visits, declined any testing, and left it all up to fate. She had almost convinced herself one Sunday, on her knees in front of a cold marble altar, that another boy might not be so bad, when she went into labor. Ten hours later, she gave birth to a daughter. A tiny, blue little girl.

The birth had been difficult. No one blamed Nell when she failed to give any immediate attention to the baby. The doctors called it postpartum depression, prescribed rest, tea, and warm baths.

Robert told her, "It's just a phase. You'll be fine. We'll be fine."

But when he brought them home and rolled the baby in her bassinet into the master bedroom, into Nell's sanctuary, filling it with noises and smells and tiny, strange things, Nell responded by pushing the bassinet into the adjoining bathroom and letting the infant cry. She told Robert that the baby must be sick, that they should send her back to the hospital. After all, she was so small, so pale, so breakable.

Robert felt it would be best to take time away from the lab and stay home with his "girls," as he called them. He rose at night to feed, change, and soothe Roxie. He sat by Nell in the afternoons, encouraging her to hold her daughter, to please just look at her. But Nell only resented the baby, resented the fact that the tiny thing had such control over Robert. Apparently over everyone—they no longer looked at beautiful Nell, but instead, their eyes flashed over her and settled on the baby. Even the checker at the grocery store.

"Oh, she's precious! How old is she? A month! My, you must be so proud."

But proud wasn't what Nell felt.

She began to wonder why she even bothered to fix her hair, apply her makeup, or change out of her pajamas. She was just the lady with the "precious" baby.

Nell whispered in Roxie's tiny, perfect ear, "I wish you had never been born."

Robert eventually went back to work. But he'd changed. He was no longer the husband Nell desired. He hardly spoke to her when he came home each night. Instead, he was drawn straight to the bassinet. When he wasn't with his bugs, he was attached to Roxie. A baby always needed something.

Nell felt a twinge in her heart when she saw the two of them together. Roxie made Robert smile. Roxie cried for Robert in the middle of the night. And Robert left his wife's warm bed and climbed the stairs to a nursery Nell had never completed to comfort, to soothe, to love another girl.

Raised ten tears later, Roxie would have been the child snatched at the bus stop or kidnapped from the crowded lobby of a resort in Cancun. She was keepable in a doll-like way, as if you could take her home and put her on your shelf, show her off to people, dress her up, and play with her forever.

Nell saw none of the beauty in her little girl. She

continued to ignore Roxie, instead filling her day with activities. She joined every club the town had to offer. She spent weekends gardening and practicing calligraphy. She met with authors and history buffs, dressing up once a month to take part in Civil War reenactments. When she wasn't sewing costumes or reading, she was studying for online courses in art appreciation.

Robert called this a phase too, and waited patiently on the sidelines, raising their daughter, filling her head with pleasant stories of the woman Nell used to be. He said, "Your mother loves you very much. She just has a hard time showing it."

For years, Roxie chose to believe him.

As Roxie grew she became less adorable toddler, less precocious grade-school child, and more awkward adolescent. She began to blend into the world, and as she became less dependent upon her father, she became more bearable to her mother.

As long as she was quiet and stayed out of Nell's way, Roxie's home life was fine. Her father dropped her off at school every morning in a gleaming black Bentley that was the envy of the other parents. They lived in a great neighborhood, went to the most popular church, and took regular vacations—always joined by the brothers and their clans, resulting in a multitude of ill-posed photographs that ultimately graced someone's Christmas card.

On the outside, it would have appeared her life was perfect. And that was all anyone knew. Roxie never brought friends home. She never had a sleepover or a birthday party at a pizza place. She was complete on the outside: a kind, slim, pretty girl, but hollow as a cheap chocolate Easter bunny.

One summer, Robert and Nell went on a church marriage retreat. They left Roxie home alone with a list of instructions. When they returned, they acted like sappy lovesick teenagers, unable to keep their hands off each other. Roxie called her brothers and told them how weird their parents were acting. They said it wasn't weird. They had fallen back in love.

Roxie couldn't help wondering how and when the falling out part had happened and whether it happened to everyone.

After a few months the three of them settled into a happy coexistence with Roxie as the roommate, the nosy neighbor. She thought sometimes that it was sweet that her parents spent a lot of time together, that they were obviously still in love, but when she looked at it sideways, she thought it was bent. She swore she would never ever get married, never share that much of herself with anyone.

Roxie spent hours reading biographies and interviews of people she admired—strong, confident, single women. She approached her life as a cultural project and began to design and alter herself, creating an act that was her life, a character that was Roxie.

While her parents had noisy sex in the boys' old playroom, Roxie would spend her afternoons meditating on quiet thoughts, which usually started with the words, "What if?" and "How could I?" Questions that led to choices, decisions, and changes that could transform an empty shell into a complete person.

By the time she graduated from high school, Roxie had become the girl every girl wanted to be around and the girl every guy wanted to be in. She knew both sides of the equation and figured out that she liked being wanted much better than being forgotten.

She was popular with all the cliques: stoners, jocks, nerds, even brownnosing brainiacs. Roxie earned her way in, paying with glorified untruths, wasted moments, and a tiny part of her soul.

***

In her first—and only—year of college in San Diego, Roxie's English professor pushed her up against the wall after class and said with his coffee breath in her face, "I know your kind." Then he winked and stepped back, running his eyes over her body, giving her a feeling not unlike mosquitoes alighting and drawing blood.

Roxie wasn't at all sure what "kind" she was—never had been—and almost wished he'd tell her. It would be much easier knowing what was expected of you if you knew who you were. But the professor never had a chance to tell her, as the moment was lost when Matt Bryant walked in, saying he'd forgotten his notebook. He snatched it from the table in the second row, where he'd sat for the last hour collecting fallen strands of Roxie's hair, then shoved it in his backpack and tapped his watch.

"Don't want to be late," he said to Roxie, who quickly gathered her books and backed out the door, not wanting to give the professor the benefit of a view of her ass. Matt and Roxie walked out together looking like a couple, which was what Matt wanted people to think.

"Thanks," Roxie said.

"No problem. So, where are you headed?"

Matt wanted more than anything to put his arm around her, kiss her, and call her "Babe." Then he'd tell her he'd be thinking of her when he was in his biology class, but that would be a lie, because all he'd be thinking about in biology was how much he hated his fat-ass instructor and the smell of formaldehyde.

Matt forced himself to focus because the hall was coming to an end and this was do-or-die time.

Roxie said, "I don't have any classes until two. I was going to go to the library and study. What about you?"

"What a coincidence. I was on my way to the library

too." Matt said, wondering if his ears were turning red like they did when he lied to his mother.

"Cool."

"Yeah, cool."

Then, because Matt was a good kid—albeit a bad liar—and because he saw something in Roxie, something inherently special that might even go deeper than the intoxicating scent of her perfect hair, he said, "I have to tell you something. I didn't forget my notebook. I left it there on purpose."

"You did?"

"Yeah, I know a girl that got hit on by that same professor last semester. She filed a complaint with the department. He's supposed to be on some kind of probation."

"She filed a complaint? What did she say?"

"I don't know. But maybe you should file one too, you know, just to make sure."

"Oh, I don't know. He seems harmless enough." Roxie thought the words sounded trite as they left her mouth and wondered how many neighbors had said the same things about serial killers. She started walking. Matt fell in beside her.

He said, "Yeah, well, a guy like that should never become a teacher."

Roxie looked at him sideways, wondering what Matt meant, wondering what he thought he was protecting her from.

He asked her to lunch that day, then dinner and a movie, and eventually he asked her to go away for the weekend. Roxie said yes and spent the next four months learning just what "kind" she was and how much a man like the English professor could have ruined her.

She enjoyed her time with Matt, and their relationship grew from a damsel-in-distress feeling of appreciation and devotion to her savior to a comfortable pairing of two young kids who—from what everyone told them—seemed perfect together. Roxie felt safe and protected, desired even.

But something was missing, and in a short while she began to see Matt as more of a damsel than she was. He'd call her from biology class, weeping for the life of a fetal pig. Stuck on the side of the road with a flat tire and no jack, he'd ask her to come pick him up; when she got there and changed his tire, he'd felt appreciative instead of embarrassed. She began to hate him.

When Matt sent her crappy love poems and recorded sappy songs on cassettes, then taped them to her windshield, Roxie thought Matt might have more estrogen than she would ever be capable of producing. She worried that if the relationship continued, she'd become cruel and callous and he'd melt into a fleshy, soggy, teary mash of almost-man.

She broke up with him on the phone at the end of the semester and had to lay the receiver on the pillow to hide the sound of her leaving the room while he cried and begged and pleaded, then threatened to take his life.

Roxie knew he'd be as incompetent at that as he was at giving her head. She went away for three weeks to visit her parents in New York. When she returned, he was gone. Someone said he'd quit school and joined the Peace Corps.

Roxie hoped he was happy.

Now that she could date whomever she wanted, it turned out that she wanted men who were nothing at all like the boy she'd had in Matt. Roxie wanted hard-bodied, dumb, insensitive jocks. Father figures for abused children.

There was Steve. He was cool like Elvis was cool, even when he got fat and bitchy. Steve could have been one of those movie mob guys with bad teeth who wear cheap shoes that turn up at the ends, but who classy women driving Jaguars still want to blow under the table at The Palm. Steve was all Roxie needed until their third month, when the steroids really kicked in and his balls shrunk and the hair on his chest began to grow back, thick and red and prickly like a cactus against her breasts.

Roxie plowed her way through relationships with college boys, steak house waiters, an insurance agent, and even her boss's boss at the golf course. She dated as if it was a contest, racking up numbers and statistics, always keeping one or two men on the line. She was the girl in the center ring, spinning plates on sticks.

Until Don, no one came close to winning her heart, partly because Roxie hadn't been using her heart in those informative years.

After all the men were catalogued and dissected, she figured that what she'd been filling instead of her heart was maybe just a kidney, or an armpit, or even a lymph node. Because when she met Don—when she kissed Don—her whole being soared. Every nerve ending tingled, every cell was jolted into life. She felt like she could funnel herself out of her skin through the tip of her tongue and wriggle right into him. She felt *present*—and for the first time, desperately, joyfully, giddily in love.

Maybe it was the intensity of the love that burned it out. Maybe Don was right when he said he wasn't a marathoner, he was a sprinter. He'd looked sorry when they broke up, when he left her that card with the lame quote about birds in a cage and leaving the door open. Didn't he know roosting birds always return?

Roxie tried to forget him. She put a tattoo on her ankle of comedy/tragedy masks and spent weekends driving slowly past his house at midnight trying to peer in the windows, guess whose shadow was whose. And when she read in the paper that he was getting married to his ex-girlfriend, she tore up the last note she'd wanted to give him—the one where she quoted all the things he'd whispered in her ear while making love. She burned it in a pot on the stove along with his favorite pair of boxers she'd found under her bed.

That kind of love changed her. For the rest of her life, Roxie would compare other men to Don. She'd size them up, test their first kiss against a memory that gained favor in direct proportion to her dissatisfaction with her current conquest.

With Barry, the busy day trader, Don became the King of Siam for the manner in which he had pampered Roxie.

When she woke up next to Jake, the personal trainer, her feelings for Don were so strong that she wept. She lied to the massive man by saying she had been dreaming of a tiny, sad kitten mewing in a box on the side of a highway. Jake nodded knowingly, then pinched her breast and said, "Fuck me hard, baby." And Roxie knew he had no idea what she needed or desired.

She almost started dating women, thinking they would fill the void of Don. But the one botched night with Laura only served to solidify her desire for men—all men.

It went on like that for years, no matter what part of California she lived in, how many cocktails she served. It was the wrong man after the wrong man after the wrongest man ever. Her brothers and her parents left her to her vices, left Roxie to confess everything to the priest behind the screen, earn her absolution, and move on.

When her parents finally decided to join her out west, Roxie broke the news that she was returning to Syracuse, said she'd decided she was an East Coast girl after all. She wished Nell and Robert well on their second-chance life, secretly hoping someone would come whisk *her* away and that she would be the one living on a coastal cliff with eight successful coffeehouses and just enough Microsoft stock.

Weeks later, hungry and almost broke, Roxie passed Flannigan's. When she saw the Help Wanted sign, she felt a bit of the old Don tingle return. It was a gauge she couldn't ignore, so she opened the door and walked in. It was just another bar in just another town, but it felt like home. It felt like a hot meal on a starched placemat in a clean kitchen. It felt like a yellow room full of unused baby furniture. It felt like the perfect combination of a broad chest and strong arms spooning her from behind.

And when the owner approached smiling, introducing himself as James Smith, holding out his hand, Roxie took it. When their eyes met, she told him, "Take down the sign."

TEDESCO ON THE JOB, IN A ROOM WITH A VIEW

Chapter 5

My cell phone rang, nudging me from a nap I didn't know I'd needed. I dug the phone out of my pocket, ran my tongue around my mouth trying to get a little saliva going, then answered it.

"Tedesco."

"How's it going?"

It was Tommy Bane, my protégé.

"Good." I yawned. "What do you have for me?"

"You were right, the rest of the staff checks out. Just normal working Joes. I did get a hit on the weekend dishwasher, a trip to juvie when he was thirteen. But he's been clean since. Might have just been one of those things."

"That it?"

"So far, but I need a better name on the Moon woman. She's invisible."

I looked through the folders. "Moon, Crescent aka Crescent Moon Brigade," was on the bottom.

I said, "Let me call you back." I hung up with Tommy, then opened the file and started reading.

The picture attached to the file looked nothing like the third girl in the crime scene photo. It wasn't what I expected for a girl named Crescent Moon Brigade—a moniker that seemed part Little Debbie, part Frank Zappa. Part commune, part crackhead stripper.

I had to look twice, and I'm good with faces. Names not so much. But crash your cart into mine at the grocery store then walk past me a month later and I'd recognize you. I would definitely remember all the details of our meeting if prominent tits or big blue eyes were in the picture. It was something I prided myself on.

With the Moon girl it wasn't so simple. First I had to get past the fact that in her file photo she was alive. She was upright. Not splayed across a dirty bar floor. There wasn't a hole in her chest. She didn't have blood smeared across her long, regally pale neck. Her eyes weren't rolled up in her head, zombie whites glaring back.

The poorly photocopied, expired driver's license showed a girl with bushy black hair, low brows, a wide nose, and chipmunk cheeks. Her pursed lips looked as if she'd been ready to argue with the photographer—or spit. I was pretty sure Miss Moon hadn't been happy to hand over this document.

I pulled the newspaper clipping from my breast pocket and looked at the photo of the girls leaning on the bar. The only one with blue eyes was the blonde. Now that I looked, I could see the resemblance. Like seeing twins: one who'd lived the party life and the other who probably knew the public library intimately. The blonde version of Crescent Moon looked like she'd been modeled after Barbie—which was not altogether a bad thing as far as most warm-blooded men were concerned.

I wondered why an innocent young woman would do that to herself—change everything. People running from something did that. They transformed themselves.

But young girls in a small city like Syracuse? What did they have to run from? And who around here did quality work like hers?

SHE GIVES A WHOLE NEW NAME TO COAL MINER'S DAUGHTER

Chapter 6

Crescent Moon Brigade applied the fader cream to her arms and legs. She worked her way over every inch of her body methodically, lovingly. It made the other women in the gym locker room uncomfortable. They were okay with changing next to strangers, even tolerated the occasional towel slip in the sauna, but did she have to rub cream all over her body with those long, slim fingers? Did she have to hum as she did it, looking so damn pleased with every perfect curve, so damn happy with herself?

If asked, most women would be eager to write off Cress's appeal, saying, "If I had the money, I could look that good too," in the same way people downplayed the lives of celebrities, calming themselves by whispering lies and assumptions—things that made the insides of beautiful people ugly and by their whispers ricocheted all the ugliness back on them.

People like that would only ever see Cress as an enhanced beauty, the product of a capable, expensive plastic surgeon. They had no desire to look any deeper, and certainly wouldn't invite her over for dinner, not with their sexually deprived husbands sitting across the table.

Cress ran a hand down her arm, the skin warm and firm under her touch. She liked herself this way: china pale, light all over. Bread-dough colored, as if in this incarnation she'd been kneaded then set on chilled marble to rise under a warm cotton cloth.

She finished dressing, then went to the mirror to put on her makeup. The first glance could still startle her. Maybe in time she wouldn't even remember the old Crescent Moon Brigade. There weren't any pictures—except a few ID cards—and no one left from her past.

As Cress leaned in closer to line her eyes, a tall brunette in a red suit stepped up to the mirror, blow-dryer in hand, staring. When Cress met her eyes in the mirror she stammered, "You . . . you have the most beautiful eyes."

Cress smiled. "Thanks." She ran her tongue over her lower lip. "I get that *a lot*." The woman blushed and turned quickly away to plug in her dryer, missing the outlet twice.

Cress's large eyes had never lost the clear blue of babyhood. Instead they'd gained in intensity until they were the color of a turquoise sea, ringed with litmus-paper blue and dotted with tiny pupils, as if someone had added them later with a black felt pen.

Growing up, people had always noticed her eyes first, but their pleasure would turn to disappointment as they scanned the rest of her. She grew up feeling like the blind date who was always described as "having a great personality."

Fed up and turning twenty-three, Cress saw her first TV makeover show and cried with empathy. She spent the next three months convincing her boyfriend, Rodney, to use money he'd earmarked for a new Camaro to buy her a nose job. She told him she wanted to be beautiful for him, that this was about their happiness, and if he loved her he'd understand.

Rodney gave up his hot car dream and helped Cress through the procedure, driving her back to their apartment afterward, tucking her into bed. He pretended to be happy when the bandages came off, happier still that she'd lost twenty pounds during her recovery, but really he hated that she was getting hit on by guys everywhere. He hated how she spent hours staring at herself in the mirror, that she started wearing tight clothes and makeup and going out with the girls—something she'd always dismissed as false and bourgeois. Rodney smelled the impending death of another dream.

He would never forget the humid Wednesday morning when he stood in the doorway with his duffel bag and handed Cress the spare key. She'd coated her hair with a coconut-and-plantain conditioner the night before, pecked him on the cheek, then rolled over to her side of the bed and promptly fell asleep. Rodney blamed the odor emanating from her turbaned head for giving him bizarre dreams of deserted islands and manic monkeys. He still felt a bit jittery inside.

She stood there, dangling his key, head cocked, shiny egg-white mask on her face, feet coated in paraffin. It was too much for Rodney.

He said, "You have always been beautiful to me, Cress. Inside and out. But I can't do this anymore. You've become obsessive about this . . . this whole thing."

"Obsessive?" The egg white mask cracked over her brow and split around her lips. "I don't think so. I mean, what's wrong with wanting to look good?"

Rodney shook his head. "It's not right. I can't do this anymore. I'm sorry."

Cress would have cried at his leaving, but she didn't want her eyes to get puffy and she knew what her nose looked like when it was red. Instead she ran five miles on the treadmill and confessed her feelings to the DVD aerobics instructor. She took the woman's smile to be encouraging. In another hour, drained, sweaty, and toned, Cress served herself a vegetable smoothie, slid into a hot tub, and managed to convince herself that she'd be fine. Mr. Rodney Stimp was making a big mistake. A huge mistake that he'd regret forever. He had no idea how extraordinary she was meant to be.

Born in Granny's four-poster bed in Windrock, North Carolina, on the luckiest day in the state— the birthday of Juliette Gordon Low—everyone knew Crescent Moon Brigade was special.

When news of her birth was announced—relayed by Bobby Joe, the cousin on the porch, to old Mrs. Wilkins, who knew everyone—it only took a few hours for the truckload of local Girl Scouts working on their bronze award to pull into the forgotten coal town with a trailer full of presents and an envelope full of cash.

Hopeful people of the mountain town came out to greet the girls from the valley. They all knew of the Girl Scout tradition, but it was a first for Windrock. They posed for pictures, not really understanding the whole fancy camera thing, but they counted the boxes of loot the Brigades received and decided to use this occasion to start believing in miracles again.

Little Crescent's picture appeared in the paper that week, introducing her to the world. People saw the Girl Scouts from Asheville huddled around a mussed iron bed, dwarfing Mamma Fiona, Daddy Lloyd, and a tiny baby swaddled in a thick-knit blanket, tags still attached, smiling in her sleep.

As time wore on in the simple mountain town, Crescent's life continued to be magical. Special things happened only to her, like presents dropping out of the sky. It would have been a charming story if it had been a fairy tale with a happy ending. If the presents had been diamonds in satin boxes tied up with golden threads. Instead, the magical things were slippery, with people dying and leaving, with houses collapsing and futures cut short. Times of plenty were balanced by days more black than fortunate. Traumatic situations that somehow, magically, ended in joyful circumstances.

Even if she didn't turn out to be Girl Scout material, Cress made the best of her life. Being a famous orphan wasn't all bad. In the beginning, Cress lived well off the money from the insurance settlement. Her father had owned more land than she'd thought, including a few shares in an untapped coal mine.

Eventually, all the mines dried up. In the spring, they closed the road to Windrock, knocked down all the shacks, and she and the rest of the town had to move down the mountain and into the valley, where life got expensive.

Someone always had their hand out. If you didn't watch it, she knew, the funds would dwindle down to nothing and then you would be left with peanut butter—not even the good brand-name stuff, but the generic kind—and you'd be cutting the moldy part of the bread away and telling yourself that was okay because you needed to lose a few pounds anyway. But then you'd realize the rent had gone up and your income hadn't and the bra you're wearing was only held together with a weak safety pin. When you realize that, you know you have to make some changes.

Cress thought about her life in the mountains and what it had prepared her for, then took a job at the city hospital dumping bedpans and mopping up vomit. She eavesdropped on nurses and doctors, watched a lot of soap operas and news programs, and began to model herself after anchorwomen and fake daytime divas with five names and no hyphens. She took Internet classes in psychology, literature, and finance, and got a night job cleaning a renowned plastic surgeon's private clinic. An employee discount and the surgeon's eagerness was all it took to convince her to go in for liposuction to reduce her mountain body to a sleeker city shape. By Christmas, she'd bought herself a pair of large, symmetrical breasts that she called Twin Peaks.

In time she found a decent man—married and hardly available—which suited her fine. She had no desire to settle down or, for that matter, share her life. Cress was in love with herself and needed no one else. It was nice to be fawned over, even if the men who often accompanied her were as inconsequential as the socks under her thigh-high boots—and as easily replaceable.

Reinventing herself, Cress grew farther and farther from the coal-town girl, the Juliette Gordon Low birthday baby everyone had called "lucky." One day, she closed the door to her past permanently by hiring a voice coach, expressing her desire to lose her North Carolina accent and replace it with something softer, more subdued—perhaps with a European lilt?

Everyone had a past, Cress figured, but not everyone chose to stay there, wallowing in what was, wishing for things that would never happen, imagining things that never were. Sometimes you just had to say "fuck that," and move on.

In her apartment, a white-walled, stark place where nothing was reminiscent of the greens, browns, and blues of the mountains, Cress adorned the walls with oversize portraits of herself.

She had posed at an art studio, not for the twenty bucks they usually gave their models, but simply to share her body with others. To share beauty. The canvases and sketches had been conceived with artistic freedom, but all were in agreement on the loveliness of their subject, a petite blonde with a model's cheekbones, a porn star's body, and unique blue eyes that were frighteningly empty.

People who saw only her name, *Crescent Moon*, might expect less of her, she knew. But once she was introduced, it was simple to surpass their expectations. She taught herself well, becoming a successful social chameleon with survival instincts. She fell short in only one area: romantic relationships. No matter how much she told herself she deserved a good man, a successful guy with everything going for him, no matter how many times people told her she was fantastic and could have any man she wanted, she found herself wanting the wrong ones. She found herself falling for weak men.

Cress was a magnet for confused, hurt, broken little boys with mommy issues. They were usually dark-haired and handsome, and exuded a professional competence that they lacked internally. Some hid behind glasses and books, which she found charming. Others quit jobs that were too demanding, too materialistic, and gave themselves up to a higher power, offering their lives to a God that Cress was sure expected more of His creations.

Each time a new guy washed out, Cress reminded herself she'd done it again. She'd fallen for a guy she thought would fill the missing piece of her, a guy who ended up being the missing part she never needed to begin with.

Weakness begat weakness.

Cress sometimes thought about what would happen if she put all the sorry men from her past into a locked room for a day. The one who cried after sex because she was too beautiful. The one who claimed to be unfixable—he was. The one who said she was too smart for him. The religious one who admitted that she scared the hell out of him. The dark, dramatic ones who were all talk and no action, who made promises to save the world while they could barely make their own rent. The sad, poetic, artistic, music-loving, cinematic ones who lived not in the now, but in a land of Hollywood rom-com make-believe. And the sad, lazy ones who believed because of past hurts and disappointments they were owed something wonderful in life but had no fucking clue how to get it or what *it* was, even when it was standing, five foot four inches tall, right in front of them.

If she put all these losers in the same room together, Cress was certain the room would implode, leaving only a mushy, granular debris of self-pity and unmet desires. Something she could hose down the drain, then step over in her stilettos.

They were air, water, and sand.

She was hot molten earth, red clay, and fire. She needed a firmly rooted redwood. She needed a granite boulder.

Cress went through enough therapy to understand why she chose weak men and why she was now done with them. She got so good at analyzing relationships that she even started a blog offering intelligent insight to men suffering from multiple inadequacies. She began by advising them to set their sights lower. Much lower.

Women followers appreciated the "Dr. Moon" replies, especially when she explained to these querying men that until they faced the truth of what little they had to bring to a relationship, they would never have a successful one. Of course, she'd explain, those skirt-chasers who seemed to get as much ass as they wanted but still managed to moan about how inadequate their lives were, well, they needed to embrace bachelorhood and buy a cat. Because then they'd always have at least one pussy in their bed.

When Cress walked into Flannigan's on a cloudy, cold Syracuse morning on the heels of a deliveryman struggling under the weight of a crate both wider and taller than he, she had one thought on her mind: Where's the bathroom?

When James Smith called to her from behind the bar,

asking if she was there for the job, she hesitated. Before she could answer, he told her to follow him to his office. The way he said it, the way he took control, she felt for the first time in her life that she didn't have a choice, that for once *she* wasn't the one in control. And it felt good.

A few minutes later, behind the closed door, when she tried to explain that she was only there to use the bathroom, he smiled and said six words that changed Crescent Moon Brigade's life. "Start tomorrow. Be here at five."

Cress had grown up used to hearing the word "lucky." Men used it as their excuse for being drawn to her, as if they thought *her* luck, *her* shiny fortune, would rub off on them and they would be given all the things they felt they deserved in life.

But luck wasn't everything. No matter how much she had of it or how shiny it was, luck couldn't stop a bullet.

TEDESCO GETS NOSTALGIC. SORT OF.

Chapter 7

I sent a text to Tommy about the Moon-Brigade girl, telling him to start his search with area plastic surgeons—the good ones. I closed with a riddle, knowing how much today's youth enjoyed a good laugh, and though my joke had nothing to do with farts or inappropriate sex, I thought Tommy would like it. I typed, *What's the difference between a liar and a lawyer?* Hit a few return spaces, then added, *The pronunciation.*

My phone buzzed a few seconds later with Tommy's reply—a smiling devil emoticon and his own riddle. *Did you hear about the new sushi bar for lawyers? It's called Sosumi.*

The kid had to always one-up me.

I took a last spin in the leather chair, allowing myself a brief respite from the outside world. Sometimes I'd get nostalgic thinking about the life of the old-fashioned sleuth, imagining myself as one of those burly, crooked-nosed gumshoes in a brown fedora with a buxom blonde on my arm. But my nose was straight and I knew the only way a hat looked good on me was when I hung it south of my belt buckle—like during the bare-assed cowboy show that me and the boys put on in Dallas in '79. *Stripper Cowboys: Foamed and Deranged.* (A twisted version of "Home on the Range.")

Our promoter, Axle Feagin, was definitely an artist before his time. Before anyone's time, we figured, as on more than one occasion his ideas tanked. It was either that

Axle was more advanced than the rest of us, or so European that Americans didn't understand him, especially local reporters.

We usually ended up having to explain our act, repeating Axle's words: "Nudity is an analogy for societal trappings. The penis has become a weapon in the expression of freedom. To strip is to speak the language of the Universal Soul." We'd bring up Salome, King Herod, and the Old Testament until questions moved onto the dancers' physical attributes, with one person always asking if it was true what they'd heard about Fifi, The Italian Stallion?

I'd have to stop myself from saying, "What? That he jerks off twelve times a day? That he has a perpetual hard-on? That when he comes he screams, 'Mommy!'" Because all of that was true. And, yes, it was twelve inches.

I can't remember everything Axle used to say, but I remember thinking at the time that he sounded a lot like that irritatingly happy guy on late-night TV who sold the "You Deserve It All" series of self-help audiotapes from his castle in Kauai.

Axle's happiness wasn't induced by money. It was induced by copious amount of drugs and caffeine. The guy never slept. He drank coffee all day and ate his applesauce laced with psilocybin mushrooms. But we loved and trusted him. Maybe that was the demise of our troupe, even of the whole approach to exotic dancing as "art form."

But who am I to say? I was just a guy found on amateur night at the Squat and Gobble. A half-drunk kid with a nice body and the confidence to move the way most women wished their husbands would. While it lasted the money was good, the travel great, and I had experiences stored up for a lifetime.

At Flannigan's, I left the office and went down the hall to another set of stairs. I pushed open Smith's apartment door. It wasn't locked. A quick jiggle of the handle revealed a broken spring—it hadn't worked well in a while, if ever.

Whoever this Smith guy was, he wasn't the lock-up type. Some people were born *lockers*. I know. I'd lived with one. My wife, Michelle, couldn't even pee behind an unsecured door—or if you spoke to her when she was in there. She had a worrisome evening routine that made me uncomfortable. Window latching, curtain drawing, and the double-bolting of every door. Michelle brushed it off by saying, "It's how I was raised. In the city you *have* to lock up at night."

She wouldn't let me crack open the window in our upstairs bedroom because she thought someone might drive sixteen miles off the beaten path, happen upon our cul-de-sac in the back of an unlit neighborhood, scale the dying oak tree, traipse through a bed of poison ivy, and scramble over our sloping roof, where they would have to remove the double safety screens, then drag themselves over a splintered windowsill to slit our throats. My only reply was to say that even if a killer did make it in, rest assured, he'd never escape.

But that was no comfort to Michelle. Her paranoia made me feel like a prisoner in my own home. It got so bad, I'd started getting panic attacks at bedtime. My heart rate would elevate at the slide and "thunk" sound of her throwing the double bolt, my throat dried up when she slammed shut the windows, and my balls drew into my body like a frightened turtle when she tied the curtains together, eliminating all natural light.

I tried to hide my sweaty palms and panting when she slid under the covers and reached for me with her long, cold toes. I tried to think about sex, about tits and ass and bumping and grinding, but felt like I was breathing underwater, slowly drowning in heavy, stuffy air. I was suffocating, going blind, and she had no idea. As soon as Michelle pulled her warmed feet back, rolled over, and started snoring, I'd steal my way to the window, opening it as far as I could, pushing the curtains aside, then turning on the ceiling fan. A few deep breaths, a few glimpses of the moon, and my heart would begin to settle back into my chest.

I don't how or why I'd let it get to that point, how I'd let her continue having her way. It must have been love. It weakens a man's resolve. It's another kind of death.

I figured Michelle was happy living alone now, peeing uninterrupted behind a locked bathroom door, slipping into her dead-bolted bedroom and breathing all that stale, uncirculated air every night. Feeling safe, sweaty, and secure.

Growing up, we never locked the doors to our house. My dad's theory was that the people who held onto their shit too tight were the ones who got ripped off. People who put an importance on things like money and possessions; those were the ones who drew the burglars, the thieves, the scams and snares that cost them their car, bike, stereo, or life savings.

He might have been right, because I left my bike in the front yard every night for a week hoping it would get stolen so I could get a better one, but no one touched it.

We rarely closed our garage door, which created a sleeping spot for stray cats and the occasional opossum. My dad left his car keys under the driver's seat. Our windows didn't even have locks. I don't remember owning a house key.

So maybe Smith with his unlocked door was a small-town guy like me, or maybe he had nothing he couldn't stand to lose.

My friend Eddie was like that—rich in material possessions—not like a celebrity, just a guy with nice things, but still a guy who figured it's only *stuff.* As if by opening his palm and saying, "Go on. Take it. It's yours," he relinquished control. If he got ripped off, he could feel good about it because it wasn't stolen, but offered. Hell, he could always buy more.

Was Smith like that? If he was the kind of man who put no stock in possessions—or possibly anything else—that would explain some things. Not all, but some. I had seen the signs before when I spoke to families of suicide victims, of confused teen runaways, of depressed jobless men and drug abusers.

And once I'd seen it in someone who made forever promises that were as airy as the clouds hanging over a three-bedroom fixer-upper on a dead-end street in Utica.

JUST GOOGLING AROUND UNTIL I NEED GLASSES

Chapter 8

James John Smith V had been doing a lot of thinking lately. It had nothing to do with the way his wife, Angel, had yelled, "You've got some thinking to do, Jimbo!" as she backed their brand-new BMW out of the customized garage and down the flagstone drive, flipping him the bird before she sped away.

The sound of her shifting the car from first gear right into third had made him yell, "You're gonna drop the gear box doing that!"

His words landed hard and heavy in the empty garage—a garage so clean you could eat off the floor. He pulled the string on his pajama bottoms and pissed in the Beemer's empty parking spot, smiling at the sizzling sound of urine meeting heated concrete. It was almost as pleasant a feeling as the day he'd dropped her little Pookie off at "the farm," aka the landfill two towns over. Fucker had squealed like a piglet the whole ride—a most annoying sound—even through two black plastic Hefty bags.

After a while, Jimbo got tired of the house—*her* house, *her* things, *her* presence, which was everywhere, even in her absence. So he went out, taking long walks to nowhere, sitting for hours practicing his stare. He had money, but it all belonged to her and he wasn't surprised when he returned home one afternoon to find the locks changed and his stuff jammed into his mother's old Chevy. It was the only thing the woman had left him, not counting the medical and funeral bills.

He banged on the door and yelled for Angel, pleading with her to forgive him, begging until he was hoarse, but she refused to open the door. She just said, "Go away, asshole, or I'm calling the cops."

Jimbo drew a drippy red heart on the front door of the house with a lipstick he found in the Chevy's glove box. Then he drove to the library, because that was one place in his shithole town where no one could ask him to leave.

Arranging himself in a computer carrel, Jimbo logged in and waited for the chirping welcome message. On the drive over, he'd come up with an incredible idea. He supposed with all those other people out there wondering, pondering, musing, and fantasizing, that someone else had already thought of his great idea. Somebody, somewhere might have already done it—surely somebody had written about it, made a movie even. There weren't any more unique ideas, not since Leary's psychedelic-induced high ideas of the sixties or Dr. Mengele. And even then, you could argue the point.

Jimbo might have burst a few brain cells hatching his plan. He hadn't come from a family of thinkers—or doers, for that matter. They were tall and pretty, which was usually enough in a material world. The common Smith moniker made life even easier, with no need to spell or correct or explain one's name.

His mother, Sandra Wykowski, had embraced the commonality of Smith, happily advancing a few letters in the alphabet when she married Big Jim. She moved to salads on the church rotation and out of desserts, leaving all those Polish jokes and cream pies behind.

The newly wedded Smiths bought a house in the suburbs and filled the rooms with plastic plants and overstuffed furniture, thinking that was what made a home. In a few years, when Sandra was fat, clumsy, and pregnant, it became an unbearable place for Big Jim. He tried to look past the big TV and the private yard, but saw only projects he could never finish, a long list of to-do's that he didn't remember writing. As Sandra sat crooning, stroking the growing bulge under her smock that would soon become their son, Big Jim escaped to the basement. He drilled holes in planks of wood, then sanded them smooth. If asked, he might say he was making a doghouse, a shed, or an entire miniature kitchen set, complete with working plumbing.

The baby, James John Smith V, was born in the spring of 1965. His name was proudly abbreviated on the hospital's plastic bassinet as "JJ #5." Another James John. The new heir to anything monogrammed: luggage, cigarette holders, desk sets, and mismatched pieces of silver serving ware.

Jimbo Five, his daddy started calling him when the nickname "Fifth" got too confusing— Sandra would hand him the baby when what Big Jim wanted was bourbon.

Bourbon. That was what killed him. Not cirrhosis of the liver or anything as invisible and lingering as that. No, James John IV went out the way he lived—loud, messy, and unprepared.

It was a cloudy Monday in 1971. Big Jim did all the things he normally did before leaving the Smith household. He kissed his son on the top of his head and planted one on his wife's cheek. He said, "Do something wonderful today, people."

As Big Jim walked out the door, Sandra murmured, "You bet I will," then wiped his kiss from her cheek with the back of her hand.

Jimbo ran to the window to watch his daddy drive away. He waved and waved but, like always, Daddy didn't wave back.

Big Jim pulled into his assigned parking spot at Smith Company. Most days at work were tough, as he was never sure what was expected of him or where he was supposed to be. He had a constant fear of being called into the boss's office (occupied by a second cousin), and being pegged an impostor. He was afraid they would admit their mistake in promoting him to head the department, that they'd find the last six months of work shoved in his bottom drawer instead of filed with corporate, like he'd told them. He was sure it was only a matter of time before they'd find the stacks of incomplete forms with bogus data, his reports ringed with coffee stains and smeared with ashes, the graphs drawn in crayon.

Big Jim had not slept well in months. He'd wake panting and sweating from nightmares where he was running naked through the office corridors as his coworkers pointed and laughed, not taunting his nudity, but his ineptness. "Jim doesn't know the difference between the CMP report and the CDP!" "Jim had to ask tech support to upload the ROD for him!" "Hey, Jim, what's your day to year plan on the ASTAP?"

He knew he should quit, but it was his grandfather's company, and as the sign on the wall continually reminded him: A SMITH NEVER QUITS. Instead, Big Jim left early most days and tried to avoid screwing anything up too bad.

Rushing out of the Smith Building at ten minutes before noon, Big Jim decided to skip the soup-and-sandwich part of lunch and go right to the liquid part, treating himself to a few cold ones at Ghilley's Pub, then a few warm ones. Eventually he forgot to eat at all.

Later, Big Jim walked out into the sunlight, feeling like the King of the Smiths. He had grand thoughts about his department—heck, the whole company—and couldn't wait to get back to the office to share them. He grinned as he pulled out in traffic, popping in his favorite Johnny Cash 8-track. He was imagining his name engraved on the coveted Employee of the Month plaque as he sped around the corner, tires squealing, belting one out with the Man in Black. He reached under his seat for a bottle of mouthwash and never saw the blinking yellow school zone warning lights, never heard the whistle of the crossing guard or the screams of the girls.

The impact forced the car left, and when Big Jim looked up all he saw was concrete. Even with two heavy feet on the brakes, the LeBaron was unstoppable. It accordioned itself into the wall like 3-D graffiti, except with the smoke and blood and the sound of Johnny singing about a boy named Sue, it was more like 4-D.

The cops came and the teachers cried, and when the paramedics couldn't pull Big Jim from behind the steering wheel they cut right through it and laid him on the stretcher with the shaft of the column protruding from his chest like a vampire's stake, his face frozen in bug-eyed wonder.

As the ambulance pulled away from Greenwood Elementary, the driver talked with his partner about what to order from the NY Deli—smoked ham sandwiches, no mayo—while the cops pulled sheets over two little girls in pigtails.

Most families would have moved. Most moms would have gotten counseling for their sons or at least offered comfort. But Sandra, now Sandy, thin and blonde, was too pleased with her new lease on life to care much about the little boy who woke up wet and screaming. The little boy who slept curled up in a ball at the foot of her bed, who rocked in front of the TV set and refused to eat anything but hot dogs—and only after she peeled off the skin and dipped them in ketchup. This same boy captured tiny green lizards, named them Jim, and sealed them in glass jars until they died, then lined up their dehydrated corpses on his bookshelf under picture books of sad puppies and fuzzy ducklings that no one loved.

Every month Sandra said, "This was the only good thing your father ever did," as she slit open the envelope from the insurance company and plucked out the check, waving it in the air. "The *only* good thing your father did."

"Except make me, right Mom?" Jimmy would ask.

Sandra looked at the little boy, who was just another Smith to her, and nodded slightly with watery eyes. "Right, kiddo. Except make you." Then she turned around before he made her too sad and tucked the check into her new purse. She primped in the mirror, smacked her lips to spread the red, then tied a silk scarf around her head.

"Don't want to mess up my hair. I just had it done," she said, patting her cotton-ball hair and pushing her sunglasses into place.

"You could put the top up, Mom."

But Sandy shook her head and sighed. "Jimbo, Jimbo. A lady needs to be seen to be noticed."

There were so many things Jimbo didn't understand. His mother was just one of them. He was baffled in the math department, had read that birds could puke but not burp, and had no idea why caterpillars would even bother turning into butterflies.

He didn't understand the men his mother brought home: the nerdy guy who challenged him in Atari, the guy with the perfect left-sided part and pressed shirt who called him "Little Buddy" whenever Mom was in the room and "Dumbshit Punk" when she wasn't. Jimbo sort of understood why he put the carpet tacks under Pressed Shirt's Porsche tires and why he added Syrup of Ipecac to the nerd's perfect Manhattan, but even those things didn't help him feel much better about his own mother.

She used to want peace, quiet, and a hot dinner. She used to be happy with a dress from Sears, a fresh coat of paint on the front door. Now she wanted diamonds, a house on a golf course, a four-car garage, friends with family estates in the Hamptons. She wanted to belong somewhere else, and seemed willing to do just about anything with just about anyone to get there. Jimbo might still be a little boy, but he understood liars. He understood manipulators, fakers, and bad, bad, people. They were *his* people, and he could smell them a mile away.

Jimbo unzipped his jacket and leaned back in the uncomfortable library chair. Apparently, his tax money had been enough to upgrade the computer monitors but not the furniture. He raised his arms and stretched, resisting the urge to sigh loudly. James John Smith V realized he'd spent the majority of his forty-three years attempting to understand the female sex. He'd read books on how they were uniquely wired, how they had different needs than men, that they wanted to feel desired and loved, and how important a gentle touch was to most women. He came up with a game plan, a course of action for each woman he encountered, one in which he identified, satisfied, and fulfilled their needs and desires. He became the missing link. Jimbo: The Completer.

He gave love. And he took everything that he could—their money, their pride, their humanity, their dignity, their purity, their confidence. Unlike in the real world, the one of bosses and paychecks and rules and regulations, in the world of women, Jimbo always got what he wanted. Sometimes it was power. Sometimes it was control. Sometimes it was just plain old sex. But always, it was a game. And he needed to win.

Jimbo figured this thing with his wife, Angel, was an anomaly. It might be his midlife crisis. But unlike other middle-aged men, he wouldn't be buying a sports car, having sex with prostitutes, or getting plugs of hair from his ass implanted on his forehead. He was going to change. He was going to make the next half of his life better—way better.

Because right now, he had shit. No kids—that he knew of—his wife hated him, and his only claim to anything was that he was still recognized as "The son of the guy that killed those precious little girls, God rest their souls."

At the table beside the computer carrel, a dirty homeless guy scribbled on scraps of paper then arranged them across its top like he was the General of Something Really Important on his way to fight a Nazi group of THEM.

Jimbo thought about the way the BMW had looked as Angel backed down the drive. It had been like the grille was grinning at him, smirking, calling him a loser.

The homeless guy rocked back and forth, mumbling, "Cocksucker, cocksucker, cocksucker."

Jimbo closed his eyes and saw his hands around the guy's scabby throat, saw him yanking the bastard across the demure insulating carpet, through the romance section, and out the back entrance, saw his hands slamming the worthless piece of shit into the steel door. He grinned, imagining the satisfying twang of homeless-crazy-person-cranium kissing metal.

The computer pinged. Jimbo leaned in as the monitor's blue screen changed to Internet green. Jimbo cracked his knuckles, then typed into the search box: *library evil stamped out, hero rewarded millions.* He hovered one finger over the enter key, then backspaced, deleting the words. He typed instead: *James John Smith.*

With the high-speed hookup, the page came back in .60 seconds with 172,000,000 hits. Jimbo smiled.

An hour later, he'd read about John Smith and Pocahontas—the real story—on a website that invited visitors to experience the pleasures of loin cloths and smoking huts on a chilly Friday in October, loin cloths optional. He skimmed the list of John Smiths and found a shoemaker, a gynecologist, an author of engineering books, a congressman, the president of Pfizer, and a sad little boy on a sadder-looking pony.

Then he narrowed the list even more by using constraints—because every game has rules, after all. Jimbo eliminated through those who didn't make at least $100,000 a year (tax records), had debilitating diseases (medical insurance claims), and those who'd had a run-in with the law (criminal records and background check, $9.95).

James John Smiths didn't make the list if they lived in an extremely cold climate or a non-English-speaking country, because Jimbo couldn't deal with either of those things.

He could afford to be picky. This was his life, after all—at least it would be.

He stopped by the bank and helped himself to some traveling cash before the wife cut him off. He made pit stops for a suitcase and some clothes, then dumped the Chevy and took a bus to the train station, buying a ticket before he could change his mind.

In the station café, he watched a chic blonde in a cashmere coat choose a seat by the window. She balanced a miniature pie and a large coffee on a too-small table.

Jimbo tossed his chin in her direction and winked. He liked women who ate dessert. It said something about them—as long as they didn't excuse themselves to go puke it up in the bathroom before the calories landed on their hips.

She looked away when he caught her eye. Jimbo knew the part she was playing. But who was he? A businessman afraid to fly? A journalist on assignment? A man hurrying to his lover's home on the coast?

He leaned against a dusty pillar, waiting for the train to begin boarding, his manner unhurried, seductive. He stirred his coffee with the striped straw, drew it to his mouth, all the while watching her face. There it was. She was filled with desire to touch him, to soothe and comfort him.

He angled his pelvis in her direction, feet planted wide, and sucked the straw dry.

She rolled her eyes, as if she'd already made the conclusion that he was lacking something she thought necessary, that he wouldn't be able to handle her, that he'd be the kind of man who said "sorry" all the time. She might have figured he slept in matching pajamas and ate alone in Chinese restaurants—never tipping more than 10 percent—or that he didn't check out library books but tucked them under his arm, took them home, and never read them, never returned them.

She might have seen in Jimbo none of the things she wanted and all of the things he would never be—successful, happy, respected, enough—for her. She held his gaze as she poked a fork into her tarte aux pommes and led it to her mouth, her pleasure as she chewed making it obvious she found the pie far more appealing than the man across the room.

Jimbo gave up the game. He knew her type. A money-hungry whore. A cunt with more shoes than brains. The kind of woman who'd hardly know good champagne from bad, who probably wouldn't understand the implications of an arsenic-laced pie until it was much too late.

On the train, in a crowded compartment, Jimbo's lips moved as he repeated "James." James Smith. James. As if he was auditioning for a Bond movie. He jammed the empty coffee cup into the space between the seats, then gazed across the car until his eyes landed on a classy older woman in pink. He almost got up to introduce himself, but stopped. What would he say? "Hi, I'm James John Smith. I've decided to swap out my old life for the life of another James John Smith. The life I was meant to have. How are you?"

He shook his head, thinking the whole thing would sound crazy, when the train lurched and a brunette fell into his lap.

"Well, hello there," James said in a voice he hardly recognized as his own.

WHO ARE YOU?

Chapter 9

Six months ago, when Angel backed her BMW down the driveway and left Jimbo standing in his pajamas in their garage, she never thought he'd pull the stunt he did. Never thought he'd have the balls to actually leave her. Who the fuck *did* that?

She'd handled it fine in the beginning, too pissed off to think about where he was or who he might be with. She told herself she didn't care, and a few weeks later, when she started to miss him, started to go soft, she upped her workload, took on as many tasks as she could, planned her days down to the minute so that she had absolutely no space for anything Jimbo.

Maybe it was the sappy movie she'd watched, or the ridiculously unbelievable novel she'd read, but one morning she woke up and knew one thing for certain: she wanted her husband back, and wasn't taking no for an answer.

Instead of packing and leaving for her week-long vacation, Angel drove to Erica's house—a woman who'd traded a life of corporate ladder climbing for an equally messy life as a parent and homemaker. They'd been friends for eight years and Angel had never once called before dropping in.

She pulled into Erica's driveway around the empty trashcan, stopping just short of a bicycle lying in front of the garage. She made her way to the front door, stepping over popsicle wrappers, a soda can, and a mashed pile of sidewalk chalk that had been left out in the rain.

She didn't bother ringing the doorbell. It hadn't worked

since last spring. She put her shoulder to the sticky door and pushed.

"Hello?" Angel called, stepping inside and closing the door behind her. The sound of a TV droned in the background. A dog barked, but it may have been the neighbors'—she didn't think Erica had a dog.

"Erica?" Angel stepped over a dumped bucket of Legos and a smashed pizza box. Clothes were piled on the sofa. Toys littered the floor. Papers, catalogs, and mail were stacked on every flat surface. If she hadn't seen Erica's house before, she might think her friend had been kidnapped, skirted away while in the middle of a major housecleaning, a room-by-room overhaul. When in reality this was how the family lived every day.

It made Angel nervous, all that stuff everywhere. The idea that you'd have to deal with it again and again, instead of just one time. She thought sloppy people made their lives so much harder.

Erica came around the corner, phone jammed to her ear. She still had one of those phones on cords, the kind that attach to the wall. Angel thought it might even have a rotary dial.

When she'd met Erica at a local wine tasting, she thought they had a lot in common. They were both wearing Chanel, and Angel could actually envision herself borrowing Erica's shoes. They were that nice. The husbands got along—as well as husbands do when forced into social situations they'd never have chosen for themselves. Angel allowed herself a "suburban housewife moment," one in which she bonded instantly with the new couple, invited them over on Sunday afternoon for brunch and a game of Scrabble. They'd sip cabernet and discuss recent travels abroad, share their love of art while jazz played softly in the background. Angel would be pregnant when her friend was pregnant and they'd be each other's doula. She'd be happy with her confidant, beautiful woman-friend. Someone who understood her, a woman who could shop in the same departments at Saks and wouldn't blink when the bill came.

It was weeks before Angel found out Erica had been dressed by her sister-in-law—a woman who worked in a bank and had lots of letters after her name that meant something really important to people who knew about things like that.

The real Erica thought a put-together outfit was two pieces of clothing—regardless of shape, style, or texture—but of the same color, preferably black, or jeans and a rock-and-roll T-shirt.

Angel forgave her this fashion infraction, because Erica was a great listener. She was interesting, and the woman made the best martinis.

Some things were forgivable—never a bad martini.

"Holy crap," Erica said, hanging up the phone after untwisting herself from the long, mangled cord. "Sears must be outsourcing to Kentucky for their customer service reps. I felt like I was talking to Jeff Foxworthy's mother."

Angel laughed as Erica went off on a you-might-be-a-redneck riff, starting with the jab that the broad had probably spent more money on her pickup truck than her education.

"Yeah," Angel said. "She probably thinks genitalia is an Italian airline."

Erica laughed, a deep chortle. "Oh, I've got to write that one down. Come on in. I've got Kahlúa. Oh, yeah. I've got coffee too."

In the kitchen, Erica served coffee in chipped mugs, then slid into the seat across from Angel. Pushing the bottle of Kahlúa in her direction, she said, "Should I ask?"

Angel shrugged.

"I'm going to ask. Why are you here instead of heading to the beach?"

Angel took a sip of laced coffee. "I know. Vacation. Woo-hoo. It's just that . . ." she sighed. "He's an asshole."

"I'll drink to that," Erica said, raising her cup. "Oh, wait. We are talking about Jimbo, right?"

Angel nodded.

"Well, honey. Hate to tell you, but that's nothing new. I've been telling you that for months."

"I know," Angel said. "But maybe I'm *supposed* to be with an asshole."

Erica laughed. "He might be an asshole, but he's *your* asshole? Is that what I'm hearing?"

Angel nodded and added more Kahlúa to her coffee cup. "I love him. I'm going to find him and bring him home. Bring him to his senses."

"First of all, you're assuming the man *has* senses. Second, I'd love to help, but the hubs is out of town and I've got the kids—all of them. Though they do love a good car ride."

"Oh, no. I couldn't impose," Angel said, getting sweaty palms just thinking about being surrounded by all those sticky hands, all those poopy diapers, all that screaming and whining. "I'll figure it out."

A loud thump came from upstairs, followed by the wailing of a child.

"Damn kid fell out of the bed again," Erica said, reaching for the Kahlúa.

"I'd better go, so you can, you know," Angel said, watching her friend down the drink then rub her hands over her face.

Driving down Pacific Avenue, past the Mom-and-Pop beach motels—flea joint throwbacks from the sixties—

Angel wasn't at all surprised when she pulled up in front of The Cavalier, as if her car had been on autopilot, bringing her home.

The hotel reeked of old Virginia money tainted with the perfume of nouveau riche. The Cavalier had been around since 1927, earning iconic status with visits from celebrities, politicians, and Presidents in every decade. Angel's daddy ran the place and her mother had practically done the recent multimillion dollar remodel herself—at least that's what one would surmise if they spent an hour with the woman.

The valet called Angel by name as he opened her door. The girls at the front desk had a key in her hand before she was halfway across the lobby, and the concierge rode up in the elevator with her, making a list of clothes and toiletries she'd need, noting his boss's daughter had arrived sans luggage.

Alone in the room, Angel pulled out her phone and made a list of the places she thought her husband might be, and with whom. She called her father and left a message that she needed to see him. Needed his help. His assistant arranged a meeting, then suggested she pass the time with a complimentary massage—she'd send a masseur to the room.

Angel didn't argue.

When the man arrived and set up his table in the sitting room, she told him she didn't want to engage in any idle chatter. She'd hold up a hand if the pressure was too much, and that would be it. The man nodded and turned away as Angel disrobed and climbed on the table, slipping under the cool sheet.

Lying there with a stranger's hands giving her more love than she'd felt at home in over a year, Angel thought about the couple she'd seen from her balcony in a disgustingly sweet moment, a young man and a woman in love—holding hands, swinging their arms, laughing, stopping to kiss—the way it seemed like they'd just rolled out of bed, and were ready to roll back in. Usually, Angel would have written off a scene like that with a snide comment, "Ain't love grand? Yeah, until *she* gets fat, and *he* starts to drink."

But on this day, she felt something different well up. She felt desire, and regret. She wanted what they had. She wanted love.

"That's enough," she told the masseur.

"But I am not done, Miss Angel."

"That's all I need from you."

"Are you certain? I could . . ."

By the way he said it, she knew he could. She hesitated, part of her wanting to say yes, roll over, and open the sheet to him. But she waved him off, waited for him to leave and close the door behind him.

There was no sense putting it off any longer. Angel was going to get her man back.

TEDESCO THINKS STANDING IN SOMEONE'S KITCHEN IS BETTER THAN WALKING A MILE IN THEIR SHOES

Chapter 10

Smith's apartment was sparsely furnished—not like the guy didn't care about what he had around him, but like he hadn't had time to shop.

I stood in the front room, a combination of living, dining, and kitchen areas. It was clean enough and relatively organized, but not overly so—as if he had something to hide. There were a few lame decorating attempts: a landscape painting over the couch; fat, dusty candles that ran the length of the coffee table; and a blank beer distributor's calendar on the fridge.

The emptiness didn't bother me. I'd been in houses where there was more floor than furniture. I liked the feel of it, though I wouldn't call myself modern by any means, it just felt better to me than the cloying, packed rooms I grew up in, where every wall had a mandatory picture or shelf of trinkets and every chair had arm covers and a matching pillow, even if it ended up on the floor more often than behind one's back.

A few years ago, I had been on an educational ride-along in Buffalo with a cop pal, Drake. We answered a domestic disturbance call, and when he had opened the door there was a distinct echo. The house was at least seven thousand square feet and three levels, (I paced it out while Drake calmed down the angry wife in the voluminous kitchen), but the total amount of furniture would have fit in my single-car garage.

The man of the house was laying on a stack of mattresses in the great room, yelling, "She ain't taking the fucking bed! She's already got the car. She ain't taking the bed!"

Drake said, "Sir, you have five mattresses there. Why don't you give her one? You don't even have to give her the best one. Come on, what do you say?"

By the time I got back from my tour of the terrace level, also empty except for a well-stocked bar and assorted pink-and-blue inflatable furniture in the theater room, Drake had dragged one of the mattresses to the front hall and was using it to keep the battling spouses apart.

Drake talked to the guy like he was two years old. "Nadine is leaving now, and she wants to say she's sorry. Don't you, Nadine?"

The woman looked like she was going to shoot fire from her eyeballs, burn a hole right through the mattress and into her loving spouse. But she gritted her teeth and said, "I'm sorry."

"See?" Drake said motioning to me while pushing Nadine and the mattress out the door. "She's sorry. Now she's leaving. You need to get some rest. Don't make me come back out here, okay?"

I looked back to see the man sitting on his tower of mattresses, tears in his eyes. "Oh, she's sorry, all right. She's a sorry piece of shit who'll rip your heart out and stomp on it! She'll sell everything you own and blame you when your company shuts down and moves its plant to Costa Rica—like that was my fucking fault! I got nothing left, Nadine!"

I shut the door, but could still hear him howling, "I got nothing. Nothing!"

I didn't know for certain that there was a Nadine in Smith's past, but he didn't have much life baggage from the looks of things. He either traveled light by choice or circumstance.

I pulled open a few drawers in the kitchen: ordinary silverware, a black bar corkscrew, a paper sleeve of chopsticks from the Chinese takeout place on the corner. It could have been my own kitchen. I was beginning to think of James John Smith as a friend, an old college roommate who'd let me crash at his place, then up and died, kind of like in *The Big Chill*, except I wasn't here to mourn his passing or bone up for the eulogy.

Most folks say what they will about a man while he's alive, but few people have the balls to speak ill of the dead. Except my ex-girlfriend, Kitty. I remembered our second date, when she'd stood in St. Mary Magdalene, Church of Lost Dogs and Loose Change, and told the entire congregation that she was sure her father was burning in hell. That he was a no-good, gambling, child-abusing alcoholic, who didn't deserve a funeral or a grave and certainly not this fancy coffin, and maybe she ought to save her dear mama a few dollars and get started on the cremation part right now.

The priest paled as Kitty reached for the sacrificial candle.

I had been reminded of the time I'd marched with protesters at the Right to Light Streetlamps Rally and a guy with an overgrown 'fro in front of me lit his hair on fire by mistake. One glance at Daddy's crappy toupee held in place by so much hair spray, I knew I had to do something. I snatched the wine carafe from the stuttering altar boy, made a trade with Kitty, then led her back to the priest's chambers, where she decided after drinking the blessed wine that getting laid would make her feel better than burning Daddy. Who was I to refuse?

Pushing the images of naked Kitty on the priest's cot and burning corpses out of my mind, I headed for the bedroom.

It was a good-size room with plain walls. It felt like a room I'd sleep in, done in browns and tans, with a wood floor. I knew there hadn't been a woman doing the decorating, as the bed was draped in a simple tweed comforter and held only two pillows.

I stood at the curtainless window and appreciated the view. A small green space over the neighbor's fence was about as rural as it got downtown, not counting the occasional rooftop garden or grass-topped building—some idiotic attempt to overthrow global warming or provide bird food—I wasn't sure which.

I scanned the room, zeroing in on the dresser. A small wooden box next to the lamp held a serpentine silver chain, a well-worn raffia-and-shell bracelet, and thirty-nine cents. Beside this, I saw a mark in the dust that looked like the shape of a cell phone. The bottom drawers held the usual assortment of jeans, T-shirts, and sweatpants—all from local department stores, all size large.

I saved the best for last—top left, underwear. I tugged the drawer out of the dresser and set it on the bed.

He was a boxer man, our Mr. Smith. I could appreciate that. Giving the boys a bit of room was always a good thing. A beer-cap keychain with three keys was in the front right corner, as were three condoms with an expiration date six months away, and a gold wedding band. I replaced the ring under the stack of boxers, but put the keys and condoms in my pocket. You never know.

Smith had a few pairs of dress socks with the tags still on them stuffed in the back and one pair of tube socks—they looked too bulky. I shook them open. A cassette tape fell out, the small ones that go in hand held recorders.

It wasn't labeled, but I could see where a sticker had been. I put the drawer back, then went out to the living room to look for the stereo when my cell phone rang.

It was Tommy. "Tedesco, you almost done there?"

"I could be," I said glancing at the cassette in my hand. "Why, what's up?'

"I want to run some things by you. And also, I have some questions about Buffy and her kid. I saw some of her work."

"Whose work?"

"Chamonix's. It's . . . let's say . . . *unusual.*"

"What does that mean?'

"It means I'm wondering about mental illness in that family, but hey, let's talk about it when you get here. I'm at My Place."

"Your place, or *My Place?*"

"Don't go getting all Abbott and Costello on me, Tedesco. I'm at Francie's."

WHERE, OH WHERE COULD YOU BE?

Chapter 11

Angel had sat beside her husband on the couch for years watching old detective movies, those black-and-whites that Jimbo loved. She knew how they did things back then, how they would follow the bad guy's sedan down empty streets, how they eavesdropped on conversations in hotel lobbies while hiding behind newspapers. But none of that was going to work for her. She couldn't follow a car she couldn't find, and she didn't remember the last time she'd seen or read a real newspaper. She was going to need to take this to the next level.

Angel knew her father was her only chance. If Daddy couldn't fix this, then Marshall Todd could. Daddy always said that a wise person surrounds himself with even wiser people, people who know things normal folks don't and who know how to keep a secret. Marshall Todd was one of those people. Angel had heard unbelievable stories about the man's life before he came to work for her father, and after meeting him, she was pretty sure they were all true.

He ushered her into the office and motioned to a chair in front of her daddy's imported rainforest-wood desk.

Her father almost looked up from the stack of papers when he said, "Speak to me."

Angel knew the drill. You had twenty seconds to make your point, or at the very least to intrigue your listener to get the chance to further make your point. Twenty-one seconds, the deal was dead. And sometimes, so were you.

She said, "It's—"

"Smith. We know." He touched his ear where the Bluetooth headset was permanently attached, then pointed to Marshall and swirled a finger in the air.

Marshall crossed the room and pressed a series of buttons on the wall panel. "White noise engaged, sir."

Angel was a little impressed. It was hard not to be. She liked all that spy crap, thought it was sexy, and here she was, about to step into it full-on to find her husband.

"One question," her father said, scrolling his eyes down one of the computer monitors on his desk.

"Yes?"

"Do you really want him back?"

Angel waited until her father looked up. "Yes. But on my terms this time."

Her father raised a brow, then shot a look toward Marshall. "You were right. Plan B it is."

He turned back to Angel, offering his version of a smile, more smirk than grin. "Marshall's already working on it from the list you gave him. A few details we were able to . . . ascertain. Give him another hour and he'll be ready to leave."

"No, Daddy. I want to do this myself. I just need a few things."

As Angel drove away from Virginia Beach, she clicked on the navigation system, noting the red dots on the screen. Her plan was to take them in order, with the first stop being an ex-girlfriend's apartment. A girlfriend Jimbo tried to hide from Daddy for years, but in the way Jimbo did everything half-assed, with his own needs put first; the trail from Internet conversations to phone texts and calls to lingerie store receipts had been pathetically obvious. Angel knew the girl was nothing special, not bright enough to cause any problems, and from her medical charts—Thanks, Marshall—an unwanted pregnancy wouldn't be an issue.

If anyone had asked why she never did anything before, Angel would have said that she figured her husband would lose interest soon enough and move onto the next conquest. She would have said that she didn't really mind, she knew there were worse vices a man could have. And that was true. What she did mind was feeling like she was being taken advantage of, feeling like she was getting duped.

Angel didn't like being on the short end of anything, especially if it appeared that another *woman* was pulling the strings.

She touched the navigation screen, selected Fastest Route, and said, "Bring it on, bitch," as she accelerated down the highway.

BUFFY-NOW-BARBARA WONDERS IF GOD'S IN THE RETAILS

Chapter 12

Barbara took the long way to the mall, avoiding downtown and Flannigan's. She wasn't sure she'd ever be able to go there again. Earlier she'd decided that since she didn't have any plans and her husband wasn't answering his phone, so there was only one thing to do. Shop. When she was younger and struggling paycheck to paycheck, the mall only reminded her of all the things she wanted but couldn't have. Now that she was older and had a little money, shopping was her social outlet.

Over the years, she'd learned how to use the window displays as ideas for her own wardrobe combinations and how to dress if she wanted the girls at the cologne counter to stop spritzing in her general direction and actually sell her something. She knew the difference between shopping in workout wear and shopping in a suit with your hair pinned up and in full makeup even if your eyes were hidden behind dark Chanel shades.

While perusing silk scarves and lounging pajamas, cocktail dresses and cashmere wraps, Barbara convinced herself that Chamonix was in a better place, that she had not suffered in her death, but been swept up in an angel's arms and gently floated through the pearly gates.

Though Barbara hadn't been to church in a long time, she was pretty sure they were still calling Heaven's doors "The Pearly Gates." Unless the Pope had become as politically correct as the rest of the people and now used the term "Equal Opportunity Entry."

She thought about the unfairness of a life cut brutally short, about young women who'd never grow old, never complete the tasks they were put on earth to do. Barbara hardly knew the North Carolina girl, Cress, but surely she had been as special as Chamonix and Roxie. If only the good die young, then why was Smith dead too? How was that fucking fair?

Right there, in the crowded shoe department of Neiman Marcus, Barbara Leonard started crying, dripping tears onto a very expensive alligator pump and drawing stares.

"Are you all right, dear?" an older woman in a mauve sweater set asked.

Barbara cried louder.

The woman patted Barbara's back, waved away the nervous clerk, and made shushing, soothing sounds as Barbara murmured, "I'm sorry. Sorry, sorry, sorry."

The woman said, "There, there," like a kind stranger in a fairy tale talking to a lost child in the woods. She handed Barbara a tissue, but when the crying didn't abate she slipped a small oval pill into Barbara's palm and closed her fingers around it.

Barbara looked up to see mirrored pain in the woman's eyes, laced with understanding.

The woman smiled. "Try one, sweetheart, it works for me."

Barbara watched the woman walk away, then blew her nose, swallowed the pill, and bought the alligator pumps with a matching handbag, thinking that's what Chamonix would have wanted.

Barbara wished she was as sure of herself as her daughter had always been—or even half as determined or comfortable with her life's choices.

There was never a moment in her youthful incarnation as Buffy that Barbara had felt absolutely positive she was doing the right thing. Even on bubble tests, she'd mark A, then change it to C, then see a pattern of dots on the paper and erase all the B's. Her tests were a disaster. Labeled an "anxious tester," she earned the right to take exams in a quiet room off the library, a room that was seldom monitored, allowing her to cheat her way through algebra, science, and two years of German.

It wasn't that she was stupid. She was just easily distracted. In her senior year, the distractions were boys. Boys on the football team. Boys on the baseball team. Boys in ski club and theater. Boys who played in garage bands and skipped school and hung out on the smoker's path, and even smart boys who knew all the answers in biology class and weren't afraid to slice the dead cat splaying its legs wide and removing the organs one by one.

Boys were everywhere. Lounging at her locker, waiting in the cafeteria to queue up behind her. A group of them fought each afternoon for the honor of walking her home. Buffy figured it was the same for everyone and was surprised to learn during a girl's birthday sleepover most of the girls had an entirely different view of boys. Odder still, the boys they wanted to get close to weren't even on Buffy's radar.

She couldn't figure it out. She didn't even know if she wanted to. Everything seemed so complicated at the time. The trauma of teenage years where you truly believe you're the only one in the whole world who's ever felt some way, done some thing, or had that much bad luck. Drama and angst, blended with love-struck joy and thrills of first time everythings.

As tough as those years were, and as glad as Barbara had felt to leave them behind her, she knew now those troubles were blessedly simple.

Therapy helped her understand she'd made the best choices with the knowledge she'd had at the time, but it was still hard for her to sit in the shrink's office and admit past mistakes. From stealing to dating married men, to the abortion "for medical reasons." Most days, if it came right down to it, Buffy-Barbara felt like a goddamned failure, except for the day she'd given birth to Chamonix.

Barbara could wish all she wanted that she'd led a life that was kinder and more giving, that she'd recycled, donated, and volunteered more. She could wish she'd been the kind of person who went to church regularly. Maybe that was what was missing. Though it was easy to suck up to God now that her only kid was dead and her marriage was falling apart.

Buffy-as-the-new-Barbara figured God probably hated mercy-seeking cop-outs, those losers who used faith as a last-ditch effort to make up for a lifelong list of fuck-ups. He probably put people like that at the end of His salvation list.

CHAMONIX. SAY IT THE FRENCH WAY.

Chapter 13

She was young by most people's standards, if numbers could tell everything about someone's life. But the way her heart felt cracked and empty, the way her soul ached on cloudy Wednesdays in June, made Chamonix old in every other sense.

After high school, she ran to college and kept running, blazing a trail across the campus. From the volunteer center to the Olympic-size track, from the sorority houses to the library and art studio and back to her dorm by way of the frat houses. She lived as if experience—in whatever form—would expand her, increasing the single space she'd been allotted in the world to a space for three.

Chamonix's roommate, Jolie, liked to say that Chamonix grabbed life by the mane, squeezed her thighs around it, and rode it until it was sweaty and spent. But that was the way Jolie talked about everything—sexually.

Back up. There's the guy. There's always a guy, isn't there? The same one who's in the picture when "love you" is offered up as a question and the "I" is nowhere around.

The guy was Jolie's big brother in the fraternity, a sweet boy with a tough-man look, the kind of man-child Chamonix thought might challenge her, or if her parents were right, tame her.

After their first date, a cafeteria dinner followed by a movie at the dollar theater, she wrote, "It's the beginning of my new beginning. I'm going to be good now," in her black journal—the one she hid when Daddy visited, not wanting to know what he would think of his baby if he knew what his baby was thinking.

But the one date didn't lead to more. By spring, Jolie and the frat brother man-child had hooked up and moved off campus, leaving Chamonix alone in a dorm room that used to feel small. She immersed herself in obscure classes. Her favorite was an art history lecture called Images of Women in Western Art. There wasn't an instructor, just a video that ran and ran in an auditorium where a naked mannequin in a cowboy hat leaned against the podium.

Chamonix realized there was no reason to be good anymore.

She started sleeping around, on campus and off. She held little respect for men—or anyone for that manner—and grew tired of dates that ended in silly games of "Just the tip," and "I promise to pull out." She hated that she frequently traded a lay for a dinner and hated how most men thought there was absolutely nothing wrong with that.

Chamonix yearned for a relationship with the kind of man she read about in books or saw in foreign films. Strong, confident, independent, passionate men. She figured she was fantasizing some reality she'd never know and blamed it on artistic preferences. She'd been spending most Sundays at the art museum on a bench in front of Tissot's *The Artist's Ladies*, praying that she'd dissolve into it and become one of the mysterious women at the white linen-draped tables, a woman who men would tip their top hats to.

Some nights she begged God—if there was one—to let her die so she could jump into another soul—because if there was a God, then surely there were souls. And she wanted, if only for a moment, to see what someone else's life was like, to know if they also suffered from feelings of inadequate deportment.

With the melodramatic cloak she managed to drape over everything, Chamonix might have been a great actress, but she had trouble memorizing lines and following direction. The one frat house play she'd been in was never performed the same way twice, as Chamonix kept changing her character, showing up one night as a French magician and the next as Pippi Longstocking. She was a gifted mimic, aware of her audience, and knew that if things took a dark turn or something hit too close to home, she could always pull back, turn the joke on herself, sacrificing Chamonix over and over to make people laugh.

No one was surprised when she dropped out of school—least of all her parents. But when she waited a month to tell them she'd turned in her ticket to Paris, where art school waited, for a one-way bus pass to Seattle and the first month's rent on a loft in the arts district, a flag was raised.

They gave her space to find herself and waited, credit card in hand, secretly hoping their daughter would fail and return home to them.

Chamonix took a job at a gallery as an assistant to the assistant. She pierced her nose and dyed her hair different colors every week, but kept old pictures of herself looking as innocent as a freshman at an all-girls' school to send to her parents twice a year. She dressed in mismatched clothes from thrift stores and garage sales, with the fashion sense and attitude that made ugly look good.

She threw theme parties at the loft, which she shared with half of an ex-grunge band —pajama night, beach blanket bingo, come as your favorite carnivore—and invited everyone from the gallery.

When her boss, Guy, drunk and draped in a tiger pelt, knocked over Chamonix's easel and saw her latest painting—one ruined when she'd cut herself with the canvas knife and splattered blood across the pristine landscape, he said, "Sweetheart! Why have you been keeping this from me?" Followed by, "I love it. Do you have more?"

It wasn't as easy as it seemed. To keep painting with blood meant you had to keep bleeding. Chamonix, though never a squeamish girl, was beginning to get a bit apprehensive every time she sat down with a knife in one hand and her own flesh in the other. There were only so many places you could cut without leaving scars, only so much you could take before growing anemic, and she certainly didn't want to get a rep of being a "cutter."

She tried painting with cow's blood from the butcher mixed with an oxidizer to maintain its reddish hue, but it was too thick and the rank smell choked her. She brought home a guinea pig from the pet shop, but it squeaked pitifully when she grabbed it so she ended up giving it to one of her roommates for his birthday.

The first time she asked a date to play rough, he was cool with it. The second time, she cut too deep, collecting more pints than the Red Cross normally allowed. When he almost died, she figured at least she wouldn't have to do that again for a long, long time. A thought that oddly depressed her.

Guy acted as her agent and her encouragement, telling her how important her work was. Pressing her to think bigger, do more. He gave her uppers and hooked her on energy drinks. He sent Wiccans to clear the negative energy in her studio when she was blocked. He took her to a hypnotist the one time she professed she'd like to try painting serious portraiture.

"The world needs your work," he told her. "I need you," he said, dollar signs in his eyes.

But the words were the right words.

Chamonix needed to be needed.

Guy said that people who bought art bought stories. They wanted to hear about the vegan artist who only wore blue, the one who collected frogs, the sculptor who lived in an old bomb shelter. There was a perceived romanticism surrounding the soul of the artist, something ordinary people believed unachievable. Something paranormal.

When Guy began a new client's campaign, he usually had to recreate them. The Jewish good-boy sculptor from Brooklyn became a troubled dyslexic from a broken home in Chicago who'd been living in a dilapidated cardboard box in the shadow of Oprah Winfrey's high rise before Guy discovered him.

Guy knew how to take someone from humble beginnings—the second son of a Poughkeepsie metalworker—and transform him into a misunderstood, genderless, passionate soul depressed by the industrialism of the new America, an artist who yearned to bring life to a dying art while carrying on the grand traditions of his heritage by welding confiscated airport nail files, corkscrews, and pocketknives into warriors battling giant insects. An artist who could now ask twenty times the going rate for airport art, and appear on both Letterman and CNN.

Chamonix hardly needed Guy's help. They simply mounted her name and photograph on the wall next to her paintings.

Her work sold better than the imported stuff, better than big local names—better than anyone expected. The people who bought her paintings said they understood where she was going and what she was saying. Some said they could hear her scream. They said they felt something—a pulsing life force. Chamonix never told them how close they were to the truth, and she was certain to always seal the paintings with coats and coats of polyurethane.

Enjoying all the liberties of a successful artist,

Chamonix moved a lot, finally making it to Europe. She kept in touch with her parents in Syracuse, sending them expensive gifts from abroad, inviting them places she knew they'd never go. She shipped her paintings to the Seattle gallery. Guy took care of all the business details, leaving Chamonix alone to create.

Too much freedom can be a bad thing. It can lead to thinking and plotting, cataloguing and sorting. With too many choices and the time to explore each one, freedom became a noise in Chamonix's head she needed to silence.

There was only one way to quiet the panic. Fill canvases. And for that, she needed blood.

In Philadelphia, Chamonix had created alter egos with intricate backstories, usually giving herself names that ended in *y* because those girls were always the cutest in high school, always the most innocent.

She'd choose the bar in the daylight, never going in, never talking to anyone. It might take a few visits, but sometimes she could feel it at the first pass. Something about the light when the door opened, the strain of music that filtered out. If it felt like misery, it felt right.

Once, after a ride into the city and after she'd stashed her bike in an alley, after she'd changed her jacket and tugged on a curly brown wig, Chamonix found herself standing outside a dingy South Philly bar. A man brushed her sleeve as he passed. He didn't say anything, just opened the door to the bar and disappeared inside, but she knew. This was the place. He was the one. Just like that.

She could tell he was the type of guy who needed a drink before heading home, his idea of wrapping up the day. She walked around the block and was waiting fifteen minutes later when he came out. He looked less tense—his wrinkled forehead relaxed, his cheeks flushed, tie hanging loose around his neck.

Chamonix let him go a few steps, then called after him. "Hey!"

The guy glanced back but kept walking.

"Hey!"

The man stopped and turned around.

She bent to the sidewalk to place, then pick up, a palmed hundred-dollar bill, then dangled the money. "I think you dropped this."

He was about to shrug her off and keep walking until he looked a little closer. She might have reminded him of a drawing on an animator's board, some artist's version of feminine perfection in her shiny black jacket and tight pants, except the footwear was wrong.

When Chamonix put her hand on her hip and smiled, he smiled back. He might have been thinking about the whiskey the cash would buy, or how having a young lady like this across the table might help him forget what was waiting for him at home. He stepped toward Chamonix, patting the rear pocket where his wallet was, then shoving a hand into the front empty one, adding a hint of surprise to his face when he caught her eye.

"You're right. I think that might be mine."

Chamonix winked and handed him the bill, then waited as he held open the door to the bar.

Four hours later he said he really, really had to get going. It had been great fun and all that but, shit, he had an important meeting in the morning and, Christ, was it really that late?

As they stepped outside into the rain, Chamonix smiled.

Perfect. Just as forecasted.

She said, "Yeah. You gotta go. Me too."

He started to walk away, then a tiny part of his nice-guy brain kicked in and he looked around. "Hey, do you need me to . . . I mean, it's not the safest neighborhood, you know."

Chamonix smiled. “That would be nice. I’m just around the corner.”

Giggling and tripping, acting more drunk than she was, she grabbed his arm to steady herself and a moment later pulled him into the alley.

“Whoa. Hey there,” he said as Chamonix pressed up against him. He stuttered like a ten-year-old forced to stand next to the cutest girl in fifth grade and recite the Pledge of Allegiance over a school loudspeaker.

“If . . . if you want to we could, you know . . . we could get a room.”

Chamonix kissed him hard, sticking her mouth on his and sealing off his air. He went weak in the knees and she pulled back. He opened his eyes, dazed.

She whispered, “I don’t think so,” then jabbed the syringe into his neck.

The bags in the satchel filled fast as the jugular vein released two of the body’s ten pints of blood so quickly that the man convulsed, slipping into hemorrhagic and then hypovolemic shock. Chamonix removed the cattle syringe and pressed a gloved finger on the puncture wound. The last bit of blood ran out the back of the syringe and through the tubing to the sterile bags in the satchel. She eased the man to the ground, capped and stowed her tools, then jogged to the other end of the alley where she’d hidden her bike behind a Dumpster.

Chamonix was thirteen miles away, riding in the rain, adrenaline pumping almost as fast as her legs, when twenty-year-old Sarah McClaren stepped into the alley to puke up five beers and three shots of tequila, and stumbled over the victim.

WHEN MY PLACE ISN'T MINE. OR YOURS.

Chapter 14

Tommy was sitting at a table in the back when I walked into My Place. The décor had changed again. In the last two years it had gone from sixties cool to shabby-chic retro, and now it felt like a tropical beach scene.

I sunk into a wicker chair across from him and said, "Before you start talking, I need to eat. I'm starving."

"I know. I already ordered." He pulled napkins off identical sandwich plates and pushed one toward me. It was like having the wife order lunch, only Tommy always remembered what I liked.

"How's everything?" I asked, trying to be expeditious while appearing as if I cared.

Tommy shrugged. "It's okay."

I swallowed a bite of the turkey BLT, and asked, "Who's the guy?"

Tommy looked at me. "You really want to know?"

I lied. "Of course."

He told me about the new love interest, a guy who was kind to animals and his mother, someone who had the same taste in music, who finished his sentences, a guy who might be *the one*.

I nodded as if I'd been listening. "What does he do?"

"He studies the triangle of affinity, reality, and communication on the bridge to total freedom."

"What?"

"He's a Scientology counselor. An auditor. He's really good at it."

I tried to hold back but the laugh escaped, in the form of a bray or maybe more of a guffaw. I've never been known for my polite titter. My outburst earned me a headshake and sigh from Tommy and a glare from Francie behind the bar.

This was pretty much her business. She didn't own My Place, but ruled it—had since Randall got sick. Apparently he was barely hanging on. No one believed Francie's stories of tango dancing at midnight and long weekends in Paris. Randall was dying in their bed at the B and B in Elmira—not that it was an operating B and B at the moment. There aren't many people who'd consider a vacation in the countryside with a man dying in the bed upstairs a proper getaway.

Francie sipped her drink through a twisted pink party straw while turning the pages of a glossy magazine with her enormous hand. She hadn't been a feminine male, and the lady part was hard for her. Maybe Francie had been Frank too long. I still saw her as the boy in the plaid pants who got shoved around a lot in elementary school. That was the problem with never leaving your hometown. Your past was right in front of you.

I held up my empty glass. She raised a perfectly waxed brow and gave me the finger.

I looked at Tommy and said, "How many Scientologists does it take to change a lightbulb?"

Tommy sighed.

"Come on," I said.

He looked away, lips pursed in a thin line, jaw clenched. Finally he said, "I don't know. How many?"

"None," I said. "The lightbulb must find eighty thousand dollars to become clear, then it will have the self-determinism to change itself."

Francie arrived in time for the punch line. She gave me a smile, placed another ginger ale in front of me, and was still chuckling as she lumbered away.

Tommy didn't find it amusing. "Honestly? I think Buck's only into it because of Tom Cruise."

I thought he was kidding, but I saw tears in his eyes and wondered how much this guy Buck was going to break Tommy's heart and where the shithead lived so I could pay his *Dianetics*-loving ass a not-so-cordial visit.

"Hey, look. I'm sorry I joked about it, okay? It takes all kinds, right?"

Tommy wiped his eyes, sat up taller, and said, "Yeah. All kinds. Look at you."

"Me? What's the matter with me?"

Tommy smiled.

"All right. All right." I held up my hands to ward off the verbal blows I knew I had coming. "Let's get back to the important stuff."

Tommy said, "I thought we weren't going to talk about me anymore."

"Cute. I'm talking about the case."

"And Bu-uh-ffy." Tommy sang like a taunting second-grader.

I stopped him before he went on to "the k-i-s-s-i-n-g song."

"She goes by Barbara now."

"How's she look? Did she . . . ?" Tommy made an expansive gesture around his torso and puffed out his cheeks.

"No," I said. "She didn't. She looks beautiful, despite everything she's going through. She still looks like the girl I used to—"

"The girl you used to what?" Tommy asked.

I shook my head, not wanting to think about it, definitely not wanting to talk about it. How the ones we used to love can come back and hit us the hardest, how they can remind us of all the things we were, the person we dreamed we'd become, sometimes with them by our side, and how our biggest fear is that in their eyes, we would be found to fall short.

Tommy, being Tommy, read the shrug. "Yeah, I get it. I've had a few of those *used to's.* myself. I was only asking because her daughter, the artist? She was a real pretty thing. Shame."

"Yes," I said, "A shame."

"She wasn't gay, was she?"

"Who?"

"Chamonix."

"I don't think so. Why?"

"There was something about her work. A guilt or feeling of not belonging. I can't describe it."

"Try," I said.

"Maybe it's just me, but there was a sadness in her paintings, an incompleteness. It's something I would expect from someone who's battling their choices, someone who isn't sure who they really are. Does that make sense?"

It did. It reminded me of a certain girl named Buffy.

"I'll send you the gallery website and you can see for yourself."

"Sure. Meanwhile, let's see what else you've got. Buffy, I mean, Barbara's a real paying client and we owe her a complete report, right?"

"Riiight." Tommy reached into his bag and removed a silver laptop. He lifted the lid and pressed some keys, inserted a disc, pressed some more keys.

Tommy was good with all that techy stuff. A real gay geek, you might say—but not me, I'd never call him a geek.

I admit all those clicks and beeps and wires and shit sticking out of people's ears intimidate me. I wasn't my grandpa, but I still was in no hurry to zap around the world with my eyes on a blue screen or to have someone buzz me in the middle of a Hitchcock festival, telling me they knew I wasn't really camping in the woods because the GPS on my phone had led them to the Syracuse Cinema.

I leaned back in the booth, still wary of cancer beams, and said, "So you said you talked to Smith's neighbors down there by Flannigan's, right?"

"Yeah. One sec." Tommy paused his frenetic typing, finger dragging, and thumb tapping and looked up at me as if to say What the hell—I'm working here!? But he saw me sweating, saw me staring at the laptop, so he slowly turned the monitor my way and said. "It's okay, Tedesco. I'm going to go slow." Like I was some kind of computer retard—which maybe I am, but unlike me, Tommy is too fucking nice to say it.

The screen changed from a black rectangle to a shot of the exterior of Flannigan's, then panned to a street shot. "The consensus was that James John Smith was a quiet guy who seemed harmless enough."

"Isn't that what they said about Ted Bundy?" I asked.

Tommy looked at me with his are-you-done-yet face. The one that made me feel like I was talking to my father.

I said, "Sorry. So, did you talk to everyone in the brownstone?" For the record, I had no idea if the building was a real brownstone, but it sounded like something a mature, intelligent man would say. It sounded like boss-speak, so I went with it.

Tommy said, "That's affirmative," volleying with cop-speak. "No one saw or heard anything that night or any other night. Apparently sleeping with noise machines or headphones is the cool thing to do if you live downtown." He pressed some more keys, bringing up an image of the building with black iron railings to the left of the bar—the same building whose garden I had admired from James John Smith's window.

The next shots were of people outside the same building. An older woman with a high, wide forehead pursed her lips as she sorted through a stack of mail on the stoop of the brownstone. In the next shot, she slipped a white envelope into her pocket as she glanced toward the dark interior of the building. The last photo showed her turned away from the camera, returning the rest of the mail to the box.

Tommy said, "That's Adele Tibbs, the owner and manager. I gave her your number, told her you might have some questions. She lives here." Tommy pointed to the ground floor of the building. "There are three more apartments: two on the second floor and one penthouse."

"Penthouse?"

"Well, top floor. Anyway. Adele's parents bought the building forty years ago. She does some kind of botanical research, never married, no surviving siblings. She's kind of a homebody."

"Homebody? Is that urban slang, some new street lingo?"

Tommy gave me a look. "You know what I mean. This building's all she has."

"What about the other tenants?"

Tommy pulled up another picture. A bald man wearing tiny rectangle glasses was frozen in time, rushing through the door, suit coat flapping behind him. He had a phone jammed to one ear and a bagel in his hand. He didn't look happy.

"There's your penthouse. Benjamin Rathbone. He's never home, some kind of money manager. We might need to catch him at the office. Police report shows a solid alibi, but said he was uncooperative—probably their fault."

I knew what Tommy was thinking. He didn't like the

cops in this town, maybe any town. The kid had illusions of TV cops—the pensive, softhearted redhead who'd tilt his head, speak hesitantly, then slam you up against the wall. He thought Syracuse cops lacked charisma, chutzpah.

"Don't get going on that again," I said. "I don't want to hear how you could have done it better. You want to be a cop? Be a cop."

"Two words, Tedesco," Tommy said. "Navy. Polyester." He waggled his finger.

"Don't do that," I said. "It makes you look gay."

Tommy smirked. "Whatever. Oh, you're going to love this." He tapped the keyboard. "The second-floor tenant, Ms. Bartlet, is in arrears with her rent and missing."

"Is that right?"

"Yeah. When a tenant stops paying for two months, a landlord tends to notice."

He enlarged a page on the screen and pointed. "That's her."

A wallet-size photo on the left side of the page introduced me to Sassy Panda and her blog: Days of Sassiness.

"What's this?" I asked.

"Our Miss Bartlet's a blogger." Tommy leaned back with a satisfied look on his face.

"Excuse me?"

"Come on," he said.

"What?"

"We've been over this before."

"I forgot then, okay?"

"Honestly, you never listen to me."

"What? Is it important? This blogging thing?"

He rolled his eyes and huffed.

"Why do I feel like we're having a lover's quarrel? Listen, Tommy, don't get testicle with me, just give me the basics."

"Ha-ha. Very funny. Trust me. You are not the type I get testicle with."

I was offended by that remark. No one likes rejection.

Tommy said, "A blog is a web log. An Internet journal. They are really, really popular. Some people who write them get book deals, some get on TV shows, some run advertising on their site and live on the income. They sell T-shirts and coffee mugs and actually garner a cultlike following."

"Fascinating," I said, yawning.

"Asshole," Tommy said and punched my arm, surprisingly hard.

I punched his arm back, thinking how much better he faked the "Ow," than I did.

"This is blogging," Tommy said. He pulled up three windows at once, splayed them across his computer screen. I saw photos of kids in hospital beds, family vacation shots with travel tips, puppy growth charts, workout videos, and food diaries.

"Who the hell reads this stuff?" I asked.

"Depends. I prefer to think of it as a collection of support groups. You can find anybody writing about anything and commiserate, or just hang out in the backyard and peek in the window, so to speak. Actually, they probably have blogs for those people too."

"Really?" Now I was interested. Tommy went on to explain where you log in, who runs these things, how you get one, and the rising price of tortillas in northern Mexico. At least I think that was what he was going on about. I was too focused on the page and the pictures our little Miss Bartlet had posted to listen.

She was not a great photographer, an even worse

writer. She seemed to be one of those people who thinks everything they say is witty and that folks really want to hear about the amazing birds they spied on vacation while learning how to open up to the universe. Yeah, she was one of *them*. I skimmed the most recent posts—a tirade against the new morning blend at the local coffeehouse, a sad bit about missing her mother, and quotes from a popular movie with a few photos of the cast. Boring. Where was the illicit sex? The honest reveal of someone's lies? The panty parties and drunk, topless friends? I thought the Internet was supposed to be fun.

"When did our blogger go missing, again?" I asked as I clicked the down arrow, browsing the dates of each post.

"Two months ago, give or take," Tommy said.

"So why is there a picture of her apartment's windowsill garden with yesterday's date?"

"Let me see," Tommy said, angling the laptop back toward him.

He skimmed and clicked, tapped a few keys, then did that thing with his finger on his lip that meant he had an idea.

Tommy grinned. "She pre-posted."

"Pre-posted?" I asked. "Is that like pre-pulled? How you never wait for me to unlock the passenger door before you pull the handle?"

"No, Tedesco. Our blogger wrote these posts at some earlier point in time and set a future posting date. It's quite simple . . ."

Then he said some techno-babble stuff that I really didn't hear because I had swung the laptop back to face me and was clicking through photos on the site. I stopped at one that had caught my eye earlier.

"Can you make that bigger?" I asked, touching the screen with an apparently greasy index finger.

Tommy slapped my hand away. "Okay. Just don't

touch the glass. You'll leave prints."

"Gee-sch. Picky much?"

Tommy snorted. "Gee-sch. Dorky much?"

The picture I'd pointed to was of a bird on a windowsill, not any windowsill, but Miss Bartlet's windowsill. The windowsill of the window that faced the alley. The alley that separated her apartment from Smith's.

"See?" I said, as the image grew, was pixelated, and grew again. Beyond the bird, beyond the alley space, there was another window. Smith's window. A man was caught in profile and behind him was another figure, fuzzy and hard to make out. The man was probably Smith, but the figure behind him could have been anyone. It was impossible to tell.

There was something about the way the frozen images spanned the screen. Something unsettling, like looking at pictures of your mom when she was eighteen, pretty, and half-undressed. Like you'd caught her being bad, though the pictures were about fifty years old and the last time you saw your mom half-undressed you'd been giving her a sponge bath at The Home.

"Save that," I said, flicking a hand at the screen, then turning away.

I felt in my pockets for gum, candy, something. While I was feeling around, my phone buzzed and scared the shit out of me. I hate buzzing phones almost as much as alarm clocks.

Tommy grinned when I snatched the phone from my pocket.

"Asshole," I muttered as I answered the call, wondering when he'd had a chance to bugger my phone.

"Mr. Tedesco? This is Adele Tibbs. Your assistant said you wanted to talk to me? I don't know how I can help you, I hardly—"

"Miss Tibbs. Thanks for returning my call. I just had a

few questions for you."

Tommy turned the computer toward me and pointed. I felt like the president reading the national address from a teleprompter when I asked Adele, "When did you first meet Mr. Smith?"

"Well, I guess it was a few days before he reopened the bar."

"Had you ever seen him before?"

"No. I mean, not to my recollection."

Great. I had an Ollie North. I strayed from the Tommy questions and went with, "How well did you know Mr. Flannigan?"

"We were quite friendly," Adele said. "As you might expect of people who have been neighbors for over twenty years."

"Twenty years? Is that right?"

"It would have been twenty-two years this November."

"I see."

"We've seen a lot of change on this block, but no one was more surprised than I was when Mr. Flannigan told me he was leaving and asked me to hand over the key to Mr. Smith."

"You had the key?"

"We were neighbors. That's what neighbors do."

"Did you know that Mr. Flannigan lost the deed to his building in an online poker game, Miss Tibbs? Don't you find that odd?"

"Mr. Tedesco. I am eighty-two years old. I find a great many things odd."

"Did you know your neighbor was a gambler?"

"I was raised to hate the sin, not the sinner. Mr. Flannigan was a good man."

"Was?"

"I'm sure he still is."

Tommy typed something, then swiveled the laptop to

face me.

I read, "I wonder if Flannigan ever played poker at his bar?"

Tommy rolled his eyes and pointed to the phone near my lips. Oh.

Adele Tibbs, unaware of my faux pas, answered me. "I doubt that. There are plenty of local in-home games Mr. Flannigan could go to, if he wanted."

I said, "In-home games? Like friends getting together for a friendly game?"

"No. More like a business. High-stakes poker."

"How does that work?"

"I'm not sure exactly. My nephew tried to explain it to me once, right before he asked for a friendly loan. Would you like to talk to him?"

"That would be great."

I repeated the contact information for her nephew, Hunter, to Tommy, who quickly pasted it all into the report he was keeping on his computer, then I hung up with Miss Tibbs.

"Still no word on Flannigan?" I asked Tommy.

"I don't think anyone's going to get the guy to come back from his Tibetan mountain trek just to confirm that he lost the deed to his bar in a poker game. I mean, really."

Tommy had a way of settling things definitively. A way of shining the light, so to speak.

I dropped some bills on the table and stood to leave. Francie was fooling around with the sound system in the "Karaoke Korner." She raised the volume on a Hawaiian song as we walked by. She looked nice there, in the twinkle lights on the palm tree. Her deep voice was perfectly suited for that ukulele version of "Somewhere over the Rainbow." I joined in as we walked past, pausing long enough to finish the chorus, harmonize with my old singing partner. She smiled, a real smile for the first time all day.

When the song ended I gave Francie's upper body a hug. I still couldn't get used to the manly parts of her.

"That was refreshing," Tommy said, holding the door for me.

"Glad I could humor you," I said, still humming as we walked to the Lincoln.

"Do you sing in the shower?" Tommy asked. "Isn't that the reason they have karaoke? For the shower singer?"

"And the drunk grandma," I said, buckling up.

"I thought that's what weddings were for."

"That too," I said as I pulled into the street, cutting off a minivan and nosing up to the rear of a shiny, efficient Prius.

"So where are we going?" Tommy asked.

"To play us some poker, son."

THE DEVIL YOU KNOW IS BETTER THAN THE DEVIL INSIDE

Chapter 15

You could only run so far on anger. Angel pulled off the highway into a rest stop. Tired and hungry, she parked the BMW at the end of the mostly empty lot.

A woman with ratty hair was walking a dachshund. Angel bet she belonged to the heavily bumper-stickered truck hauling motorcycles, or maybe the red minivan with the towels hanging in the windows. She grabbed some money for the vending machine, got out, and stretched.

With the drone of the highway behind her, Angel made her way to the main building. The food selection was shabby to say the least, but the restrooms were clean and the drink machine fully stocked.

Returning to her car, she noticed the truck with the motorcycle trailer was gone. In its place was a long, black Lincoln, its engine still running.

She set the food and drinks in the front, then climbed into the back, locking the doors and setting the alarm on her phone. She tucked the gun she'd borrowed from her daddy under her shirt, then made a nest with her coat and snuggled in.

She thought about the black car across the lot, the Lincoln with the mean-looking grille. It reminded Angel of the limos that pick you up from the airport, like the one Daddy had sent for her that summer she returned from France. It had been early July, warm but not too humid. She had asked the driver to hurry as she called Jimbo to tell him she was back, then agreed to meet him at the bar, as they'd planned.

When Angel replayed the day in her mind, everything moved slower and was much clearer as if over time she'd perfected the memory making it more like a nostalgic film than reality. She arrives before Jimbo and makes her way to their table. The door opens. She turns and watches him walk into the room. He takes off his sunglasses, letting his eyes adjust to the darkness. When he sees her in her yellow dress, sitting in the same place where they met a year before, he crosses the room in three long strides, reaches for her and pulls her into his arms, pressing her against his chest. He's sweaty from the ride over, and she's sure he can feel her heart thumping through his shirt, that he can read her Morse code message beating dots and dashes: I. Missed. You.

He smells too good, and fits against her as perfectly as she remembered. He trails his hands down her back, making a path to the top of her ass, then lower. The silky fabric of her dress rides up when she raises her arms to encircle his neck. She thinks for a minute that he will spin her around in the center of this bar, that she will pull the clip from her hair and shake it free while kicking up her heels. But the moment passes and they're still standing there in front of the other customers—she hears them now, scraping back their chairs, resuming their conversations as if to say the show's over—but still Jimbo holds Angel.

He presses his cheek against hers, then tucks his head into her neck. His breath is warm and cool at the same time, as if he's just brushed his teeth. He reaches for her chin and tips it up toward his. They are almost the same height, she in her high heels, he in his cowboy boots. She opens her eyes and slowly blinks. A tear runs from the corner of each eye. She doesn't try to wipe them away.

He smiles then, as if that was what he'd been waiting for, as if that tear told him everything. He looks at her so intensely, his gaze moving from eye to eye. It's a test, a confirmation, the solution to the puzzle. She rolls her chin in his hand and, when he meets her eyes again, his lips part and the angle is perfect. When his lips touch hers there is nothing else in the world but them.

She doesn't want to break the kiss. She wants to climb up his body and wrap herself around him like a python, she wants to slither down the front of him then lie at his feet, sucking on his toes. She wants to stick her tongue in his ear and reach her hand down his pants and ride him barebacked through town with hair as her only clothing. She thinks all these things in one foolish moment and then allows herself a small giggle.

He looks at her with a question in his eyes and she pulls back, just a little, so she can focus on his face, on his grin. She sees the man she loves. The man she needs.

Angel awoke remembering all the reasons she fell for Jimbo and all the reasons she wants him back. The parking lot was bustling: people walking dogs, kids running on the grass, a slew of minivans with assorted license plates overloaded with suitcases and bicycles. She glanced around, but there was no sign of the Lincoln.

After double-checking her route to Tammy-the-girlfriend's place, Angel reentered the highway, telling herself that soon she'd either have her husband back, or, at the very least, she'd have some answers.

TEDESCO TAKES ON THE HOUSE OF ILL REFUTE

Chapter 16

Hunter Tibbs not only took my call, but invited us over. He offered to enlighten me and Tommy on the finer points of in-home poker games, Syracuse style. I figured the fifty bucks I spent for the info and the brief lesson would be worth it, especially when he threw in the blond wig.

"You know where you're going?" Tommy asked as I pulled out of Hunter's driveway and headed down the street.

"Sure. No problem," I said, switching lanes without looking, pissing off someone else's mother.

Tommy consulted his magic phone. "This time of day, I think we should use back roads. Turn left up here."

Though "up here" looked like an alley to nowhere, I knew better than to question him. If there was one person I wanted to be stranded with on a desert island, it was Tommy, and not just for his survival instincts or witty banter, but because he'd be the one to tell me which way to paddle the palm-frond, coconut-shell MacGyvered raft he'd whipped up overnight.

But the kid was too intense. He was in such a hurry to grow up that he didn't realize it wasn't all it was cracked up to be.

I wished I was still his age. I'd be in my dancing prime, touring forty-eight states and Canada, making thousands a night and blowing through it the next day.

It had been easy to live in the moment: none of us thought we'd make it past thirty. We didn't bother planning for a future. We barely planned the next day's lunch. What we did plan on was getting our egos stroked while we took off our clothes—in the most artistic way possible, mind you.

Our clientele lived on the best side of whichever town we happened to be in. We had a regular following, a group of ladies who traveled to see us, including one guy who sewed our costumes. Once he made me a stuffed-pantyhose schlong that hung to the floor, for my flasher routine. The girls loved that. I never could figure that guy out. He was straight. Married and everything, but he loved us boys and would do anything for us.

Tommy's back roads got us to the poker neighborhood right before dark. Syracuse traffic was nothing like real city traffic. We knew how lucky we were. Local commuters who complained about a twenty-minute delay were scoffed at by folks visiting from LA or Atlanta. But to Syracusans, twenty minutes in the cold and snow sucked way worse than two hours in any kind of sunshine.

I turned onto the appointed street and slowed down to a crawl. I made my usual scan for exits as Tommy commented on each homeowner's landscaping and house color choices.

"That mailbox planting is so seventies. Railroad ties? What were they thinking? Can you believe someone would paint a house peach? And add those turd-brown shutters? Please! Someone needs to report them to the homeowners association. Fine them for bad taste."

I passed the poker house.

"Three," I said.

Tommy shook his head. "Four, if you count the motion sensor behind the gutter on the north side.

I grinned. "Nice job."

"Learned from the best," he said.

He had counted four security features we could see just

from one drive-by. I was sure there would be a lot more.

Adele's nephew Hunter told us how the basic setup worked. All you had to do was form a meet-up group online, sell memberships to access the local games, then buy a cheap house in a decent neighborhood, preferably one toward the back of a development so the traffic would be less noticeable. Strip it down and hire in some dealers, maybe offer something to draw the talent.

"You want in?" Hunter had said. "I can make that happen."

After he shoved my fifty in his pocket, he called a guy named Buzz, who ran the game. He wrangled me a spot at one of the lower-end tables. All I had to do was show Hunter's card and bring cash. Hunter said Buzz included a home-cooked meal for every player. From the BBQ smell, I figured we were having chicken tonight.

I parked at the end of the street, pulled on the blond wig, popped in a set of fake teeth, and said, in the worst Southern accent I had, "Hey y'all. Let's play some ca-ards."

Tommy busted out laughing. I popped him in the arm, not too hard. I needed him to be able to drive later.

I got out of the car and adjusted my outfit. "I'll text you."

"Good luck," Tommy said, sliding over to the vacant driver's seat and immediately adjusting the seat position. I hated when he did that.

I gave my fake name at the door, said Hunter sent me, then walked through the metal detector and tossed a wad of well-worn bills to a lady behind a Plexiglas partition. She popped her gum, passed me a rack of chips, and I went off to find the bar. I bought myself a two-dollar Coke.

The house had been gutted of any extras. There were cheap commercial carpets in all the rooms, rolling task chairs and game tables in two back rooms, recliners and flat-screen TVs across the front rooms, a bar in the middle. All they needed was a few hookers, a pass for upstairs, and I am sure some of these guys would think they had died and gone to heaven.

This was the house that Jack built. Straight poker, five hundred bucks a hand, and nightly payouts. For guys that wanted the real thing without flying to Vegas, this was where they came.

Three hands in, I heard Flannigan's name.

"You kidding me? That asshole, Flannigan?"

Perked up my ears, that did. I reached down to scratch my ankle, a well-rehearsed eavesdropping technique, one which gave off that certain "Who, me?" feeling and also allowed me to cock my head at such an angle that I could see the speaker. He was a thin, pointy-nosed dude with pale skin who looked like Tin Man without the silver makeup.

Tin Man threw his cards away and shook his head so hard I thought he was going to need a little WD-40 in his neck. "You picked a helluva time to get lucky," he said to everyone and no one and maybe to the little voice in his head. He rolled back from the table, more eloquence pouring forth. "Goddamn. I need a drink."

The cards came around to me and although I had a passable hand, I tossed it and made a grimace, then headed to the bar.

I pulled up next to Tin Man, ordered another Coke, and said, "Just not feeling it tonight, you know?"

He grunted.

I pressed Mr. Talkative by saying, "Might need some of what Flannigan had, huh?"

"What? Herpes?"

"Hah!" I laughed, too hard, too loud.

Tin Man slammed his shot glass on the bar and motioned for another.

I pushed the change from my soda back to the bartender. “I got it,” I said. “Pour me one too.”

It was cheap whiskey, the kind you didn’t dare sip—even if I still had been sipping the stuff. I raised my glass. “To Lady Luck.”

Tin Man added his sentiment. “That fuckin’ whore.”

He downed his and I tossed mine over my shoulder. Another round later, he told me how Flannigan had been the kind of guy bookies loved.

In Syracuse you could bet on just about anything. Our demographic was 40 percent Italian, 40 percent Irish, and 20 percent Latino. We were good with numbers, coercion, and praying.

“All those years,” Tin Man said, “The guy would lose his shirt. No matter what he played. Horses, the numbers, sports, everything. Finally, when he loses the last thing he had—that goddamned bar—he tells everyone angels came to him in a dream and he’s going off on some spiritual fuckin’ journey—that he found enlightenment in having nothing. What the fuck is that? Do you have to lose everything to win?”

He raised his face to the ceiling, but when no answer came, he met my eyes. “Would you listen to me? My mother, God rest her soul, would get a kick out of this. Ke-rist, what am I saying?”

“I think what you’re saying is something we all think but are afraid to say, ‘What are we really chasing?’ And ‘Will we know it when we find it?’”

Tim Man stared at me, watery eyes unblinking. He did one of those “aww, shit” neck rolls, so I tried another approach. “Or maybe it’s just time for another drink.”

“Yeah,” he said. This time he didn’t even notice that he was drinking alone.

By the time I left I'd dropped enough hints about our boy Smith that someone should have bit, but I got nothing back. These guys seemed more homebodies than bar hoppers.

Someone did mention The Leopard Lounge. I heard that loud and clear.

SO THAT'S THE WAY THE OTHER HALF LIVES

Chapter 17

Angel pulled to the curb in front of the graffiti-defaced apartment building. She was pretty sure her car was in more danger than she was by the look of the drugged-out kids on the stoop. She reached into the duffel bag Marshall had put together and slipped a blue DEA hat on her head, then tucked the gun in her waistband.

As soon as she stepped out of the car, the kids scattered. She yelled after them, "One scratch on the car, and I'm coming after you!"

There was a row of buzzers for the apartments and a single security camera at the entrance to the building; one buzzer was dangling by a single wire, another had so many names written on top of each other there was no way to know who you were going to get on the other end.

Angel pushed through the door and held her breath. Number 206 should be upstairs in the back. "Get in and get out," she whispered, like a video gamer.

She paused in front of the apartment, took off the ball cap, and tucked it under her arm.

The woman who answered the door might have been fifty, or a hundred and two. She was one of those mixes of Asian, Black, and Mexican, where you're sure no matter what you say or do, you're pretty sure you'll end up offending her. Angel's solution was simple. Do not engage.

"Is Tammy here?" she asked, trying to get a look around the shriveled old woman.

"No Tammy. She working." The woman stepped

forward, holding the door closed behind her. "You bring money?"

"Did I . . . yes, of course I did." Angel started to reach into her pocket.

The old woman offered a jack-o'-lantern grin and let Angel in.

It could have been a scene from one of those drug-deal-gone-wrong movies, with the high girlfriend laying half-dressed on the torn couch, piles of pizza boxes and porn mags on the floor, overflowing ashtrays, holes in the walls, and Disney-character sheets for curtains.

The place was just like that, minus the girlfriend, and with the added scents of weed and bleach.

"Jesus," Angel said. "Erica would love you."

"What that, lady?" The old woman said, coming up behind Angel.

"Never mind. So, Tammy? She lives here, right?"

The woman nodded.

"You know this guy?" Angel showed her a picture of Jimbo, a decent one taken in the backyard as he was grilling steaks. A picture in which he wasn't grabbing his crotch or throwing gang signs, and his gut was where it should be, not sucked up in a pose.

The woman reached into her pocket for a pair of Coke-bottle glasses, perched them on her nose, and squinted at the photograph. "I don't know. You got money?"

"You're a broken record," Angel said. "What about the guy? You ever seen him with Tammy?"

"What about money?"

"Christ. Here." Angel pulled a wad of twenties out of her pocket and fanned them for the woman. Before she could snatch them, Angel asked again, "What about the guy?"

"Yeah, I seen him. He come to pick up Tammy. Not lately. He kinda dick."

Angel smiled. “Yeah. Kinda.” She peeled half the fan off and handed it to the woman.

“Where can I find Tammy?”

“Gentleman’s club. Three block down. Tell them Miss P. send you.”

Mario’s: The Club for Gentlemen. What a shithole. The only kind of gentleman that ever would have gone to this club probably died in 1965. Angel used the “Miss P.” line at the door to get in, and instantly regretted it. She tried to see past the dark, sticky interior, past the smell of skank and Brut. But it wasn’t working—for that she’d need a hypnotist not merely rose-colored glasses.

“Get in and get out,” she mumbled, keeping her distance from the abandoned stage, noting where the muted music and happy sounds were coming from in the rear of the building.

Taking her cue from one of Jimbo’s old movies she swaggered to the bar, ordered a shot of whiskey, and bummed a cigarette from a biker dude whose jacket read: SET FREE SOLDIERS.

She was pretty sure the dancers wouldn’t be wearing nametags, but she thought she knew her husband’s type enough to pick out Tammy in a stripper line-up.

“Hey.” She called the bartender over and tapped the wad of bills she’d placed under the ashtray. “How about a private party?”

“How about it . . .” he said, leering.

“Sorry, sugar. You’re not my type,” Angel said.

The biker dude laughed the raised his shot glass to the bartender. “Call the girls, Jeremy. And give this lady another drink on me.”

Angel guessed right. The busty brunette with a permanent deer-in-the-headlights look was Tammy. On stage and off.

Once Angel had her behind closed doors, in a most embarrassing bent-over-at-the-waist, ass-in-her-face kind of position, she pulled out the Jimbo picture and waved it around until she had Tammy's full attention. All ten braincells' attention.

Turns out there really are some sensitive strippers in the world. Maybe even some who are working their way through medical school. By the time Angel left, Tammy was practically her BFF, swearing on her life she didn't know the guy was married, and honestly, he wasn't really her type anyway, you know? Angel said she knew, and thanked her for the new address to enter into her GPS. Apparently Daddy and Marshall didn't know everything after all.

TEDESCO, CHASING IT

Chapter 18

I was dragging a bit from the late night at the poker house and, admittedly, I didn't have Tommy's internal map, but I knew how to get to The Leopard Lounge and where to park to make sure I'd still have a vehicle afterward.

When I was dancing with the boys, this place was ours on Wednesday nights. We kicked the guys out, let the ladies in, and hung a banner: Hump Night Special: $1 Screaming Orgasms. Yeah, those were the days.

Even before the door opened, I felt the pounding bass vibrating like a large bell in my chest. My sinuses loosened, the headache at the back of my neck moved a bit north. I stepped in, tipping my chin to the bouncer, a beefy, faceless guy who could have been perched on a stool at the door of any number of bars in the county. They all had the same angry look, the same bushy, black mustache and bald head, as if they'd gone to bouncer school to learn how to dress like a European hit man, how to cross their arms at the correct angle and pressure to highlight already-bulging biceps. It was all designed to make a statement: "I don't take no shit. Especially from you, creep."

I could dig it. The guy nodded back and I walked into the dark. There was a smell to the place, Lysol and musk, like clean and nasty were competing for top billing. I was glad for the dim lights.

Two more bouncer types leaned on the bar, though the place had less than a handful of customers. I ordered a beer, then sat at a table near the stage. Purely for research purposes.

The music changed from head-banging to something bluesy, smart-sexy, not as much of a slap in the face. A white screen dropped into place and a spotlight snapped on behind it. It was too bright until my eyes adjusted, then it felt like it was the only thing in the room. No chairs, no tables, no sticky-topped bar, no tough-guy bouncers or squirrelly men in baggy pants. Just me and the glowing screen.

The dancer appeared in shadow segments, like a stop-motion film. A pointed toe. One leg. A muscular, arched back. Long hair trailing. She posed like the chrome girl on a truck's mud flaps. Fit and trim, her legs were two-thirds of the package, topped off with a high, tight ass and tits that were not big or perky enough to be fake. Either she was smart or young and new, strapped for cash. She reached offstage and pulled a rolling chair and hat into the frame. She bent over, ass to us, and pushed her hair into the hat, then straddled the chair.

The music swelled—and so did something else—as the girl writhed and gyrated. I would never look at office furniture the same way again. As the tempo slowed she rose, spinning the chair out of the picture and snapping open a retractable cane. She tipped her head to the side and removed her hat. Her full mane of hair tumbled out. Someone sighed. This was better than Basinger in *9 1/2 Weeks.*

The shadow girl continued telling her wordless body story. A swivel of the hips, a shimmy of the breasts, a hair flip, and a torso roll. We were hers. She might have been our girlfriend, our wife, the girl next door, or the missed opportunity on that island in our twenties. She took the music as her partner, exciting and full, deep beats, ramming drums, mixed with prancy piano runs and some sort of woodwind trilling a promise—something she might have whispered in our ears, a sound that could have come from between her thighs.

She captivated us with a simple black-and-white bump and grind. A nipple was an exclamation point, the curve of her ass a question mark. Her dance told a tale that we didn't want to end.

It was magic.

A single moment in a strip bar in Syracuse, New York, in the middle of a nothing afternoon. Magic. I could almost have believed I was in a better place, a classy place, a place where they paid you in diamonds and gold for giving the world that kind of art. A place where the scent of sweat and semen and stale beer was considered the fragrance of gods. A place where men never hit women and women never grew old.

The song ended. Collectively, the room held its breath, waiting for the screen to drop, for the girl to reveal herself. I closed my eyes, not wanting to ruin the perfection my imagination had wrought.

I didn't need to worry. The sounds of displeasure that came from the front tables assured me our mystery lady had chosen the backstage exit. The music changed again as the screen rose, disappearing into the ceiling. A large black woman in hot pink took the stage—the whole stage.

I put a napkin over my glass to indicate I'd be right back and the waitress shouldn't take my drink, then wandered back toward the restrooms. As I remembered, the dressing room shared the same narrow hall. I could hear voices behind the door, snippets of the strippers' conversations.

"He wasn't fat but he was really, really big and I couldn't. I just couldn't."

"She tells me—she tells *me*—that I need to step off! Can you believe that shit?"

"You was great, Yolanda. Hardly couldn't even tell you wasn't Chamonix."

I leaned in closer. What were the chances that there were two girls in town named Chamonix? I was here because I already knew there was some kind of connection, I had just expected the connection to be more Flannigan-Smith oriented than dead-girl oriented. I also couldn't help feeling a little protective of Buffy's kid—and curious as to why the kid had been dancing here and who might have been coming here to watch.

The DJ came down the hall, ear to his cell phone, eyes on me. I tried to look drunk, confused, stupid—all things I've been at least once before. I pushed myself into the men's room as he knocked on the dressing room door.

"Ladies, Two minutes. Customer Relations Time in two minutes."

The way the guy said "Customer Relations Time," he made it sound important, like they were part of a mighty marketing machine that could change the way consumers thought, the way money was spent, the way wars were fought. Like what these girls were doing out there was more than offering a few kind words to a bunch of immature losers who still lived in their mother's house, like this was the real deal, not at all like they were making their living objectifying themselves for the big shot who needed to think girls really liked him, not his money.

But for me, "Customer Relations Time" meant a free opportunity to ask questions without looking like a cop.

I returned to my table, tried to figure out which of these dancers Flannigan or Smith might have been into. For the sake of research, I decided to work my way down the line, starting with the blonde in the pink panties.

I motioned her over, paid for a lap dance, and let her lead me to the "interview area," a sticky red pleather booth with suspiciously dim lighting.

"Hey, you know a guy who owns a bar called Flannigan's?"

"Why? Is he hiring?" She asked, pausing in her thigh grinding to reach up and adjust her breasts. One seemed to be stuck in the left-turn position. Not that I was noticing.

I wanted to ask her the name of her perfume so I'd be sure to never make the mistake of buying it for my mother, or anyone else. I also wanted to ask her who the big guys were at the bar, but I didn't want her to think that I wasn't giving her my undivided attention, though by the look in her eyes she wasn't fully in the room or even on the planet. She swung around, whipping me with her weave, and shoved her ass in my face with a glance over her shoulder to check her aim. I caught the tail end of what she was saying, but the music was pretty loud. "Say it again?"

She stopped wiggling and twisted around a little more. "I said, there's a girl who comes by sometimes who works at a place that sounds like that, but I think it's called Shenanigan's."

"What's her name?"

"Um . . ." She shook her butt some more, like she was trying to jiggle the name out of it. "I think Shangri-la? Or is that a song?"

Realizing this could take a while, I took another ten out of my pocket.

The girl gyrating in the next booth leaned over. "Turn that into a fifty and I'll fill in the blanks of *Spacey.*"

"Hey!" My dancer jumped up and pushed out her chest even more. I was mildly surprised that was anatomically possible. "It's Stacey! Not Spacey!"

"What. Ever." The new girl looked at me. "Well?"

"Sure," I said and reached for my warm beer like I was the coolest dude in the place.

She smiled. I could hear the guy she was grinding

against moan. She rolled her eyes and, for the first time, I saw life in The Leopard Lounge. I tucked the ten in Stacey's garter and gave her a little smack on the butt, part "nice job" and part "move on, now."

I peeled another ten and two twenties off my bill roll and showed the new girl. She whispered something in her client's ear, then pushed off the banquette and came around to my side of the booth.

I patted the seat. "Take a break."

She looked around, hesitated.

I said, "I know, same price. No problem."

She sat, flashing a brief smile and revealing more wide pink gums than I thought was normal, though I've been told *I* have a gum issue.

She bent down and, for an awkward moment, I thought something was going to happen. It didn't. She reached under the booth and came up with a pack of cigarettes, tapped one out, and lit up without asking.

"I'm Candy, by the way." She offered her hand.

I took it. "Tedesco." Her hand was dry, the handshake professional. "Are you sure you can smoke in here?"

"They let me," she said, exhaling a plume over my head. "If I'm working. Some guys think it's sexy."

For me, cigarettes were about the farthest thing from sexy. If you had to put anything in your body to make you feel better, then—according to every health article written—it was poison. Add in how that particular poison stunk up your house, car, clothes, body, caused yellow teeth, bad breath, and cancer? Yeah, not so sexy.

I let the girl smoke and bought her a glass of what passed for wine in this place.

She said, "Her name's Chamonix. She usually does that song behind the curtain, the one Yolanda did earlier? That's her gig. She hasn't been around for a while. It's not unusual. Some of these girls go missing for months, then show up like a prodigal child."

She noticed my expression.

"Don't be so surprised. I went to college. Used to work a nine-to-five. Just couldn't make the bills without a little extra. Then it got so the extra was better than the real job." She shrugged, then elbowed me like she was letting me in on a secret. "I still wear a suit a few times a month, sensible shoes, the whole bit. Guess you could say I clean up good. Anyway, you aren't here to talk about me." She waved her hand in the air, stubbed out the cigarette on the bottom of her stiletto, and drained her wine. "Chamonix? She's a good kid. I've seen it before. They do it for the thrill. Then it might get so they need it. Like a validation. Like the performer in her needs to be let out to play. Maybe she's acting out a fantasy, or running from her reality."

What the fuck? Who the hell was this stripper? Freud? I looked closer. The broad was close to my age, though in the dim light you really had to concentrate to see it. She had something beneath the surface, something that said she had seen enough to know what she was talking about. I listened closer.

"We pay her in cash. The owner, Duke? He doesn't care as long as he doesn't know anything about it. One time a lady came in here, said her friends dared her. She offered us cash to let her on stage for one song. We acted like she was putting us out, like the five large wasn't enough." Candy laughed.

I motioned the waitress for another wine for Chatty Cathy. She held the glass correctly, by the stem, and sipped—didn't chug this one. I almost thought she was going to raise the glass and admire the hue or reflect on the grape's viscosity or whatever the hell wine people do. But she didn't. She kept talking.

"Anyway, Chamonix is really good. She could make some decent cash here if she wanted. You tell her that."

"I would, but I can't."

"Don't tell me. You were hired by her family to bring her home, to set her right, to fix her."

"Nope."

"You're doing this for her own good?"

"Nope."

"You see her potential, want to marry her and take her away from all this?" She drew her arm across the room, in game-show-model fashion.

"Nope. But I think I saw all those movies and read all those books."

She smiled. "Touché."

We clinked glasses. I watched her when I said, "I want to find out who killed her and why."

She reacted like an innocent person would—and I knew people.

"Killed? Oh my God."

She did that female thing, clutching her chest, her heart. It would have been more effective if she had been wearing a top. To me, it looked a little too sexy to be taken as shock, fear, or the realization of one's mortality. But what was I thinking? I'd just told a stripper that another—albeit part-time—stripper was dead. What did I expect? I know what part of me hoped for: that she'd burst into tears, allow me to comfort her, maybe even sweep her up in my arms and take her home to finish the comforting. Like we were reenacting our parts in *An Officer and a Gentleman*, which in my head segued into *Behind the Green Door.*

But there was no time for any of that. One of the bouncer types at the bar noticed that I had made the nice stripper lady cry.

He rumbled across the room, tanklike. “Everything all right here, Candy?” Each syllable punctuated as left, right, jab.

I raised my ginger ale and took a sip, unsure where this was all going but fully aware of the opening on his left and how if I tossed the soda in his face I could make the lunge-leap-and-roll escape I had practiced and perfected quite a few assholes ago.

Candy put her hand on the bouncer’s arm. “It’s okay. Just some bad news. We’re fine. Really. See?” And she tried one of those overcompensating smiles like you find on portraits hung in mall photo studios, except her nose was running and she was almost naked.

The guy bought it and backed away, but not before he gave me one of those I’m-watching-you looks, complete with the two-finger-eyes-to-me gesture.

I sent him the “oooh” face and a fake little shiver, even though it was something I’d seen Tommy do and was probably a gay thing. Then I finished telling Candy what I knew about Chamonix and watched her move to the second stage of bad news, the part where you realize, holy shit, it could have been me.

I asked her if there was anything she could tell me that might help. She stubbed out her cigarette then said, “One time Chamonix came in with another girl—a really sexy thing, beautiful as a movie star. Had quality work done, you know what I’m saying? One of the girls asked if she was looking for work. She would have killed on stage, looking like that. But she said she was in a complicated relationship, said she had a man who’d never approve. She looked a little afraid when she said it. I know that look.” Candy got a little dreamy-eyed.

“Do you remember her name?” I asked.

“Yeah.” She laughed. “That was the thing—she already had a stripper name. Crescent Moon.”

I almost said the name at the same time. Instead I asked, "You said sometimes girls go missing, then they come back. Anybody lately?"

"None of the girls from the day shift. I wouldn't know about the night girls. I'm first off, so I don't run into any of them."

The waitress glided by, slipping a note to Candy.

Candy read it, then looked past me toward the door. "I gotta go. Some of my regulars are here. But listen, if there's anything else you need . . ?" She slipped a card out of the pack of cigarettes and handed it to me, then bent down and pushed the pack and lighter back under my chair, her breast grazing my thigh.

I watched her saunter over to the newly arrived group of men—bankers or money managers, white-bread guys with power ties—then left with Candy's card in my pocket: Susan Harrington, Realtor, Your Lakefront Property Specialist.

THE WAY IT HAPPENED, OR MEMORIES IN JIMBOLAND

Chapter 19

Jimbo knew there was a lake nearby, from the way he could hear those ducks—no, loons. James had been keen on explaining the difference. Damn things creeped him out, yodeling like that. Fucking made him wish he had a shotgun.

"Jimbo does not like loons," he mumbled, pacing the wall of windows. He had to stop talking about himself in the third person. He had to stop thinking of himself as Jimbo. That wasn't his name-o. He had a week to become James John Smith, the new James John Smith of New Hampshire.

The guy had been a total loner. Single, never married, no children, and no family in the States. He had worked as a commercial freight pilot most of his adult life—until the crash. When he pulled out of the coma six months later, he got news that his parents had died while skiing The Alps. The hits kept coming. The doctor ordered him to never fly again, and that was followed by a visit from his company's attorney, a man with some paperwork that he said would make Smith very rich if he'd just sign on the dotted line.

Smith signed away, cashed the check, and bought up all the empty land around his house in the White Mountains. It quickly became his hermitage.

He became dependent on delivery drivers, satellite TV, and the Internet. Packages piled up on the porch, food was left at the door. He paid all of his bills through a global trust account.

This was a man no one would miss. He would be leaving a world where no one could tell one James John Smith from another anyway. They were like Mexicans to black people.

Jimbo had come to New Hampshire with a plan, and—except for the sex part—it went exactly as he'd envisioned it, like some sort of divine karmic happening without the robes or Kool-Aid.

From the moment Jimbo invaded James Smith's space, he was in control. Borrowing a line from Calloway in *The Third Man*, Jimbo whispered, "You were born to be murdered," as he limped into Smith's mountain home.

"What's that?" the man said.

Jimbo answered, "I said, 'You sure have a nice place.'"

"Thanks. Don't get much company."

The rest of the conversation might have gone something like this:

"I'm Arnold. Sorry I fell and twisted my ankle while trespassing on your land, but thanks for putting me up.

"No problem. Somehow my Internet connection and phone lines have gone down and I am lonely and hopped up on pain pills and welcome the company."

"So what do you want to do now?"

"I don't know. What do you want to do?"

Or maybe it didn't go like that at all.

Jimbo liked to think of the whole ordeal as one of those action-packed extraction movies. Injured hero swoops in, surveys the land, picks off the bad guys, befriends the rich man and his money, then saves him and moves on. Just insert con man with self-inflicted shin wound instead of hero, and kill instead of save.

"This all you ever do?" Jimbo-acting-as-Arnold had asked James as they sat reading one day.

"With the Internet down and the cable out, it's about all you can do. Besides, I like it. It's quiet and I can go anywhere in my head."

"You can go anywhere, for real, can't you?" Jimbo-Arnold asked.

"No."

"Sure you could, James. I mean, I'll bet you could."

"I guess I could afford to go anywhere, I just don't think I could handle it physically. I'm not as strong as I used to be."

Or as thin, Jimbo thought. "Nah. You'd be fine. Look at all these travel books. Pick one. Where do you want to go?"

They'd been playing that game for two days, the where-do-you-want-to-go game when James told Arnold-Jimbo about his online poker addiction, the Syracuse bar, Flannigan's loss, and Flannigan's impending Tibetan trek.

Jimbo swore he heard angels sing. He said, "You ever meet this guy, or been to Syracuse?"

James shook his head. "Nope. Not much for the bar scene. Thought I'd just sell the place, or put it up in another game. Sweeten the pot, you know?"

"I hear that. Hey, you want another beer? I'm heading that way."

"Sure. Thanks. You're a good listener, Arnold."

"That I am," Jimbo-Arnold said, reaching for James's empty beer bottle, brushing the man's fat fingers as he did.

Jimbo played another game while James slept. It was the watch-me-shed-my-old-life-for-this-new-one game. He wrote the name James one hundred times. He practiced answering the phone as James, made miscellaneous calls imitating James's voice and walked around James's house, making up anecdotes about all the things he saw.

"Oh, that chair? I brought it home from Mexico, as a memory of my night with Ensenada Juanita."

He stood in front of a poorly executed painting of a red barn in a wheat field, posed as though he had a glass of Chardonnay in one hand and a cigarette in the other.

"That? I picked it up in a little shop in Boston. Pathetic, isn't it? I like to close my eyes and imagine my grandmother rocking on the front porch of a farmhouse as grandpa painted beside her. God, I loved my granny."

Jimbo flicked his imaginary cigarette, then downed and tossed his fake glass of wine and moved on to the next knickknack in the room.

"Oh, this old thing?"

He picked up a wooden implement laced with thick rope, turned it in his hands. "I don't even know what the fuck this thing is! But it charms me."

Jimbo never lasted long at that game. It wasn't that he wanted to become James John Smith of New Hampshire, he simply wanted what James had. Sure, they were both Smiths, but they couldn't even have passed for distant cousins, much less the same guy. Where Jimbo had stringy, lean muscle and a hungry tiger, urban cowboy kind of look, James was more pasty and flabby, in a retired opera singer, puffer fish kind of look. And in the end, Jimbo figured the game didn't matter because he wasn't planning on hanging around—or inviting anyone to visit.

His own life as James John Smith V, had been easy to leave, easier than he would have thought. There was freedom in living for the moment, in refusing to plan for a future that you had no control over anyway. It seemed so simple to Jimbo. Like those brilliant ideas that came to you in your teenage years, revealed in a pot-induced stupor. Peace equals cool. Less is more than more and better than nothing. Water is good for you. Feet are necessary.

But Jimbo knew this feeling of harmony, this carefree lifestyle couldn't last. There were downsides to every good thing, but he fucking refused to think about that. Instead, he loaded up a day's worth of porn on James's computer, opened a bottle of wine, and made himself a frozen pizza.

By the time the week was out, Jimbo emerged as an improved version of James Smith of New Hampshire. Formed by the pieces of people he'd never met—film noir movie stars Richard Widmark and John Dall, and some people he *wished* he'd never met, like Randy Amis, the handsome bully in grade school—the new James was sly, charming, and sexy with a mysterious allure. He no longer thought of himself as Jimbo, but as James, the new owner of Flannigan's bar in Syracuse, New York. He could almost see himself inserting the key in the lock and placing a Help Wanted sign in the window.

"Trust me. I'm doing you a favor," Jimbo said just before he shoved James John Smith off the cliff. "Only thing you had to look forward to was gout, Type 2 diabetes and a slow, lonely death."

If the fall, bounce, and tumble down the mountainside failed to kill James immediately, the fat fuck might have survived for weeks, his body feeding off itself in a bizarre weight loss regime.

Jimbo forced himself to look over the cliff. His namesake had landed on an outcropping of rock and lay broken and tattered, staining the snow crimson—a chilled meal for a passing carnivore family of four.

BEAUCOUP DE CHAMONIX

Chapter 20

The blood stored in her refrigerator was still deep red, thanks to the oxidizing procedure. You could learn anything from the Internet, especially when you befriended chatty doctor types who suffered from insomnia. Chamonix pushed aside orange juice and a Chinese takeout box and reached for the Tupperware container. Inside were two baby-food jars of blood, one marked "R," one marked "J." There was less than an ounce in each. Chamonix never used much in her paintings. It might be the stripe of an umbrella, the shoes of a girl waiting in line at the library, a Frisbee dangling from a tree in an abandoned park. She always tried to pay homage to the donor, but in an obtuse way. She wasn't one of those guilty criminals asking to be caught, wanting to pay penance. She was an artist.

The way she had worked in Seattle in the beginning of her career was different from the way she painted now. She'd been less controlled, more passionate. Dumber. Now, living in Syracuse via Vegas via Shreveport via unnamed towns she'd rather forget, she was the retooled model of the original Chamonix. Smarter, calmer, more self-assured. She painted with more purpose than passion. Instead of the roller-coaster thrill of the past, she began to feel satisfied when a canvas was completed, like the moment after you scratch an itch.

Some days, Chamonix wondered if her feeling toward her art could change. What would be next? Her feelings about food or exercise, her desire for sex? Would that become mundane? Forgettable? Skippable? Chamonix was afraid she'd wake one morning and decide to buzz her head or wear muu-muus or speak Italian or raise Shetland sheepdogs in Utah. What if she lost herself? Surely not everything could go away? What if she lost the first kiss? That was the one magic thing Chamonix felt everyone could agree on.

The first kiss, when it's real—not the trial kind—when you're testing the chemistry, but the true first kiss when you can feel the electricity, that's the kind of kiss novels were written about, futures planned upon, those were the kisses immortalized in songs.

If that kiss had magic, Chamonix would feel it expand into a rolling patter, releasing a line of tension, a drumming at the base of her spine, touching her in all the places the nuns had said were bad. If the kiss was too wet or too hard or too tight or too stiff or premeditated, if she couldn't feel the man behind the kiss or if she peeked through her lashes to see him staring over her shoulder, then she'd shut her synapses down—pull the plug on the kiss and anything it might have led to.

A kiss could make her feel foolish, as if she was exposing herself, especially if it wasn't reciprocated. Chamonix didn't do vulnerable. She didn't do soft. She didn't give herself away. She understood why hookers never kiss, and how you can have sex without kissing and call it sex, but if you kiss—even once—it's making love. Unless it's rape and the kiss was one-sided and made you spit afterward.

Chamonix was thinking all this as she coasted downhill, returning from her morning bike ride. She'd logged over forty miles and would have gone more but she couldn't shut off her brain. She tried again to get lost in the music, cranking the volume on her iPod, easily matching the rhythm of her pumping quads to the bass beat of "Suicide Blonde."

She was smiling when she turned off Main Street and onto Bonanza, raced into the pseudo-courtyard of her building and yelled, "Hold the door!" to a guy in navy peacoat.

The guy barely had a second to react. His first instinct might have been to let go of the door and jump out of the way of the bike, but when Chamonix called again he turned, pulling the door open wide.

She barreled past, hunkered down over the handlebars, and zipped into the building's foyer. Standing on the pedals, she charged the bike up the stairs, hooked it around at the first landing, and skidded to a stop in front of her loft door. The guy followed her inside, staring up at the place where she stopped.

Still in the saddle, she unclipped her helmet and grinned. "Thanks!"

He raised his hand to wave, but she was already rolling her bike inside.

"Hi. I'm Adam," he said as the door closed.

Chamonix stripped, leaving her clothes where they fell—shoes and helmet in the entry, jacket, T-shirt, sports bra in the hall. She was nude by the time she entered the white-tiled bathroom. She pulled the elastic from her hair, releasing a long ponytail. She shivered as the strands of hair swept across her back. Pipes clanked before the cold stream warmed. Hot water sprayed from the old nozzle, halting and jerky, something she'd talked to the landlord about—twice. The guy was only interested in the shower if Chamonix was in it. Asshole.

Twenty minutes later, wearing coveralls splattered with dried paint, wet hair dripping, Chamonix stood in front of a painting. The background might have been Cape Cod, or any seashore with sand, surf, sea grasses, and a dilapidated fence. She uncapped the jar marked "J," held her breath against the sharp scent, then dipped her brush and gently touched it to the canvas, adding a bloody line to the horizon, an accent to the setting sun. The transformation was instantaneous, turning an ordinary seascape into a tainted memory.

Chamonix eyed the rest of the painting. At the forefront, a swimsuit-clad couple lay entwined, their beach blanket twisted beneath them, a bottle of wine tipped, spilling, while at the water's edge two children stood holding hands, throwing elongated shadows across the sand. She added a dash of red to the spilled wine and the hair of the girl, then capped the jar of blood and reached for the polyurethane spray.

WHEN HARVESTING DOESN'T HAPPEN ON A FARM

Chapter 21

Cress checked her watch. Early for her nail appointment, she was killing time on a bench at the park. A woman passed, furiously texting while pushing a stroller/carseat contraption. Cress stared at the ignored baby who was just as furiously attempting to grab a toy dangling just out of his reach. Across the path, mommies pushed toddlers in swings, kids hung from monkey bars. They chased and taunted one another. Children.

Cress touched her stomach. Most days she could convince herself some other girl had done it, could look in the mirror and believe it. Another girl made those children. An ugly girl. The kind of girl who studied the data and knew the facts: every female baby is born with one to two million eggs, eggs that are gradually destroyed so that by the time a female enters puberty, she may only have four hundred thousand. With puberty came menstruation, which released another thousand eggs a month, with the chance of only one being fertilized. That was where the importance of the million-egg difference came into play.

Cress had been given too many eggs. Like a collection of antique salt and pepper shakers stored in a glass display case, she had an abundance of something valuable she never planned on using. Her eggs were her true inheritance. Unlike her grandparents' mines that went dry, this gift could change lives.

Not just for Cress, but for barren women on their knees

in candlelit churches. Cress might be their answer, a paper-gowned girl in a sterile room acting in a totally anonymous and generous way—her own version of God Almighty and the Virgin Mary. Cress donated young, fertile eggs. Babies for all.

That was how she preferred to look at it. As a donation. Not *her* potential child, or *her* eggs, because all of that sounded too personal, too important to ever walk away from.

It was interesting to her only in a vague, cinematic way, that out there somewhere her biological child might live and thrive, a kid who looked nothing at all like her, but might turn to the light and for a moment remind Cress of a childhood better forgotten.

Once, she allowed herself to wonder if one of her eggs was born a girl and one a boy, what would happen if they hooked up? How could anyone stop that from happening?

She crossed the street and entered the nail salon, trying to not think that some babies weren't supposed to be born. Babies that grew up to make crucial mistakes, babies that became adults and screwed up more than they succeeded, babies that turned into psychopaths, into killers, into crazed tyrants.

When she read about the man who had donated so much sperm he fathered three thousand children and the doctor who used his own sperm in all the women he was treating instead of their choice of the Swedish triathlete's, the Italian duke's, or the nuclear scientist's, she couldn't understand why the new mothers were upset. They had wanted a baby—they got one. Their dream came true. Or did it?

As if she could read her thoughts, the manicurist paused in her filing and looked Cress in the eye. "My sister-in-law still can't get pregnant. Says she's going to look into surrogacy."

"I think that's a fabulous idea," Cress said. "A surrogate mother. There should be an award for that."

A woman at the next station laughed. "What would they call it, The Belly? The Uterus? Come on. I think sometimes people do it just for the money."

She was right. People did do it for the money. Donated eggs. Rented out their uterus. It was business, wasn't it? Albeit a secret business. Cress had only admitted her actions twice. Once, in the therapist's office, she'd whispered the truth like a child in a dark confessional: "I harvested my eggs for thirty grand so I could change my face."

The therapist said some consoling words, but none were as impactful as what her new family at Flannigan's had told her the second time.

"There are worse things," Chamonix said.

Roxie, pouring them another round of beers added, "Yeah, at least it was better than using the money to buy a new ass, right?"

"Right," said James, who had been listening from the doorway.

He crossed the room, reached for Cress, drew her into a hug. "You did what weaker people couldn't. Your actions changed someone's life. Don't ever look back with regret. Trust me on that one."

He smiled, then kissed her gently on the forehead before reaching for one of the beers and raising it in a toast.

"Besides, we all know there are more than enough asses in the world, right girls?"

TAKE A PICTURE, IT LASTS LONGER

Chapter 22

Roxie had read enough books about men's brains to know that the guy at the home improvement store would be thinking of her ass for at least three hours after she'd had to bend over that woodpile to find the measuring tape. She hated that the orange-aproned employee was old enough to be her grandfather. Wasn't there a time when the sex thing just shut off? An age when it would it be safe for every girl to bend over?

Roxie thought she'd seen it all. Holding over seventeen jobs in a six-year period, sometimes three at a time, she wondered how she could ever have thought of her California days as fun and free. She was almost to the point where she could tell stories about living there, if she'd had a few glasses of wine, but never unless someone asked—she'd learned that nobody likes a bragger and that everybody likes to hear their own stories more than anyone else's.

People liked to hear themselves talk. Roxie was cool with that. Cool with listening, unless the talker had an annoying voice like that seriously hot dentist she'd once dated. He'd had a voice like a gargle, sort of phlegmy, deep, and sad. Like the put-on voice of a pathetic cartoon character. It left Roxie clearing her own throat and swallowing all night long, until she finally she devised a way to turn the stereo up too loud for conversation. If he started to speak, she kept kissing him and kissing him so he would shut the fuck up.

Her listening and storytelling skills made the perfect combination for a job as a waitress in the tourist trap of downtown San Diego. She worked twenty hours a week at a restaurant called Johnson's, where everyone was treated like some guy's johnson, just slapped around a little more on weekends. Her boss gave her a piece of paper when she was hired entitled "The List of Appropriate Customer Insults." He wadded it up and threw it at her. Roxie had nursed a paper cut for a week where it hit her on the chin.

It included such witticisms as: "You want fresh tuna? Go see your girlfriend. At Johnson's, we fry your cod." "You want your check? Around here we call it a bill. Heads up, duckie. (Server may then toss check folder at guest.)"

Roxie had no trouble being a smart-ass. Throwing wadded-up napkins and yelling across the room was nothing compared to the crap she'd pulled off in high school. The job was easy money, good hours for a girl who never slept, and a perfect place to meet fun people.

She went into work the first day wearing kabuki makeup, her hair in a high, tight bun, and a light-up Star Wars saber tucked into a sparkly belt. She pulled out a chair, hopped up on it, and addressed a table by saying, "I'm the Queen of Siam, motherfuckers. Now what the hell do you want?" The bartender applauded and the diners tipped 35 percent.

She'd appear at work wearing battery-operated Christmas lights around her waist and trailing behind her like a tail. She recited dirty limericks in foreign accents. She took all the guys' phone numbers slipped to her in the check folder and pasted them to the ladies' room wall, next to an arrow and the words: "Rich. Hung like a horse."

On a typical night in June, Roxie had sat around the bar with the other servers counting out tips, winding down.

"What did you clear?" they'd ask.

"Ah, the usual bullshit, you know," Roxie said, shrugging.

But they didn't. The other girls were pulling a buck fifty, maybe two hundred on a Saturday, and that was if they hustled. The quicker you turned a table, the better chance you had to clear a nice bit of coin. But you still had to tip the kitchen and the bar, and sure as shit those bartenders knew what your tickets were. Most of the time the waitress could blame it on the customer, calling them cheap or saying somebody had walked, but if you said that too often it came out of your pocket. Like Janice. She had fucked up more than once.

"You aren't pulling a Janice, are you?" the girls asked Roxie.

"Who me? Shit, I sold a thousand bucks and turned in two hundred in tips, okay?"

Roxie was getting pissed. She climbed onto the bar.

"Look, fuckers!" she yelled, waving a twenty. "This is for you, Rusty."

Roxie crumpled the bill and threw it at the bartender.

"And you, and you, and you," she said as she went down the line, tossing ones, liking how the staff looked scrambling on their hands and knees for the money. She didn't care. She'd really cleared over four hundred and stashed most of it her bra.

"All right then? Are we okay? Now, can I have a fucking beer? Please."

She drank her beer and passed on a shot when the only guy Roxie would ever wait for exited the employee locker room, freshly washed and changed.

"I'm gone," she said, throwing some more bills on the bar though after hours they all drank for free.

"Show me." She pointed to Rusty.

He grinned, then pulled up his T-shirt, displaying a perfect set of rippled abs.

"Nice." She reached over and tucked another bill in his pants.

In the parking lot, he was waiting by his motorcycle. Roxie was still on the fence with the whole environmental-verses-the-cool-factor thing. What was better, a hot car or a speeding Ducati?

Not much, except maybe another Ducati.

Sitting behind Daniel, arms wrapped around his waist, the road whizzing by as they leaned in and out of turns, feeling the hum of the bike between her thighs, Roxie thought she had it all. In love, living a good life in a sunny place with her family a safe distance away, creating even more feelings of love.

Some people go home because they fail and there's no place else for them to go. Some return to spread the wealth of their success. The town gives them a key and they reunite with old friends and marry someone's sister and build hospital wings and host charity parties in their gardens each May.

Roxie had gone home because someone died.

She went backward because "forward" wasn't in her vocabulary yet. Without Daniel, San Diego wasn't the same and sunny wasn't enough anymore. Sadness is the kind of cold that sunshine can't heat.

Working at Flannigan's was her salvation. Destiny led her to that corner bar and introduced her to James Smith. Destiny, and also her car broke down right outside.

As James said, "Sometimes lives collide. And it's a beautiful thing."

"Weather sucks today," Roxie said, easing onto the bar stool that she'd claimed from day one.

"You sound surprised. Forget where you live?" Cress said. "It's another typical shitty day in Central New York. Good morning!"

Roxie yawned.

"Did you sleep at all?" Cress asked.

"Few hours. It's enough."

Roxie hated wasting her day in bed. She couldn't understand people who complained about insomnia. To her, not sleeping at all would be great. She imagined how much more people could do if they didn't have to sleep, how much more they could accomplish.

Cress said, "Whatever, Roxie. I don't care how much you want to quote the napping Einstein or Benjamin Franklin. You're supposed to sleep eight hours a night. It's good for your skin. It's healthy."

Chamonix poked her head into the bar from the kitchen. "Healthy? Who the hell cares about healthy? Shit, how old are you, Cress? I'm with Roxie on this one. I'm gonna sleep when I'm dead." She slid onto a bar stool and took a long slug from her coffee mug. "Got any Red Bull back there?"

Most mornings it was like this. They'd all come together from whatever place they had been the previous night and share a morning moment. It was like a modern version of the family breakfast, the office water cooler, the morning carpool catch-up. And it meant something different to each of them.

Chamonix needed the ruse of normality that she found with these girls, in this bar, on this street. This was her constant. A piece of life she could count on every day. Something she could cling to. She needed it as much as she needed her daily horoscope, her morning tarot card reading, her afternoon phone psychic call, and her early evening astrological alignment chart.

Cress needed these mornings too. For the comfort, the belonging, the acceptance. Things she had never been able to claim before. These girls—no, she reminded herself, these *women*—had created a family, one that celebrated individuality, but one that was stronger together.

They were a team. Like *Charlie's Angels*—with their own Charlie, in James. That was how Cress saw it anyway. Not that they were saving the world or running around with gold revolvers or anything. Though that would be cool.

Cress would be the pretty angel, the one who never had to do the dirty work, could simply rely on her looks. Vanity wasn't a bad thing. It was supersized self-confidence. Using beauty wisely meant getting seated at VIP tables in restaurants, being able to return the fancy whosamajigger at the hardware store for cash without question. It meant extra attention when you needed it and never having to wait in line and, sometimes, the ability to go places other girls couldn't—for free.

But it never meant selling out. It never meant degradation or acceptance of rudeness. All it took was one look toward James, holed up his glass office, and the offending guy would be in the street before the current song ended. Families watched out for one another.

In their family Roxie was the leader, the level-headed one, the kind of person you think is older than they really are just because they seem to know a lot about everything.

Chamonix said Roxie was the most normal one of them. Roxie had been embarrassed by the observation, almost apologetic. She knew the others wouldn't understand why she needed them, which piece of her puzzle they completed. She could hardly understand herself. They certainly didn't fit her usual MO for friends or lovers.

They made her think of what-if's, and that was dangerous. The other day on the way to work, she'd passed a group of kids waiting for the school bus. If they hadn't been holding backpacks and lunch bags she might have guessed them to be seven years older. Maybe it was from all the hormones in their milk and the stuff sprayed on their lawns. Puberty was arriving earlier and earlier, and kids grew taller than their parents. Girls were having periods at nine, sex at twelve—just like what happened in the Colonial days, except instead of getting married and moving out West to conquer land, build railroads, find gold, or make a little house on the prairie, they were becoming movie stars or running the streets ripping off strangers, doing drugs, pissing in alleyways, sleeping in abandoned buildings, and figuring out how long they had until they died or got pregnant or picked up or just couldn't take it anymore. Total despair at fifteen.

Roxie knew how that shit felt. Though for her, when she lost Daniel, it was never an option to get addicted to substances, or to become fat or lazy. She wasn't a quitter. She didn't believe that good things came to those who waited, she thought they came to the person who was first in line, the one who not only had a hand out but was yelling, "Hey! Over here!"

She didn't leave anything to chance. It didn't mean she wasn't superstitious or religious or any of those "-ious" words, but she had a strong sense of real in her "-iouses." She would not be the girl who was caught sitting in the corner on her prayer mat when the bomb struck, or the one tossing her baby out the window during the flood.

"Check it out," Roxie said, scanning her phone screen. "This guy says he can tell everything about a person with just a glimpse inside their refrigerator."

"Get out," Chamonix said.

"Think about it. What's in your fridge?"

Cress said, "Right now? A whole lot of empty space."

Chamonix and Roxie laughed.

"All right, very funny," Cress said. "What about you, Chamonix? Would you let this guy look in your fridge?"

"Yeah, right," Roxie said. "She won't even let us in her house. She's not going to let some stranger scope out her refrigerator."

Chamonix brushed imaginary crumbs from her lap. "I never said you guys couldn't come over."

Roxie said, "Well, you've never invited us."

"Why is that?" Cress said. "Aren't we good enough?"

Chamonix slid off the bar stool, took her time pushing it back, then said, "I don't know. I guess I never thought about it. You guys see me all day. Isn't that enough?"

"But we've never seen where *the magic* happens." Cress poked Roxie and winked.

"Magic?" Chamonix stared at her.

"You know, like they say on *Celebrity Cribs*. They take you on a tour through some rich asshole's mansion and when they get to the bedroom they open the door and say, '*This* is where the magic happens.'"

"Oh. Right."

"Shit!" Roxie jumped up, eyes on the clock. "I gotta go. I told James . . . anyway, I'm freakin' late. See you guys later."

When the door closed behind her, there was a silence in the room, partly uncomfortable and then, nice. Like the mother-in-law had gone to bed.

"Did she say *James*?" Cress asked.

"That's what I heard," Chamonix said.

"Strange."

"Yeah."

"So, what are you doing today?" Cress asked.

"Not much, got some errands. Just boring stuff."

"Want some company?" Cress asked.

"Um, sure." Chamonix turned away before Cress could see her face.

Chamonix led the way to the parking lot, then stopped short. "Crap."

"What?" Cress looked around.

"I forgot," Chamonix said. "I walked to work today. I guess we'll have to do it another time. So—"

"No problem. I can drive. Look, I'm right there." Cress pointed to a metallic blue bullet car. She pushed the remote in her pocket and the car whistled at her. "I'll play chauffeur. Just tell where you need to go."

For a tiny thing who seemed so perfectly put together all the time, Cress was a dichotomy behind the wheel. Chamonix almost expected her to pull on a pair of worn leather driving gloves, or some wraparound sport shades by the way she revved the engine and pushed then pulled levers and buttons like they were preparing for takeoff.

They were.

Cress zipped out of the parking lot, merged into a lane of moving cars, switched lanes with a glance and wrist flick, then turned toward the highway. She drove her Audi like the Germans had designed it to be driven—fast and with confidence.

Chamonix took in the interior. This was one of the downfalls to having an artistic side. She analyzed everything. Clean black leather, chrome accessories, upgraded stereo, not a speck of dust anywhere.

"Nice car."

"I like it. What do you drive?" Cress sped up and passed a chain of minivans, then zipped in between a pickup and a roadster without a blink.

"Normally, I ride my bike." Chamonix forced herself to stop gripping her thighs, willed herself to relax her jaw.

"I love motorcycles," Cress said. "I had a Fatboy once, and a Kawasaki for off-road."

"That's nice. But my bike is a bicycle."

"Cool. You have the legs for it."

Cress reached over and touched Chamonix's thigh, gave it a little squeeze. Chamonix jumped. Cress laughed and put her hands back on the wheel.

EVERYBODY HAS A STORY, SOME PEOPLE HAVE THREE

Chapter 23

Chamonix grabbed her bags from the trunk of Cress's car. "Thanks again for driving. See you tonight."

She held her breath as Cress pulled away. Not until the door to the apartment closed behind her did she let herself exhale.

She tried to shake off the feeling she'd been wearing a too-tight shirt, or an uncomfortable bra, something she could finally pull off and toss on the floor, giving her body sweet release.

It wasn't that she didn't like the girl. Hell, she was better than most of the chicks Chamonix had to deal with on a day-to-day basis. There was something damaged in Cress that appealed to Chamonix, something she thought she'd like to paint someday—which reminded her that she owed three canvases to the gallery in Vegas, and hadn't started any of them.

"Nothing like a little pressure to get the creative juices flowing," she mumbled.

The guy upstairs, the one she'd seen when she came back from her last forty-mile ride, was playing his guitar. At least she hoped it was him. For all she knew it could be his gay lover or a really good sound system pumping out a crystal-clear recording.

She found a blank canvas and set it on the easel, adjusting the stand so her back was to the open window. She opened three cans of paint at random. Yellow, turquoise, and tangerine. The guitar player slowed, changing from a classical ballad to a twangy tune, then a syncopated flamenco beat.

Chamonix smiled. "That'll do."

Three hours later, two canvases were almost completed.

Chamonix was hungry and had a small headache behind her eyes. There was silence from the apartment upstairs, but if she'd been asked when the music had stopped, she wouldn't have been able to say. She lost track of everything when she was in "the zone."

She called her agent in Seattle.

"Guy, it's me. I got your messages. All of them."

"I'm sorry," he said. "I know you hate to be bothered when you're working. You are working, aren't you?"

"Yeah. I am. I can have two of the three pieces ready to ship by the end of the week. But I need some money. Have you moved anything out there? Or through Vegas?"

"Honey, you are selling just as hot as ever. You sure you only have two for me?"

The guitar music started up again. Chamonix looked toward the ceiling. "Two for now. We'll see. I'm feeling . . . productive."

"Good. Good. Productive is good. Anything else you need? Besides the money?"

"No. But thanks."

Guy started to say, "Hey, how is everything in Syracuse? Your folks doing okay?"

But Chamonix had already hung up.

She took a shower, making the water as hot as she could stand it, until she thought her bones would melt from the heat, then she turned the faucet to cold and waited for the switch to happen.

The instant icy-cold water touched her heated bones, she shivered with a rattle from her insides, like an orgasm. Her breath came shorter, in gasps. Every piece of her alive. This was what it felt like when she rode well—zipping down a hill, the buzz of wheel and air in her helmet, passing a pack in a road race, quads on fire, lungs and heart fully engaged. She was more animal than human in those moments and she sometimes wished she could keep that sensory overload and call it up whenever she wanted to. Like now, when she needed to finish the canvases, when she needed to add the blood. When she needed to kill.

She dressed carefully, digging in the back of the closet for the thrift-store bag, planning her backstory as she selected garments: a tight denim skirt, rock-and-roll T-shirt. Chamonix stood in front of the mirror and tried on a few looks, settled on a sneer and an arched brow. "Name's Nat. What's yours?"

Today she didn't feel like a cute, vulnerable, Y-named girl. Today she was a lioness, a hunter. She gave herself red lips and Goth eyes, grabbed a marker and drew two tattoos, one on the inside of her left wrist, a Chinese character that meant purity, and another on her abdomen, a road. Someone would wonder where it led.

She rolled her bed away from the wall and pried up the loose floorboard, tugged on a string, and dragged out a black, zippered bag. She checked the contents: rubber gloves, plastic sheeting, baggies, lighter fluid, and a book of matches. Beneath that were things stolen from a veterinary clinic: a yellow cattle-syringe gun, four feet of tubing, and three empty blood bags.

She shoved the bag in her backpack, slung it over one shoulder, then pulled on a baggy sweatsuit over her tramp attire.

Two minutes later, with her dark glasses and her headset cranked up, she was pretty much deaf and blind. She pushed open her door, rolled out her bike, and slammed right into the guy from upstairs, knocking him on his ass.

"God, I'm sorry. Are you okay?" Chamonix asked, pulling the headphones from her ears.

His leg was cocked at an odd angle. He held a hand to his lip. It came away bloody.

"You're bleeding." Chamonix took off her sunglasses and looked around. "Shit." She leaned her bike against the wall as he struggled to rise. She tried to help him up. He wasn't as puny as he appeared. Chamonix managed to get him inside the loft and over to the couch.

"Hold on. I'll get you something for that," she said, motioning to his bloody mouth. She found an old towel in the bathroom, dampened the corner, and caught a glimpse of herself in the mirror.

"Be right there," she called, wiping off the trampy makeup, smoothing down her hair, then hurrying back to the living room.

"Here. Use this."

She shoved the towel at the guy. When he looked confused, she knelt beside him and pushed his head back gently, dabbing at his bloody lip. He had wonderful eyes, though they could never be described as baby blue or steely gray, nothing as cliché as that. They weren't any discernable color, really. It was that his eyes had no veil, they just let her in like she was the optometrist on the other side of that machine and he wasn't blinking.

"Hold that," she said, putting his hand on the cloth.

She went to the kitchen and filled a baggie with ice cubes.

"If you ice it right away, it will keep the swelling down."

His eyes met hers. Chamonix forced herself to look away.

Behind the cloth and the ice, he mumbled, "Um, if it's not too much trouble? Could I have a glass of water?"

She stared at him, then blinked. "Sure. Yeah. Absolutely."

In the kitchen, she forgot why she was there, and when she held her hand out, it trembled. Chamonix alternated between feeling disgust for her weakness, her lack of resolve and an insane desire to fall headlong into this odd feeling, to surrender completely and let it play out however it would.

Water. She filled a glass and brought it to him. He exchanged the bloody towel for the glass, but kept the ice. Chamonix took the towel to the kitchen, sealed it in a plastic bag, and put it in her freezer.

"So, you're an artist?" he said when she returned and sat in the rattan chaise across from the couch.

"What?"

He pointed at the canvases, the easel, the drop cloth and splatters, her studio space.

"Oh. That. Yes. I am."

He smiled, then winced as the skin stretched over his cut lip. "I'm Adam."

"Chamonix."

"Nice to meet you."

Like polar opposites, as she leaned forward to get up, to see him to the door, to move away from this whatever-this-was, Adam leaned back, sinking deeper into her couch, into her apartment, into her life.

Chamonix said, "So, listen, if you're all right . . . I was just . . ." She flapped her hands like they had the answer.

He looked at her. "Have you eaten dinner yet? Because that's where I was going. When we ran into each other."

"I really am sorry."

"It's okay. Accidents happen. But you could make it up to me. I've never been a fan of the whole solo dining experience."

Chamonix smiled. "It sucks."

"Yeah, it does. So you'd be doing me a favor and getting a meal out of it besides. What do you say?"

Chamonix looked at the clock. She still had time to finish the canvases before the courier came for them, and it might be weird if she said no. After all, she was responsible for him getting hurt. She surprised them both by saying, "Sure, why not? Let me throw on some jeans."

ARE YOU READY TO PLAY JAPANESE GAME SHOW, TEDESCO?

Chapter 24

I turned down the volume on the radio, even though it was The Killers and I loved that band.

"Tell me again," I said, when Tommy finally answered his cell phone. "Where is this place?"

I'd been driving up and down the same strip of two-lane highway for fifteen minutes, looking for the sushi joint where Tommy had just been dumped by his Scientologist boyfriend, Buck. Public break-up consoling was out of my realm. I had only agreed to meet him because I was hungry and curious about the place.

Tommy's phone crackled, and I heard him sniffle. "Do you see the Dollar Store sign? Turn in there. It's the second storefront."

Of course it was. "Bunya's" was spelled out in lights on a sign better suited for a Broadway theater than a restaurant. I made my way down the red-carpeted entrance and through a velvet rope queue, then pushed past thick gold drapes and stepped into the cool interior of the restaurant. A hostess stood behind a false theater box, complete with a listing of ticket prices and a scrolling marquee announcing showtimes.

"I'm here to meet someone. He's—"

"Mr. Tommy, right? You're Tedesco?"

"Uh, yes."

"Follow me, please."

Inside, Bunya's was like most other sushi places, except for the stage, emcee, and big screen.

I'd heard of Japanese places offering karaoke on certain nights, and while I thought that was best suited to crappy romantic comedy films, I supposed some folks went in for that sort of thing. Personally, I liked my karaoke loud, drunk, and food free. But this was more than karaoke, this was like being in the audience of a successful talk show.

I passed the sushi prep area and a row of padded stools, following the hostess to a plush red booth. I climbed up two steps, thanked her, then slid my way toward my dining partner, who was hidden behind a tall menu.

"Nice place. Where's Buck?"

He sniffled. "Asshole."

"Nice to see you too," I said.

"Not you. Buck."

"And that surprises you why?" I asked.

There was the sound of a sigh from behind the menu. When it dropped, revealing a newly blond Tommy, I thought it was like when Brad Pitt went blond, only Tommy was more like Brad Pitt's shorter double. From the back, from far away, if you squinted.

"I know. I know." He ran his hand over his head. "At least it's not permanent. Unlike my—"

"Jesus. Don't say it."

"Broken heart."

"Shit." I signaled to the waitress. "We need a sake and two beers. Make that a large sake."

She shuffled off, bowing and nodding. I reached into my pocket, pulled out my backup ball cap from Furman with FU lovingly embroidered over the bill.

"Here."

Tommy slipped it on.

I reached over to adjust the angle and said, "Better. Okay. I'll give you three minutes to say whatever you need to say and then this goes behind us. Got it? No more Buck and good riddance to the Scientologists, right?"

Tommy nodded sadly.

I tipped my watch face, counted down, then pointed at him.

Tommy poked his chopsticks into the tablecloth as he said, “He is an ass. I hate him and I don’t know what I ever saw in him.”

“Is there something else you want to add?” I asked, alluding to the quote he’d memorized from a relationship book after the last three boyfriends hadn’t worked out either.

He stopped poking, looked around, then said, “I deserve better. The perfect person for me exists somewhere. I am open to possibility, open to opportunity, and welcome life with open arms.”

The sake arrived right on time.

“To chance,” I said.

“To opportunity disguised as misery,” Tommy chanted.

We drank. We ate. We didn’t mention Buck or his crazy group again. We played along with the game show—by trying to guess what was being made in a factory somewhere before the real Japanese contestants on the paused TV screen could.

We didn’t win, but that was okay because Tommy was back to being a single-minded employee. Uttering a tearful version of “cross my heart and hope to die, stick a needle in my eye,” complete with hand motions for the deaf, Tommy swore off relationships—*for a while.*

As a friend, I knew I needed to keep him busy by offering him distractions. Distractions in the form of evidence that I was still carrying around from Smith’s apartment. I reached in my pocket. There was the ticket for the dry cleaner and the microcassette tape I’d found in the sock drawer.

I dangled the tape in front of Tommy’s face. “Two guesses.”

Tommy sloshed the rest of the sake into his tiny ceramic cup. "Illicit sex."

I shook my head.

He swallowed another bite of a spider roll and followed it with more sake. "A bad mix tape from the eighties?"

"Close," I said. "There's a lot of background noise in the beginning, some stuff I can't make out, then it gets garbled, but before the songs cut in, there's a part where our boy Smith says his name over and over. Like he wants to be the next Howard Stern."

"I wonder what that's all about?" Tommy stared at the empty sake cup, then looked at me. It was hard to take the guy seriously, what with his buzzed eyes and that bleached-blond hair poking out from under the FU ball cap.

"The background check I ran on Smith said he was a retired pilot living off lawsuit money," he said.

"No telling when the tape was made," I said. "Or why he kept it. You should listen to it. Tell me what you think."

I slid it over to Tommy, who carefully wiped his fingers, picked up the tape, and tried to slip it into his shirt pocket, but missed twice.

"Come on," I said. "I'll take you home."

TEDESCO, A DIRTY GIRL, AND A DRY CLEANER

Chapter 25

A few hours, one We Fix Hair salon detour, and two pots of coffee later, I told Tommy about the dry cleaning ticket I'd found at Smith's apartment.

We were at his house—a cottage-looking structure that he called a Craftsman. I had no idea what that meant, unless it referred to the fact that you should be some sort of craftsman to live there because something was always on the fritz or threatening to be. The house was just *old* to me. I'd never felt comfortable in it. There was too much history everywhere you looked. Too many ghosts.

Tommy scooped up a passing cat, stood her on the kitchen table, and began running a metal-toothed brush through her long, white fur. I had no idea where he'd been hiding the comb.

He had two cats. One was nice and one liked to bite me and piss in my shoes. I glanced at the heart-shaped tag on the rhinestone collar: DIRTY GIRL. She was the nice one. I reached out and tickled her under the chin. She turned her smashed-in face toward me and winked. I wasn't a cat person, but this one seemed to forgive me for that.

Tommy worked his way from the front of the cat to the back, his words emphasized with tugging strokes that left deep parallel lines in the cat's fur. Dirty Girl purred.

"Look, Tedesco. I understand. We have to run down all the evidence. We have to explore all the possibilities. We have to tramp down all the alleys in our hooker platforms.

We must leave no bed unturned, no chocolate uneaten, no champagne uncorked."

"All right. All right," I said. "Enough with the analogies. I get it. We'll check out the dry cleaner and leave the tape to your techie friends. Is that what you want to hear?"

"Yes," Tommy said as he finished grooming the cat. He kissed her on the nose, then set her gently on the floor. Dirty Girl walked away, swishing her tail. A small puff of love emanated from Tommy not unlike the whiff you get when you pull the wrapping off a fragrant candle for your bathroom.

He stood and pulled the hair out of the brush, pitched it in the trash, then ran the metal teeth through his own hair—once again dark and shiny. "Come on. We have to see the dry cleaner."

Somehow that sounded liked a whole new analogy, or was that a euphemism?

As I weaved the Lincoln across town through the city streets, I wondered why people chose white cars, why there weren't more multicolored cars, and why a guy would go to a dry cleaner so far away from his apartment.

"Maybe he spilled something on a jacket and decided to get the stain treated right away."

Tommy had this weird way of answering questions I hadn't even asked.

"That's something *you* would do," I said.

"You're saying Smith was nothing like me?"

I just looked at him.

"Okay. Whatever."

He wriggled a little in his seat, finally cleared his throat, and started one of his Tommy monologues. This one was sans PowerPoint presentation, but I still knew better than to interrupt or to ask for any sort of clarification.

"My parents used a home pickup and delivery dry

cleaning service," he began. "One day I was home sick from school and the driver rang the bell, hung the order from the doorknob, and left. I was sixteen at the time, and in some kind of trouble. I remember thinking I'd get on my mom's good side by putting all the clothes away. That was when I found some guy's shirt mixed in with ours."

Tommy stuck his arm out the window and did that air surfing thing with his hand. I was about to tell him to cut it out when he continued with his story.

"There was tag on the shirt with part of a last name and a phone number, so I called the guy, planning to tell him we'd send it back to the dry cleaner with our next pickup. The guy answered the phone. It never even occurred to me that he shouldn't have been there, that he should have been at work, or that his wife should have answered, or a machine with all the kids saying their names before the beep. But I stood there with this guy's blue, fitted, Geoffrey Beene dress shirt in one hand and the telephone receiver in the other and I felt something like *love* for the first time—or lust. I had something somebody wanted. And it was all under my control—whether the guy got his shirt, whether I gave him my address, whether anything happened at all. It was about more than the shirt. I knew that too. I don't know how I knew. I just did. Maybe it's how women say they just *know* when they're pregnant, or when their guy's lying . . . maybe it's like that.

"Anyway, he came over and he was good-looking. Really good-looking. Movie star features. Definitely the kind of guy people look at twice. I left the shirt in the kitchen before I answered the door so he would have to come in. He had to walk down the long hallway. He had to follow me. He had to look at my house, at my doors and the rooms beyond, at the back of my head and my ass, my sixteen-year-old body. In the kitchen, he didn't have to, but he kissed me."

Tommy ran a finger over his lower lip, then stared out the window.

I had to lower the volume on the Count Basie CD to hear what he said next.

"He was my first. Sometimes I think he might have been the best. I tried calling him once afterward, but he pretended he didn't know me. I could hear a woman in the background, a barking dog, and a baby saying, 'Da-da. Da-da. Da-da.' I never called back."

I might have said this before, but it bears repeating. I don't care about another guy's sexuality. I really don't. Some guys like women with fat asses. I don't get that either, but do I think it's wrong? Nope. It's what they like. It's what appeals to them. And I'm not them. End of story. Because who are we to say what's right and what's wrong? What's good and what's bad? Who'd make the better angel? So I didn't say anything.

Tommy lifted his commuter cup and drained his latte. He pointed to the radio with his pinkie. "Hey, turn that up."

We listened to Jimmy Rushing backed by the Count as we wound through farm country on poorly paved roads that bore no signs. It was the only route I knew to Baldwinsville. I used to date a girl who lived there, back when I was a boy and still on the kick of finding someone younger. Before I figured out that older women were much more reasonable—and inventive.

We crossed a green metal bridge, tires whomping and singing, and drove into the center of the village.

Tommy checked the address. "Should be right up there."

We pulled into a spot across the street and checked the meter. Fifteen minutes left. We felt lucky.

The dry cleaning shop was like all the others I'd been in—hot, cramped, and disorganized. It smelled like the underside of a sink mixed with the odor of the household products row in the dollar store, like fake sunshine and bug killer.

"How can I help you?"

An Indian man in a brilliant-white shirt and pressed khakis shuffled to the front, appearing from behind a rack of plastic-wrapped clothing. Shirts, suits, and dresses swayed in his wake, offering glimpses into the back where a handful of workers were cleaning, pressing, buttoning, and sorting the garments of strangers.

Snippets of an argument and raised voices filtered to the front of the store. The language could have been Hindi or Swedish. I wasn't very good at languages, and if you talked to me long enough in your foreign patter, I might start mimicking the sounds back at you, though I meant no disrespect. I didn't even realize I was doing it, until my first ex-wife pointed it out to me. She said I was embarrassing her, that I was being demeaning to Italians. I tried to explain all the ways that couldn't be possible, but I think she took it personally. She brought the whole thing up again during the divorce. It was her fault for hiring a lawyer with a Southern accent. She knew I wouldn't be able to help myself. It was a social disorder. Probably a great talent to possess if you were a salesman or a professional pickup artist—two things I've never been.

Since I wasn't there to sell timeshares or pick up anything but the stuff Smith had dropped off, I let Tommy do the talking. We waited until we were in the car before we opened the manila envelope Mr. Lee had given us. Tommy threw plastic-draped pants and a white shirt into the backseat, then slit the envelope and upended it—a pen from a bank, two paper clips, a stick of spearmint gum, and a folded receipt.

I opened the faded receipt carefully. I recognized the logo for a national gas station franchise, the name James John Smith, and when I held it to the light I could make out the location: Wolfeboro, New Hampshire. It was a start.

JUDGMENTS, EXPECTATIONS, AND DEJA VOODOO

Chapter 26

Roxie flattened the sheet of paper across the steering wheel. She'd forgotten, again, to check her pockets on laundry day. There was a hole in the middle of the page, and the handwriting had faded, but she could make out the words "Dr. Hanna" and "Professional Drive."

She drove around the hospital and pulled up to a row of office buildings. Roxie found a listing for Hanna, MD, in the third office building. She skipped the elevator and jogged up two flights of stairs, rushed into the waiting room, and tapped on the glass divider at the nurse's station.

"I'm here to pick up a friend. James Smith?"

"Still with the doctor," the nurse said. "You're welcome to wait."

Roxie looked around the empty waiting area. What kind of doctor was this? The ones she went to always had crying babies and teenagers on cell phones, a pile of plastic toys in a corner, and a stack of outdated magazines to peruse. She couldn't sit. It was a sick room and she had a thing about germs. Just standing there made her want to wash her hands.

"I'll be out there," she said, motioning to the door, the world, another place with fresh air, sunshine and normal, healthy sounds. "Could you tell him when he comes out?"

The nurse nodded.

Roxie walked down the hall to the area overlooking the lobby. Outside, banished smokers puffed away, polluting everyone's environment instead of just a bathroom or their own offices.

She read the names on the marquee, started to run her finger down the list until she imagined how many sick people might have done that before her. She shuddered, then looked around for a restroom with a sink, soap, and hot water.

When Roxie returned, James was leaning against the wall, his face unguarded, innocent, and a bit sad.

"James?"

He straightened up and switched on his usual face. "Hey. There you are." He scooped her into his side, a comforting gesture, something a father or brother would do, or a gay friend.

"Everything okay?" Roxie asked. "Anything you want to talk about?"

"Nope," he said, pressing the elevator button.

Their reflection in the metal doors was warped, twisting their faces into one mass, compacting their bodies into a senseless blob. When the doors parted, they were split in two, and Roxie felt loss.

In the car, Roxie didn't ask how he'd gotten to the appointment or what it was for or if he needed to go to the pharmacy.

"Hungry?" he asked.

"I could eat. Though I shouldn't. Girl's gotta watch her figure, you know."

"Why don't you let me watch it?" James grinned.

Roxie glanced over. Even though the guy looked a bit paler than normal and he had seemed thinner, less energetic lately at work, he was grinning at her like the old James. Like the guy who had flirted with her all through her hiring interview and always had something sweet to say. Not bullshit. Not just words, but a sentence that made her feel sexy, powerful, made her—if she was totally honest—wet.

Some guys could do that. Not many. And most of them were assholes. Hot, well-built assholes. But when you found a guy who was kind and sweet and attractive and had that talent, well, hell, you'd be stupid to pass it up. Unless of course it was your boss. Your friend. And your friends' friend. She'd be stupid to blow something like that—or him. She started to laugh.

"Want to let me in on the joke?" James asked, smiling.

"What? Um, no." She pulled up to the stoplight, looked around. "Want to get Mexican?"

"I have a better idea." James pointed. "Take the next left."

Roxie followed his instructions and ended up on a crowded street lined with junker cars. Skinny black kids sat on the steps of tenement-style brick buildings, shaking their arms and shoulders in complicated dance moves that looked to her like slow-motion fighting. Roxie clicked the door lock and shoved her purse under the seat.

"Be cool, Roxie," James said. "You're with me." He waved his arm out the window and all the kids on the steps waved back. Two removed their hats.

"How do you know them?" She shook her head. "Never mind. I don't want to know."

"Pull up there, at the brown gate," he said.

It swung open as they approached. Roxie drove into a cobblestone courtyard that reminded her of something she'd seen on the travel channel during Italy Week.

"What. The. Fuck?"

James laughed. "Yeah, that's the normal reaction. Wait till you see the inside."

The gate squeaked closed behind them as they rolled past an ornate fountain of cherubs and busty women. She parked her Honda near an artful arrangement of sculptured shrubs and trees.

They stepped up wide marble stairs to the largest doors Roxie had ever seen. Before James could use the lion-head knocker, one huge door swung inward. Roxie was certain Lurch was going to poke his head out, but no one did. James put his hand on the small of her back and guided her inside.

The gold-domed ceiling in the entry was at least thirty feet high. Chubby angels painted by a brave artist circled the lip of the dome, and trailed ribbons and stars down the walls to stained-glass windows. She was staring at the art when a short, mustachioed man appeared from behind velvet curtains. He approached, arms wide. "Buongiorno, Signore Smith!"

James returned the man's cheek kisses, said something in Italian, then tipped his head in Roxie's direction. "Signore Aldo Lombardi, this is Miss Roxanne Dupont."

Roxie leaned down to take the man's hand. He pulled her into him, saying, "Welcome to my palace, bella."

She smashed her cheeks up against his, right then left. He smelled of talcum powder and musk, like a baby grandpa.

"We are happy to have you," he said. "This way, per favore." He motioned them through the curtains into a sunken room of tables and chairs, of waiters and diners, of candlelight and soft opera arias. A very plush, very private Italian restaurant.

Two hours later, after the antipasti and the soup, after the risotto and the salad, after the pasta and the veal and the cheese and the digestives, after the sampling of the tiramisu and the torte, after multiple glasses of wine and bottles of mineral water, after all of it, Roxie cried "uncle" for the second time and James agreed. It was time to go.

"Aldo, my friend." James motioned to Aldo with one

hand while reaching in his back pocket for his wallet. "We have to go. Tell me, what do I owe you?"

Aldo brushed him off like a fly, pushed away his wallet. "No, no. We have an arrangement? Do we not? It is my pleasure."

He collected the dessert plates, bowed to Roxie. "Is there anything else I can bring you?"

"Oh, no. I really couldn't." She ran a hand over her stomach, exhaled loudly. "It was all so fantastic, really. I am just. Wow. Thank you."

"And I think that says it all," James said. "Grazie, Aldo."

"Anytime my friend, and let me know if there are any more problems with . . ." He leaned in, lowered his voice. "The other thing."

James's smile faded. He dabbed his lips with the napkin, said something behind it while pulling Aldo close. The man nodded, then smiled at Roxie, who pretended to be very interested in the tablecloth's design.

They were quiet in the car, sedated by carbohydrates, by Chianti, by the remnant of music written centuries ago. Roxie was glad for the stillness. She wondered how she could ask James all the things she'd been thinking about. They were personal, and that wasn't a place anyone went with James. She waited, hoping he'd say something to give her an in. He didn't.

So she drove to Flannigan's, pulled to the curb, and pressed button to unlock the doors, saying, "Home sweet home."

James stared out the window as if he was seeing the bar for the first time. "Yeah. Home." He reached for the handle and said, "Thanks, Roxie, for picking me up and for having lunch with me." He yawned. "I might need a nap before work. You?" He waggled his brows Groucho-style.

Roxie laughed. "Afraid not. I still have work to do. No rest for the wicked, you know."

James stepped out of the car and closed the door, murmuring, "I know that's right."

"What's that?" Roxie called after him.

"Just saying, gonna be a slow night," James said, waving as he walked away.

Roxie watched as he unlocked the door to Flannigan's and stepped in, pulling it shut behind him. Through the bay window she could see him cross the room. He ran his hand through his hair, then over his face. He seemed to have aged ten years in seconds. She watched until he moved out of view, then she pulled away from the curb and made her way down the block.

Lost in thought, she jumped when her cell phone's ring filled the car speakers. The caller ID lit up the dash as she clicked the Bluetooth. "Hey, Cress. You'll never believe where I was."

"Let me guess," Cress said. "You finally got that colonic you've been talking about?"

"Ha ha. No. I was in a real live fucking palace!"

"A *fucking* palace? You are one sick girl!"

"No! And *what*? It was a mansion on the south side done up to look like a palace, and there's a restaurant there. Omigod. I had the most amazing meal. Seriously, you would not believe the food we ate."

"We?"

"Me and James."

"Since when do you go out for lunch with James?"

"Since he invited me."

"I see. So where did you go again?" Cress asked, thinking how she and Chamonix had just said Roxie was the best one of the three, the one you could depend on like a mother, and that when they were all together—all four of them, how James was like the older brother. He was the necessary fourth, the one that made pairing up okay, because no one wanted to be the odd man out when you rode rollercoasters and no one liked being the third in a car. The backseat never felt full.

Roxie said, "I don't know exactly—you know me and directions. But the guy knew James and brought out all this food and wine and never charged us a cent! It was great."

"What guy?"

"Some old Italian dude. Aldo something."

"Aldo? Not Lombardi?"

"Yeah, that was it." Roxie put on a deep Italian voice. "Signore Aldo Lombardi."

"Holyfuckingshit, Roxie. He's a don."

"No, Cress. His name's Aldo."

"I mean he's a *don*? As in the head of the Lombardi family? As in Mafia?"

"What? That sweet old man? C'mon. I went to school with a bunch of Lombardis. It's a common name. You know, in Italy it's as common as—"

"Smith?" Cress said.

Upstairs, in his apartment over the bar, James stared at the blank calendar. The doctor had given him three months—maybe six—to live. He'd known something was wrong, that there was something dead inside him already. He wondered if he had made that dead part grow even faster with the choices he'd made. He hated thinking like that. As if he'd ever mattered.

He hung the calendar back on the fridge, drew the curtains, then laid down on his couch. TV flickered images from a black-and-white film, *Double Indemnity.* He reached under the couch for an ashtray, picked through the butts of half-smoked joints, and chose a fat one with a pink lipstick tinge. Jimbo fast-forwarded through the opening credits to a scene where Neff, played by Fred MacMurray, sat at his desk speaking into a dictation machine:

"It was perfect, except that it wasn't, because you made a mistake, just one tiny little mistake. When it came to picking the killer, you picked the wrong guy, if you know what I mean. Want to know who killed Dietrichson? Hold tight to that cheap cigar of yours, Keyes. I killed Dietrichson. Me, Walter Neff, insurance agent, thirty-five years old, unmarried, no visible scars—" (He glanced down at his wounded shoulder) "Until a little while ago, that is. Yes, I killed him. I killed him for money—and a woman—and I didn't get the money and I didn't get the woman. Pretty, isn't it?"

Neff interrupted the dictation, lay down the horn on the desk. He took his lighted cigarette from the ashtray, puffed it two or three times, and killed it. He picked up the horn again.

James played out the scene on his end, lip-synching the monologue, mimicking the hand flourishes. He smoked when Neff smoked, stubbing his joint out simultaneously. He punched the Fast-Forward button, stopping on the part where Neff goes to the Dietrichsons' house and meets Phyllis. He unzipped his pants, pulled out his cock, and spoke the lines out loud, stroking himself. Barbara Stanwyck had been something else back then.

Later that night, after closing the bar, Jimbo lay in bed staring at the ceiling. He thought about how there are certain things in life that, once you start doing them, you can't stop. Like a gateway drug. He thought about the first kiss—just a peck, but a few of those and it led to inserting the tongue, which led to groping over the clothes, then under the clothes, then without clothes, which led to trying all those same things with other people. And once you went there . . . The possibilities were endless, especially if you liked to travel. And maybe you stumble on a certain inappropriate picture or website or magazine and you think that wasn't so bad, so you go a little farther and then . . . it's no big deal. None of it is any big deal.

Until you wake up one morning totally uninhibited, your innocence compromised beyond repair, and you ask yourself, who the fuck am I now?

IF WISHES WERE HORSES, TEDESCO WOULD BE IN DEEP MANURE

Chapter 27

It felt a bit surreal, being there with her, alone. I tried to not think of the possibilities, but walking behind Barbara, following the sway of her hips, possibility was definitely one of the things on my mind.

She led me to the sunroom, a glass-walled outcropping expanding the already-too-large house. The view was spectacular. A manicured lawn rolled away to a wide expanse of field and forest beyond, like something you'd see on one of those horror movies that start out all nice and sunny, or a made-for-TV drama where the mean guy is dying of cancer and builds an amusement park in his backyard so kids will always remember him.

Barbara waved at a wicker bar in the corner. "Do you want a drink? It's not too early, is it? Mick's traveling and, I swear, I don't keep a schedule when he's gone. I don't even like cooking for myself. It seems such a waste, all that preparation and cleanup. I'd just as soon eat a bowl of cereal."

I listened to her flit from subject to subject like a hummingbird. She was still cute, still had no idea the effect she had on men—on me. I had to watch myself or I'd fall in love with Buffy all over again. I sunk back into a chaise lounge angled to take in the view, the green expanse of lawn. That was the thing about Syracuse—precipitation and clouds were good for growing grass. Also for indoor sports and fat, lazy people.

But on this day we were neither of those, doing nothing

like that. We were instead two old friends reminiscing in a fancy house in the suburbs while the hard-working husband was away.

"Why didn't you ever come back for the reunions?" she asked.

"There were reunions?"

"Stop it. You know there were. I sent the invites, made the list myself."

"Is that right? I should have come, then."

"Why didn't you, Bill? Didn't you wonder, I mean, about everyone?"

"Sure I did," I said. "But I was on the road with the guys then, and we hardly knew what city we were in much less what month it was. We did forty-eight states in ten months, made more in one night than some people make all year."

She raised her brows. I could almost hear the "cha-ching."

I shrugged. "I blew it all. Only one of us had any sense. Fifi put half his take away every month, played the market, did good for himself. Now he owns a few car dealerships in Miami, has oceanfront property, and travels to Europe with a new woman every spring." I started feeling a bit depressed. "You know, I think I will have a drink."

I glanced at a bottle of Jack, but went to the fridge instead and found a Belgium beer that I poured into a glass bearing the same name. "What can I make you?"

"Surprise me," Barbara said, lying back in her chaise, crossing her legs, and allowing the slit in her skirt to spread another inch.

I let myself think for a minute that she was *my* wife, that this was *our* house, that I had a regular job and was staring retirement down, that we had plans for the rest of our lives and they weren't the normal ones. Me and Buffy, we were going to travel to places where no one else went. We were going to spend every dime, leave our ten kids penniless, and to hell with nursing homes. When the time came, we'd know it and we'd go out in style, forget to surface on a deep dive in Belize, drive off a snowy turn in Montana, hang glide into the cliffs of Brazil. Our terms, baby.

I made her a vodka martini using the good stuff. I measured it into the silver shaker, added vermouth and ice, hummed a Bon Jovi tune as I shook it. They had been her favorite band, once. When she started singing I joined in, harmonizing with her smooth soprano. We sounded good together.

I could have done this all day. Maybe for the rest of my life, because I was still good-time Willy from the old days. This was the big game and I had the playbook memorized, but I was ready to throw it away and come up with a new play—the swing play, the take-it-the-long-way-around-while-the-husband's-away play—where I got the touchdown and the cheerleader too.

I brought the drink to her as we closed the song "You Give Love a Bad Name." She laughed and reached for the glass, and I knew I could have her if I wanted. That really, she'd been mine all along.

Until she said, "Mick hates that song."

I blinked myself back into reality. I had been unhappily married—a few times—with nothing to show for it but having disappointed yet another woman. And Buffy was Barbara now, a rich wife with monogrammed linens, a social calendar, and a condo in Boca. I pushed our past back where it belonged and concentrated on why I was here.

I had to tell her what I knew about her daughter's death.

I told her about the tape and how James Smith might

not be exactly who we thought he was, that we were still working on that part. I didn't say anything about what Tommy and I had found at the dry cleaners.

"It might be nothing," I said.

"But it might be something."

"Yes. Did Chamonix ever go on a trip with James?"

"Not that I know of."

"I know the cops have been through it, but, I'd like to check out Chamonix's apartment. Would that be okay?"

"Whatever you need, Bill." She twirled the tooth-picked olive in her mouth, then bit it tenderly.

I glanced at the family portrait on the wall behind her.

Time to go.

At the door, Barbara gave me a door key and an address. I pecked her on the cheek, took a minute to inhale the familiar Buffy scent, reminded myself she was my employer and nothing else—for now.

For the life of me, I couldn't understand the appeal of loft living. I guess it would be great if you needed a warehouse for storing antiques or housing an artist's studio. But I wasn't a decorator or an artist. To me it just looked like wasted space.

I had just started going through Chamonix's kitchen cabinets when someone knocked on the door.

The guy in the peephole looked harmless enough and I definitely wanted to talk to anyone who knew Chamonix, so I opened the door and tried to look like I belonged.

"Hi. I'm Tedesco."

He shook my hand. "Adam," he said, looking over my shoulder into the loft.

Barbara hadn't mentioned any friends or boyfriends. Though she was the first to admit she wasn't as close to her daughter as she would have liked. I backed up, still holding his hand, "Want to come in?" I asked, pulling him forward.

"Uh, no. I mean—"

"How did you know Chamonix?"

He pulled his hand back like he'd been stung. "Who are you?"

"I'm Tedesco," I repeated. "A friend of the family." I circled around him, closed the door, and used some body language to move him into the kitchen.

The kid seemed nervous. I needed to find out if that was just an uncomfortable thing or a guilty thing.

"Where do you live, Adam?"

"Here. I mean, upstairs. I didn't know Chamonix. Well, not really. I mean, not for long. I used to see her coming in from bike rides. One night we ran into each other." He blushed, touching the scar on his chin. "Literally."

The kid was an open book.

I opened the fridge. It was surprisingly clean. Most of the time in these situations—sudden deaths, disappearances—a refrigerator would be stocked with spoiling food, sometimes bought the very day the victim had died. A rotting meal no one would eat. I grabbed a light beer and a girly wine cooler and motioned to the stool at the counter. He sat, glanced at the colorful bottle then twisted off the top expertly and straightened up a bit.

"What do you do?" I asked.

"I'm a guitarist and a meteorology intern at the radio station."

"Is that right?"

"It's the only job where you're allowed to be wrong half the time. What's not to love about that?" He smiled and raised his fruity concoction.

I said, "Well, when you put it that way."

He shrugged. "My dad always had low expectations for me."

There wasn't anything I could say, other than I knew how he felt. All sons did.

"But it must be cool sometimes, right?" I tried. "People talk about weather all the time."

"Yeah. When they run out of real conversation."

He took another slug, burped softly in his hand, like a balloon deflating.

"I thought going into it, it would be exciting. Tornadoes, hurricanes, tsunamis, hail storms, extremes of cold and heat, life-and-death situations. But really it's just telling people what they already know and sometimes stuff they don't want to hear."

"I like the girl who does the weather report on the Naked News Channel," I said.

He nodded. "Well, there's always that."

We raised our bottles in a toast and reflected on the effects of weather in a whole new way.

After a bit, he said, "Chamonix was always trying to get me to see the best part of my job. I do love the research, and math was always a strong subject for me. There's this cool thing I've been working on, it's a Doppler radar algorithm called CVT, a text-based analysis tool that can be used to interrogate the radar algorithm output—"

"Hold on there, pal," I said. "I was just fine with the partly cloudy, partly sunny, bare-assed weather girl."

"Right." He finished his drink, then glanced at the open cabinets behind me, the stuff I'd pulled from the drawers and left on the counter. "So, Tedesco. What are you really doing here?"

I smiled. Kid wasn't as dumb as he seemed. "Chamonix's mother asked me to look into her death, wanted to see if I could go a little deeper than the cops had. I was thinking maybe I'd find something here, something they missed. Best to see everything as she left it, before they pack it all up."

"Are her parents taking everything?"

"I guess. Why?"

"It's just that she said she was painting something for me, and I never . . . you know."

"Never what?"

He looked toward the studio space.

"I never got the chance to see it."

We both stared at the easel in the corner. A paint-splattered sheet draped the canvas. There weren't any other pieces in the room. Everything I'd ever read about artists said they were messy and impulsive, usually had bizarre routines, odd lifestyles, as if by being artistic they had to give up a conventional life. But from the looks of Chamonix's place, she was organized, neat, almost impeccably so. And that got me wondering.

"I don't think anyone would mind, now," I said, moving from the kitchen toward the easel. I heard the squeak of Adam's chair as he rose.

It felt like we should say something—an incantation or eulogy, a prayer or a blessing, *something* before we unveiled the canvas. I also didn't want to be the guy who did it, the unveiling. It felt creepy, like a horror movie scene where the brave one dies first, the hero figure, the one who always has the right answers. Maybe he just got so annoying the writer had to bump him off.

"Go ahead," I said, elbowing Adam.

He stepped forward and grabbed a corner of the sheet, slid the fabric off, and let it pool on the floor.

The painting was of a man in a fishbowl. It was only the back of him, a shadow figure. It could have been the back of Adam. The man's arms were outstretched, touching the sides of the bowl, and his face was lifted to the sky. The fishbowl floated on a raft of matchsticks. Their red tips flared against the blue, blue water. The sky was full of storm clouds, deep and menacing. Yet behind one there was a glimpse of sun, a piercing ray of light forcing a path through, aiming straight for the man.

I felt the fishbowl man's anguish, his hope, his desire, and his inadequacy.

And beside me, Adam must have felt it too.

YOU DON'T KNOW ME FROM ADAM

Chapter 28

His fingers ached from hours of tremolo picking, but when he was like this, all lost in the sounds coming from his guitar, there was no stopping. His mother used to yell at him when he spent hours in his room creating music. She called him a fool, a dreamer, said he was someone who would never amount to anything.

The idea of that—the amounting part—bothered Adam for years. What was someone's worth? If you had to look at it mathematically, to tabulate it, would you add for every good deed, subtract the times you didn't return a call or loan money to a friend, multiply by two for your kindnesses, three if they were given unwillingly, then divide the whole by ten, if you'd ever committed a mortal sin?

If so, Adam figured he amounted to about $647.18. The odd change was his contribution to music. Fool. Dreamer. He might have been inclined to agree with his mother. Until Chamonix. She called him brave, said he was an artist—like her.

"The world doesn't get us," she'd said. "And that's okay. It's not supposed to. See, if we were as normal and predictable as the rest of them? We wouldn't be as desirable. Being odd ups your value. Trust me on that."

And when she had touched his back and leaned in to kiss him, Adam felt his worth increase.

It wasn't perfect, him and Chamonix. But what relationship is? He needed the passion. The awakening. Even when it got uncomfortable. Him wanting more than she could give. Him, acting selfish, controlling.

But she was also selfish and they were both stubborn and emotional, and would probably kill each other if they stayed together. Maybe he really needed someone to mother him and she needed a daddy and they were mismatched and the cruel reality was they *had* love but it wasn't enough. They had the one thing people all over the world seek, and still it was not enough to make everything work out okay.

Adam thought someone must be laughing now. Someone who wrote a love song. Someone who directed a love story. Someone who put those poems in those books that he'd read, believed, and memorized. They were all laughing now at our gullibility, at the private joke on humanity.

Love ain't it, people. It's agreement, it's appeasement. It's giving up what you want in order to make a peaceful existence and it's never, ever, wanting more than you deserve. Because you know what? You don't deserve shit.

Or so he thought, until Chamonix. She changed that idea in him. She made him feel important, special, lucky.

And how? By letting him know love.

They had been taking things slow, with quiet nights in—at his place, always—and the occasional dinner-and-movie date. Chamonix told Adam that she needed her space, she was a loner by nature. He didn't mind. It took a lot of pressure off him. Besides, the sex was good and the way she could share the couch and be with him, but not suffocate him like other girls he'd been with—in that way, it was better than good. It was almost perfect.

They'd been seeing each other for a few weeks when Chamonix asked Adam to make a promise. He thought it was one of those moments men dread, until she said, "If something happens to me and I can't come back to the loft, I need to do something for me. Would you promise me, Adam?"

She sounded so serious, so mature, that he sounded like a child when he said, "It depends. Do what?"

"Promise me first."

"I don't know if I can, if I don't know what it is," he said.

"You can," she said. "And you will. Because you're brave. And because you love me."

Adam said nothing. They were lying naked on their backs on his bed. An oscillating fan blew fake breezes. Through the window, moonlight splayed across his thighs, her chest. He could see Chamonix's nipples stiffen. The Man in the Moon was a Peeping Tom.

"I promise," he said.

She sighed. "Thank you."

He didn't understand why it was so important to her, the task she'd given him.

But when she didn't come back one night, or the next day, and when his calls went unanswered, even before he read in the paper that her body had been found, he knew what he had to do.

He climbed down his fire escape and slid open the window Chamonix never locked. He erased the phone messages on her machine, took back his clothes and toothbrush, and grabbed a garbage bag from under the sink. He found the towel in a baggie in the freezer and the plastic container exactly where she'd said it would be—on the lowest shelf of the refrigerator behind the Chinese takeout box.

He put it all in a trash bag, then drove fifteen miles to Hidden Acres Campground. He parked on the side of road, avoiding the main entrance, and hiked back to an abandoned campsite. He dug a trench in the circular fire pit for the bag and built a stick pyramid over it, doused everything with lighter fluid, then tossed in the can. Within minutes, the fire was blazing. The garbage bag and its contents melted and smoked a little, but in the end, it all turned to ash and glass. Adam used some bark and cardboard to scoop dirt over the remains, then covered the whole thing with branches and kindling, leaving a perfect setup for the next camper.

Back at the road, he slipped behind the wheel and started up the car. There was no one around. He sat for a moment as the local radio news announced weather, mortgage rates, and the deaths of three women in a local Irish bar. He plugged his iPod into the stereo, hit the shuffle button, then sped off. The whine of the engine was rivaled only by the angry, sexy sounds of flamenco guitarist El Rubio and the bellowing of single-again Adam.

WHEN MOMMY STILL MANAGES TO FUCK UP YOUR LIFE

Chapter 29

Sandy Wykowski-Smith would have been proud of her son, Jimbo Five, now Mr. James John Smith, entrepreneur extraordinaire.

Jimbo felt a certain accountability to his new persona, as if he'd walked into a masked ball dressed as Zorro and was expected to wield a sword with expertise, slash a Z into his enemy's shirt, sweep a damsel off her feet, then ride off on a black stallion. He did his best to be the new James. In time, he figured this would be all he knew. Anyway, there was no question of going back. He began to think of his transformation like puberty—permanent changes that yielded a better man.

One thing Jimbo couldn't change was his taste in women. He couldn't help that he was attracted to the stupid ones. God simply made them sexier, or maybe it was due to their lack of intelligence that they became sexy. They never thought about how they looked to others. They had no knowledge of mathematics, so they didn't realize their pants were too tight for their mass or that their breasts were largely disproportionate to the rest of their body or their chosen hair color never occurred in nature. He couldn't blame them for being dumb. That would be discrimination.

Instead, he loved them. He accepted them only for what they were and he took them home to his apartment through the back door and tried not to tell them that he was the owner of Flannigan's. He made sure they were drunk enough to be as stupid as possible and he always drove them home, dropped them at their door, inserted the key in the lock, and bowed as he backed away.

Except that one time.

Sylvia Ponce had no idea she was about to be seduced.

It had happened before Flannigan's reopened under Jimbo's management, before he hired the girls or fixed the rickety kitchen. He found himself in a college bar on the hill, checking out the competition, and, from habit, the women.

She was too old to be a college student. He thought she must be traveling on business. A woman as pretty as that would never be alone in a bar by choice. He waited until it looked like she was getting ready to leave, then sent her another glass of wine and waited for the bartender to point in his direction. She smiled, tipped her head in thanks, and when he walked toward her she turned to face him with body language that said, "Welcome home, stranger."

After the usual introductions, Sylvia and James drank their wine, and then had more wine until James suggested they head over to his place for something else—a nightcap, perhaps?

"Maybe some Sambuca?" he suggested.

She put her hand on his thigh. "I can think of a nightcap that also begins with *s* and ends in *a*." She mouthed her name, then reached for her purse.

Jimbo grinned, thinking he'd like having both.

He parked in the lot behind Flannigan's, kissed her in the alleyway and on the landing, each time working his tongue like a beckoning, swiveling finger. In the apartment, he turned on the stereo, selected a playlist labeled "S.E.X." Sounds of a sultry saxophone filled the room. Jimbo served the Sambuca, and when Enigma began to play—music guaranteed to turn any halfway-decent slut into a more-than-adequate stripper—drunk Sylvia complied.

After the impromptu, pole-less routine, when she was naked and Jimbo was hard, sitting on the couch, stroking himself, Sylvia suggested they move into the bedroom for nightcap number two.

It was his fault, he figured later. He never should have fallen asleep, never should have let her get comfortable on his chest, never should have had that last drink. When he woke up, he was tired, hungover, and sore—in a good way.

In the living room, Sylvia sat in an armchair smoking a cigarette and exhaling out a cracked-open window. He was pleased to see her still there, naked and vulnerable, until he saw the book in her lap. He wondered where she had found it, and why she was looking at him like that.

He played the whole chess game out in his head and knew that there were other things he would have to do, now that she had advanced her pawn on his castle. If he had been a different man he might have allowed himself to have a relationship, might have felt love again, might have made babies, raised a family, taken vacations to the mountains, learned to ski, bought a dog. But no. It was a shame—all of it.

Jimbo almost winced when she asked, "Who's Sandy Wykowski?" followed by, "Why do you have her son's book?"

The call was made on a disposable phone he'd bought a month before. Jimbo hated calling in a favor, but a dead girl demanded it. He knew it would cost him later. These guys knew him as a risk-taking gambler, a guy used to having his balls against the wall. They'd help, but they'd hold him accountable. It could mean going to the track to claim a winner, moving a mysterious car to a place it was bound to be stolen, answering a cell phone at a designated time and reading words from a note card, then pitching both into an incinerator in an industrial park—not that he'd been asked that yet, but those were the kinds of things he might expect. The payback didn't matter when you needed help, when you wanted someone to do what you needed, no questions asked, and all without looking you in the eye.

TEDESCO HEARS DEAD PEOPLE, AND SOMETIMES THEY SOUND LIKE LOONS

Chapter 30

When I work a case, I like to think the guy or girl I'm assigned to is trying to help me by slipping up, by leaving clues. Some people are convinced bad guys want to be caught and the lost want to be found. I guess I'm one of those people.

I couldn't afford to think this all the time, especially not when the cases were about dead people. That would just be weird. It's one thing to follow a living creep who's running around on his girl, lying about where he spent the night, and denying the red-haired son that calls him daddy one weekend a month in Idaho, but it's a whole different ballgame when I'm on the mound of a grave and I see something no one else does—that the day she died is her wedding anniversary and maybe the husband really wasn't on that trip to New York as he claimed, because couldn't anyone check into the Ritz, pay cash, and say he was Thomas Elton?

Maybe I'm making myself out to be more important than I really am. Maybe just being observant, being open to possibility is what it takes to hear the clues, to see the solutions. In actuality I'm no more psychic than fakers who claim they can talk to your dog—the canine who wants to be walked more.

Being as observant as I am can be tiring. Lying on my bed and listening hard to the tape that Tommy's pal "Big C" broke down for us was making me sleepy. Tommy left the tape and another envelope that I hadn't opened yet in my mailbox with a note telling me to call him later. At 9:22, to be precise. Not a minute later. He had this way of making me his alibi, his excuse. I didn't mind. Much.

I was about to close my eyes when I heard it—a sound in the background of the tape that I hadn't heard before. I sat up, punched Rewind and listened again. I was instantly transported back to the Adirondacks, the seventies, and church camp.

I love how brains can do that. I can hear a song that will put me right back into the angst of teenhood, complete with painful acne and the taste of bong water on my tongue. Aural memories were almost as potent as scent for me, and that sound, a loon crying in the background on James Smith's tape, took me back to two places where birds were that sad—the lakes of upstate New York and the White Mountains of New Hampshire. Having lived through winters in both, I understood the loons.

I'd never truly enjoyed the wintery outdoors. Sure, snowmobiling and the occasional day of ice fishing were fun, but you wouldn't catch me shushing down a snow-covered mountain for hours at a time.

Growing up with inclement weather meant lazy winters that lasted long enough for you to smell spring coming and start getting the fat off before shorts-and-T-shirt season hit. I had friends who did the whole seasonal thing well. They'd been raised in families that swapped out clothes every three months, had specific houses for specific times of the year, and routines that were celebrated along the way to usher in spring, summer, fall, and winter.

Not our family. When the Tedescos said we were "going to camp," we were talking about a one-room hunting cabin in the Adirondacks, not a million-dollar lake house retreat or a quaint, historic, shabby-chic cottage at the shore.

My dad and his buddies from the bowling league had

bought the land in the late sixties and built a cabin that they swore every year to modernize but instead left it as it was, mending it with tar paper, caulk, and cast-off barn wood when required.

The men loved that rustic place. They hauled in buckets of well water, cooked on a woodstove, pissed in the woods, and shit in a two-hole outhouse while resting their feet on a mouse-eaten bag of lime and perusing twenty-year-old *Playboy* magazines. There were windows in the one-room cabin but the huge pines hid the sunlight, encouraging the growth of moss on the roof and the burrowing of squirrels in the drainpipes. Sleeping in the cabin was a claustrophobic test. Night descended like bondage.

The place smelled like decay and skunk with a hint of maple syrup. I imagined that when the men were up there in the winter during deer season, it would smell more like tobacco, baked beans, and bourbon—with a gassy overtone.

I never got a chance to experience the place as an adult, add my own scents, since the government bought up the land with plans to expand the hydroelectric plant upriver. By that time our family had separated into two different kind of camps: them and us. And that never made good company in the woods.

For the most part, I'd forgotten about the cabin and the summers my brothers tormented me there until I was dancing with the guys as Free Willy and Axle, our promoter, decided to expand our circuit with shows in the Adirondacks—thankfully not during hunting season.

He already had us dancing at birthday parties, drunken bachelorette fiascos, and once even at a gay guy's coming-out party. Sometimes the clients wanted a pair, sometimes we went solo. It was easy money. I never felt uncomfortable and almost always segued the dancing into a karaoke session starring the guest of honor. I'd leave my card and at least one T-strap behind, assuring I'd be remembered. Sometimes a familiar face would show up to vote for me at a local contest and I'd have to think twice to remember if I'd stripped for them, slept with them, or wished their Granny Ethel a happy eighty-fifth.

When the bookings ran dry—thanks, Chippendales, for raising that bar—we played bodyguard to female strippers, or exotic dancers as they preferred to be called, even though the only thing exotic about them was their choice of career.

Axle set up a guy's sixtieth birthday party all the way out in Number Four, New York. The Leopard Lounge girl couldn't go. She had issues. It might have been that there was no one to watch her kid, or that she had her period, or any one of the bullshit excuses Axle said he had to wade through when he worked with women. At any rate, he'd booked a waitress instead, a friend of the stripper, a girl who appeared so young and innocent that she had no business even listening to the kind of music I was supposed to play for her at that gig.

As her driver and bodyguard, I was the guy who was supposed to save her if something went down. I couldn't carry a real weapon, but I was bigger back then, and sometimes intimidation was enough. Especially in Number Four, New York. I hit the weights hard before I picked her up, trying to get as pumped up as a guy could who'd spent the last week eating extra-cheesy nachos and drinking twelve-packs of beer.

I pulled up to the perfect little white house in the perfect little neighborhood and practiced a grimace in the rearview. I looked more constipated than cruel.

Mandy stepped out, calling good-bye to someone inside, then skipped to the car and tossed a small pink bag into the backseat. She was as sweet as they had warned me, and that made my stomach turn, made me feel like a pusher in a schoolyard. Next time, Axle could do his own dirty work, I thought.

I hesitated before I put the car in reverse. "You sure you want to do this?"

"Been wanting to for a long time," she said, letting her coat fall open to reveal a plaid miniskirt and gartered stockings.

I made my way up to her face. She smiled, then ran her tongue over her lower lip and winked.

"Are you Catholic?" I asked.

"How did you know?" she said.

"Just a guess."

We drove through the familiar towns of my youth, but this time I didn't have fishing and marshmallow-roasting on my mind. It didn't help that Mandy's skirt had ridden up, or that her fingers were doing a dance of their own up and down my leg, with the occasional squeeze when a wild animal crossed the road. Eventually we arrived at the Elks Lodge, parked in the back as we had been told to, and were met at the door by a crooked old man who smelled like boiled cabbage. He tried to stand a little taller when he saw Mandy, but even pulling on his suspenders and jutting his wobbly chin out, the poor guy was still angling toward the floor.

I thought I should invent something for old crooked people, like a ceiling pulley system or The Tedesco Antigravity Belt. I was thinking so hard about this great invention that I missed what the guy was saying to Mandy. I figured the gig was a surprise like they all were and that the birthday boy would be happy to see us, just maybe a little shy at first. I hoped it was only the guys, then I remembered where we were—in an Elks Lodge on the outskirts of a logging town in the Adirondacks. Yeah. It would be men.

I followed Mandy down the hall, reading the handwritten posters on the wall informing members that dues needed to be current and that this Friday the fish fry would be delayed in honor of the annual Bob Miller parade. I wasn't sure who Bob was or why he'd earned himself a parade, but I figured he must be a pretty important guy because I knew how much those Elks liked a fish fry.

Mandy stopped short and I bumped into her, catching her in the back of the knees with the swinging boom box. She buckled but recovered quickly with a little "whoopsie" and a giggle.

"Sorry," I said.

"That's okay." She looked around, started to take off her coat.

"Is he here already?" I asked.

"I don't think so. I'm supposed to wait until they start singing 'Happy Birthday,' then walk out. Do you think they'll be able to hear the music from the doorway? Or should I walk it out with me?"

"It's kind of heavy. Maybe I should just run it from here. If you need it to be louder I can bring it out to you."

"Yeah, okay." She started to stretch, legs wide, arms overhead, swaying side to side. She hummed something low in her throat and closed her eyes. It was pretty damn sexy. I had to look away. Twice.

I stepped up to the door and looked through the window. There was a big, open space with a fireplace on one wall, a bunch of windows on the other. It looked cold in there—and empty. Seven or eight guys sat behind cheap buffet tables arranged in one big rectangle. I looked at the room from my perspective, as if I was the entertainer and this was my show. You could leap over the tables into the center of the rectangle and dance inside, but the flimsy tables wouldn't hold if you climbed up on them. I'd had one collapse on me in Ithaca—gave me a bruised ass for months.

The chairs were metal folding chairs, nice props for swinging around, standing on and tipping over, or slapping closed. The sound always got a yelp out of the ladies.

As for Mandy, I bet she'd look pretty hot straddling one, showing off her gartered stockings or perched sideways, frozen in the *Flashdance* pre-water drenching moment. I hoped she wasn't too new to be able to work the room.

See, that was the thing. You were hired by the buddies as a gift to the birthday boy, but for them to feel like their money was well spent, you had to do something special for the rest of them. Everyone wanted something, and it was up to Mandy to figure out how to give it to them and come out richer for it in the end.

I glanced over my shoulder to see her bumping and grinding, running her hands down her body, warming up with an invisible audience. Yeah, she'd be able to work the room.

Celebratory singing filtered through the door—the voices of old men with secrets and hearing aids. I let Mandy through and as soon as the fat, bearded guy said, "Look what we got for ya, Vern!" I pushed Play and let the sounds of The Gap Band remind Mandy what she was there for. She pranced into the room, spun around twice like one of the Jacksons, then unzipped her skirt and stepped out of it, rotating her hips and moving her hands higher and higher, all the while shaking her nice Catholic hair. She approached the tables half-undone, kicked and spun and wriggled like a combination karate/ballet/tango instructor. She turned around and was working the buttons of her shirt when the birthday boy held up a hand.

"No, no," he said. "It's all right."

Mandy approached, swiveling her hips and pouting.

"I mean it, little lady," Vern said, louder. He held out the skirt she'd tossed in his direction and turned his head away. "You don't have to," and then, softer, "You never have to."

Something in Mandy clicked off. I turned up the music a notch, tried to get her attention, but she was frozen to the spot, her eyes tearing up. She was losing it.

None of the men there got it, not really. When Mandy pretended to laugh, threw back her head and danced away, I was the only one who saw her wipe those tears from her cheeks, the only one who saw how that old man had touched her. I figured we wouldn't be using this waitress again. She'd be back in church before Sunday.

The men paid us in full, along with a little tip, as we'd driven all that way and arrived right on time. Apparently punctuality was a big Elks thing.

That was almost twenty years ago. I wondered where Mandy was now, what she'd done with her life, if she'd ever regretted her moment with Vern and the boys, if she'd ever told anyone.

Smith's tape was still humming in the microcassette player. I rewound it to hear the loon calls again, then pulled out my wallet and fished through the receipts, balling a few up and tossing them, until I came to Candy's business card—I mean Susan, the lake property specialist. I liked to say I was a U-turn from anywhere. Now I was pleased I'd come full circle, back to the strip club.

Sometimes you know where you're supposed to be, you just have to remind yourself by fucking up a bit. That was my theory about life, for the most part. There are no mistakes if you learn from your choices and there is no such thing as a dead end as long as you can still put it in reverse. It took me a lot of trash-ridden alleyways to understand that, and though I was no valedictorian, I wished I could impart this knowledge to every college graduate.

But I wasn't Vonnegut. I was a PI with a hunch.

SHE WAS LYING WHEN SHE SAID DON'T WORRY IF IT'S NOT GOOD ENOUGH FOR ANYONE ELSE TO HEAR, JUST SING, SING A SONG

Chapter 31

I called Tommy on the way out the door, told him about the loons—told his voice mail anyway—and floated my idea about how we could provide a little legitimate work for a struggling single mom.

It was too early to find Candy-aka-Susan Harrington, the stripper-realtor at The Leopard Lounge, so I sent her a text. I punched in the little letters on my phone thinking I was taking on these technological advances pretty well, even if my spelling still stunk. I figured she'd need a few hours to get all the info I'd requested and in the meantime I'd head to My Place so I could do a little thinking.

I parked the Lincoln in the owner's slot out front, knowing Randall would want me to and not caring what Francie said. She was going to give me shit no matter where I parked. It was what we did.

As I walked into the bar I heard a girl singing, or maybe it was a guy. After all, I had to remember where I was.

I sat at my regular booth and tried to shake off the ghosts of my past as I strained to see around the fake plants to the karaoke stage. I could see Francie's back, her waving arms, and bobbing head. She seemed engrossed in her bitch-out session, but not so much that she missed shooting me a dirty look when my phone gave off a loud and jarring ring.

She yelled, "You know the rule. Mute it or lose it."

"Sorry. I'll just take it outside," I said, getting up and heading for the exit.

"Yeah? That's good," she said, walking away from the stage.

I saw the girl that had been singing—a skinny thing with glasses and frizzy hair. She was crying.

Francie shot me another glare from behind the bar, as she added, "And Willy, why don't you leave it out there?"

The guy at the bar high-fived Francie as if she'd just said the most amazing thing. She slapped him back, smiling, then slid a fresh beer his way. I wondered what Randall would think of that, then immediately felt bad for even thinking it, because this was Francie and Randall—the great not-so-American love story, and he was dying and who the fuck was I to deny her companionship, or love, even?

I let the door close behind me, glad to see Francie too engrossed with the new guy to bother locking me out.

I figured the call was Tommy getting back to me, so I was short and snappy when I answered, "Tedesco."

"Oh. Hey, it's me, Buf . . . Barbara. Is everything okay?"

"Yeah, sure." I cleared my throat. "How are you?"

"I'm fine. But, I wondered if I could see you today?"

I looked at my watch, not because I had scheduling conflicts or because I wasn't sure I wanted to see her. It was a reaction, a reflex, and in the back of my head I was calculating how long it would take me to drive across town.

"I can be at your place in forty minutes," I said.

"No! It's just that . . . Mick's home and I . . . well . . . he doesn't know I've hired you."

She sighed then, a good old-fashioned exhalation that said it all. I heard her exasperation, her depression, her desire, I heard in that escape of breath an invitation.

Maybe I was reading a little too much into a simple sigh, but they weren't all simple, were they? You didn't just go around sighing all day like it was a stretch or a blink. You sighed when a task was complete, when a problem was too big, when you were ready to admit something, when you were whooped big time.

Barbara made that kind of sigh. The I-need-you-to-take-over sigh.

So I said, "Come to me," thinking only a little that it sounded like a song reprise, or a line from a diamond commercial with a couple in silhouette and a spotlight on the glittering necklace the man dangles to his beloved in the gazebo at twilight.

Barbara was still talking, so I zoned in on that, thinking she obviously hadn't placed much importance on the "come to me" line, that she might not even have heard it.

"Mick says we need to let Chamonix go. Whenever I bring up her murder he thinks it's just a way to keep the pain fresh. Can you believe he said that? He took all her things away, stripped her room at the house when I was helping out at church last weekend. I can't even talk to him right now. Where are you?"

I heard the sound of another door opening when she said, "Can I come to you?"

I gave her directions to My Place and went back inside to wait, pausing at the restroom to make sure that my fly was zipped and that I didn't have anything green in my teeth.

I went back to my booth, saw the beer Francie had left for me on top of a cocktail napkin that said: "If you can read this, you haven't had enough to drink."

I sipped the lager, pretended it was something stronger, and thought about Barbara. As much as a part of me wanted it, I couldn't see a future for us. It would always be: *I found out the truth about her daughter's death and that was how we met—or re-met.*

There would always be a dead girl between us, and there's no happiness in that.

It was like those screwed-up relationships that came out of 9/11, the wives of dead stockbrokers and bankers that were consoled by guilty firemen who couldn't save the husbands, and later the consoling became a private thing and some of the firemen even left their own families to be with 9/11 widows. As if *that* was something you wanted to tell your great-grandchildren.

No, that backstory wouldn't work for me.

Maybe I was being too picky, or maybe I had just been out of the dating game for too long. Granted, I wasn't a monogamous person, but when I went from wife to mistress and back I never considered it dating, just time spent in bed.

Fifi, my old dancing buddy, was great at dating. He really knew how to woo a woman. Once he planned an elaborate lunch for a girl he liked, Cheryl. He drove to the mall and set up a table in the parking lot with candles, flowers, and real silverware. He buzzed the delivery button at the back door of the bookstore where Cheryl worked and when she unlocked the door he tucked her arm under his and walked her right down the loading dock to her seat. As classical music played he teased her, stripping off his suit jacket, shirt, and tie before settling in beside her to enjoy the steak au poivre he'd cooked himself.

Fifi knew how to get into a girl's heart before he got into her pants. He understood that all women liked soft music, candlelight, poetry, chocolate, and flowers, even if she was an amateur mud wrestler on her days off.

I could blame my family for my inability to understand women. I won't, but I could. My father had issues. He was a purebred male chauvinist pig. He even had a tie that loudly proclaimed his tendencies. He'd been a bona fide card-carrying member of Hef's Bunny Club, married to a stay-at-home mother who'd raised all of his sons. My father taught me that manly men were supposed to be assholes, his point driven home daily by my two jock older brothers.

It's surprising that I turned out so good with all that crap in my life. Never mind that my mother took my brothers with her when she moved to Canada to study the migratory pattern of the zebra mussel. She wooed those boys with promises of French girls and cheap, potent beer. It took my brothers years to understand Canadian girls are nothing like their French counterparts, and by then it was too late.

My brothers were close—less than a year apart—and close in our family meant competitive. So when Edgar decided the military was for him, Scott signed up too. The day they left for boot camp, a major storm passed through our town. Though the skies were clear and the woman on the Weather Channel claimed the worst was past, as the bus left New York, the storm resurfaced and grew more fierce, the winds reaching tornado levels and eventually ripping the roof off the bus, sucking out the occupants, and spitting their bones into a basin lake in Virginia.

The military managed to kill my brothers before their first "Booyah!"

Maybe remembering the past wasn't such a good thing. I might do better concentrating on the present.

Francie smacked me on the head with a bar towel. "Earth to Willy. What is up with you?"

"Ow. Nothing. I was just thinking."

"Shit. We're in trouble now," she said.

Laughter came from the bar area.

I tipped my head in that direction. "Who's your pal?"

"None of your business."

"Take your sweet pills today, Francie?"

"Yeah, only mine are stamped: Fuck You."

That made me laugh. Francie dropped the tough act enough to let one edge of one lip lift. It was as much of a smile as I was going to get, so I took it.

"Good to see you too, hot stuff," I said. "Can I get another beer? And could you put on some music? I'm expecting a friend and the ambiance . . . Well, it's a bit lacking." I glanced in the direction of the crying girl.

Francie leaned in, dropped her voice another notch. "New student. She's not taking the criticism well. You know how that goes."

Boy did I. And boy, did I know this was a good time to go mute.

"Hey, Francie," the guy from the bar called. "Why don't you sing us a song?" He was doing a total guy-from-the-bar thing, arms outspread, bleary eyes beckoning. It was like he'd stolen his act from a Charles Bukowski story. Suddenly I needed some air.

Francie caught my eye and we shrugged at the same time. I watched Francie sashay her way back to the guy. Just as I started to get up, the door opened. Barbara was standing there looking for me, letting her eyes get used to the dim. I waved and she offered me a smile, the one I could never refuse.

"Hey," she said as she approached.

We did the friendly hug thing with a bit of cheek press. It was hard to not linger.

"Hey yourself. Have a seat. You look good."

"I know." She giggled. "I'm sorry, I don't know why I said that. Chamonix used to say that to her father all the time. It was her way of assuring us everything was okay, you know? Like she had it all together, like she wasn't. . ."

I watched as Barbara twirled her wrist, swiping away an air thought or practicing tai chi.

"She wasn't what?" I pushed.

"I don't know." She looked around and I saw the desperation in her eyes as she gazed toward the pretty bottles lined up behind Francie's bar.

I tapped the table then leaned back, offering my version of nonchalance when really it was killing me that she was still so broken up. I said, "Can I get you something to drink? Francie makes a helluva martini."

Barbara nodded and I twisted around in my seat and ordered with hand motions that only Francie understood.

Barbara and I sat for almost an hour, talking and laughing and enjoying the music and the moment for what it was. It was like sneaking off to a matinee on a rainy day when you're supposed to be serving subpoenas on the South Side or following the guy with the bad back to batting practice. It was a forbidden dalliance that felt good. It made me wish I'd skipped school more often.

I barely registered Tommy's arrival until he punched my arm. "Why are you being an ass?"

"What?" Forget what I said earlier about liking the kid, or wanting to be friendlier. "What the fuck, Tommy? I'm just sitting here. I didn't even see you come in."

"The loons?"

"Yeah. So what?"

"Listen Tedesco, if you want to make fun of me, I can take it. It's just that when you bring my mother into the picture I don't think it's fair. "

"Let me reiterate: What the fuck, Tommy?"

"I should be asking you the same thing. Leaving me that message about loons and the woods. I know you were talking about my mom."

I started to laugh. "I wasn't talking about your mother. Shit, I was talking about the sounds on the tape."

Barbara was listening now. "What tape?"

"The one he found at Smith's place," Tommy said

before he saw my eyes go wide and my finger come up to my throat, slashing and slashing, a motion I turned into spastic scratching when Barbara looked back at me.

She said, "Bill . . ?"

I had nowhere to hide. I looked at Tommy. "We haven't had a chance to talk about the tape yet."

"I see." Tommy pushed his way into the booth beside Barbara, nudging her with his slender hip.

I could see what Barbara must have been like with her daughter. If I squinted, I might have mistaken Tommy as Chamonix, a little girl snuggled in next to her mom, telling secrets, whispering things that would be forgotten during the next argument, asking for things she'd never get and later realize she never needed.

My first wife used to talk about how she felt when her kid died. It was a tragedy—a misdiagnosed illness followed by a long-lasting coma. Hardly the same as a gunshot to the chest in an Irish bar. Hell, I know everyone's pain is different. But I could see the same disappointment in Barbara and knew she'd react to another young girl like my ex had when a happy, live, eight-year-old blonde would ride her bike past us on the sidewalk, or a sad, lost kid would call out, "Mom?" in the grocery store. You never stopped being a mother, I figured. Maybe that explained old ladies with lap dogs in cashmere sweaters.

I raised my hand and flapped my fingers at Francie again, ordering a round for the table, glad for the reprieve. I wasn't eager to spit out way too few facts while relying on way too much instinct, and I didn't have the damnedest idea how I was going to sell Barbara and Tommy on the importance of a road trip to New Hampshire.

KARA ANGELINA DI SARRANNO SMITH

Chapter 32

Making her way across New Hampshire toward the White Mountains, Angel Smith amused herself by performing a running monologue in the rearview mirror. Hopped up on NoDoz and energy drinks, she played the narrator in her life's story.

"Sweet Kara Angelina Di Sarranno, born the bastard child of immigrants. No, that's not right." She tried again. "It was a Cinderella story." Angel laughed, chugged the rest of her GoGo Juice, crushed the can, and tossed it in the backseat of the BMW.

"Let's get to the good stuff. Jumping right ahead to Angel's sexually active years, we meet a variety of boys who will ultimately disappoint poor Angel and make her wonder about her own mother—someone she never knew. Her father, always too busy for his little girl, takes the three-monkey approach: See no evil. Hear no evil. Fling handfuls of shit when something bad comes near. Yes, Angel loves her daddy.

"Maybe that was why she left all those boys behind in college and dated the professors instead."

Angel reached across the car and popped open the glove box. She pawed through gas receipts, gum wrappers, and broken sunglasses until her hand closed on a crumpled package of Kools. She slammed the glove box closed and drove with her knees as she extracted the two remaining cigarettes, one broken in half. "Thank you, Jesus, and your mama too."

The first drag of the first cigarette she'd smoked in over a year took her right back to the night she'd met him. Not Jimbo. The one that came before. The only other man she'd loved. The one she'd always regret letting slip through the cracks. Doctor Peter Hazard.

She'd been on vacation with two studious college pals, two girls who thought vacations were guided bus tours, museum visits, and boring literary events. Didn't they know if you really wanted to soak up local flavor when you traveled it was necessary to spend time in bars?

Angel had pretended to be asleep when they tiptoed out of the hotel room for the day's tour. She went for a run, then had a swim and a soak in the hot tub. By the time she left the pool she had a list of the best bars in the area, compliments of the cute towel boy. Scribbled on the back of list was his phone number, with a winkey face.

She took a taxi to the first bar on the list, invoking her Vacation Rule Number Three: It was always five o'clock somewhere.

"How you doing?" The bartender said, drying his hands on a towel hanging from his belt.

Angel smiled. "I'm fine. And from the looks of it, I'm in the right place."

He grinned. "Wait till you get to know me. You might change your mind."

"Don't flatter yourself, sugar. I was talking about your beer selection." She nodded toward the wall of Belgian beer taps. "I'll take a Verboden Vrucht."

The guy on the bar stool beside her spun around. "Excellent choice." His eyes slid over her. "I would say you are definitely in the right place." He stuck out his hand. "I'm Peter."

It may have been the Verboden Vrucht, but Angel fell head over heels for Peter, didn't even care that he was married. She loved the way he said her name with his

British accent, the way he had pulled her aside to kiss her in the hallway between the men's room and the emergency exit. There was something so honest in his confusion about their mutual attraction—him insisting they must have met somewhere before, known each other in another life. Angel drank it all in hook, line, and sinker. They kissed and danced and she tried to not feel the chill of the wide gold band on his ring finger as he ran his hand up her leg.

She tried to leave him that night and forget him, but he kept coming back—every time she turned on the TV and saw a medical drama, every time a man passed wearing his same cologne, every time she reached down and caressed her calf, running her fingers in slow circles and whispering in her best British accent, "You are fucking amazing."

She got his calls—and returned none of them at first. She played back his voice on her message machine and tried to discern whether he was sad, drunk, or desperate. She made a pact with herself that if he mentioned divorce, she'd talk to him again, she'd even entertain the idea of seeing him, because what if this was *the guy*? What if he was who she'd been looking for all along, even when she didn't know that she was looking?

Angel was no stranger to love. Her forays into it began with the little boy in the second grade who'd played Spock to her Uhura. Love was a challenge and she was a worthy competitor. With the married British doctor from Vacationland, it was no different. She wrote sexy poems and sent videos of herself dancing. He loved it and asked for more. He complained about the stress of his job, how his wife and friends were taking advantage of his kindness and his wealth. She sent him songs to listen to while running, a book of positive affirmations. He sent her goodnight wishes every night and told her every morning that she was beautiful, that he loved her. Angel believed him, and the game played on. They were seven states and two time zones apart but she didn't care. If he was the one, it would all work out.

As the months wore on and the messages changed from "you're great" to "you're too far away and I can't do this" back to "I have never felt this way before and it scares me, that's why I was such a jerk," to "I can't leave my wife, I need to end this" and then, weeks later, drunken midnight phone calls pleading for forgiveness, calls that were denied in the light of day.

Angel began to think she wasn't broken enough for him. She would never be a medical mystery he could solve. She began to see that she was just another conquest in a string of somebodies for the good doctor. She might be nobody after all.

She confided in her friends, the ones she thought wouldn't judge her when the "but he's married" part came out. She talked to guy friends who probably wanted to fuck her, because they all said the guy was a loser, advised her to dump him and move on. She was apparently "too good for him."

Angel had known from the beginning that it would be a whirlwind, a maelstrom. But she loved the way it woke her up, how even the bad feelings—the anger and the angst—turned on a passionate switch inside her.

She found his hospital on the Internet and searched for staff photographs, for any news clips in his city that featured emergency room situations. She stared at the backs of scrub-clad men, believing she knew which cap covered his thick brown hair, which accident victim was even now being soothed by his soft voice, his brown eyes boring into theirs.

Angel hated how her days had become soap operas. She saw an image of herself standing stoic and backlit, perfectly coiffed, waiting for an e-mail to be returned, a phone to ring, a text to chime and then appear. She ate too little, ran too far, and began hearing pieces of love songs that she had never heard before as if they were written for her, as if the doctor was sending his love in a random radio song.

She began to despise the man who had wrecked her stable heart. She hated how she felt weak and manipulated. She imagined driving to his house and confronting his wife, or better yet, meeting and befriending her, getting invited to their house for dinner. But she thought that might have already been done in some psycho movie. So instead, she sent him a message telling him to fuck off, go away, and never think about her again. She deleted his number and his messages and all the e-mails they had ever exchanged. She threw away the shirt she'd been wearing when they met. She changed her favorite satellite radio station setting to "Hard Rock" instead of "In the Mood."

She began dating the guy at her father's firm that they called The Golden Boy. She went on trips and dined in fine restaurants. She did everything you do when you're falling in love. She tried to move on, forget Peter. But it wasn't that simple. Men don't just go away. Hearts don't really heal. Especially the heart of the dumpee.

Angel caught herself imagining the doctor still in love with her, still wanting her. She imagined him calling and asking her to dinner. She played out the scenarios: telling him to go fuck himself, or meeting him and rejecting him publicly, doing something that would hurt his ego. She even took the imagining to a dark place, a place she'd never go. A place where Doctor Peter disappeared forever.

She remembered, in the beginning, praying for a do-over. Asking God to give her back that day. She'd change everything by going on the tour with the girls. And Peter would find another girl to share Belgian beer with on a sunny Wednesday afternoon, a girl he'd leave his wife for. She'd love him better than Angel ever could. She'd know how to be perfect. She'd be younger, prettier, stronger, sweeter, kinder, more of the most tender things.

Angel wished she could wipe it all away. That day and everything that followed. If only there was a bleach pen for regret.

She finished the cigarette and tossed it out the window, exhaling the last of the smoke through her nostrils as she wiped the tears from her cheeks.

"Fuck you, Doctor Peter Hazard. Fuck you! It's your loss. I have Jimbo. I've always had Jimbo."

She pushed the BMW's speedometer to the three-digit mark, screaming, "No one leaves Angel. No one!"

Angel didn't see the dog until it was too late. Not that she could have stopped in time. Not with the ice and the snow and the curving roads. Sure, if she'd been asked, she would have admitted she was going too fast, and yeah maybe she'd reached over the seat to grab a tissue, but no one was asking and no one was watching.

She hesitated, having come to a skidding halt a hundred yards down the road, and finally said, "Fuck it," as she turned the car off and reached for her red parka.

She shrugged into the coat, tugged on her boots, and trudged back down the road to where the small yellow dog lay. She nudged it with her foot. When it didn't move, she unclipped its collar and went back to the car, wrapping the leather around her fist.

She turned up the heat and pulled back onto the road, driving a little slower. Not because she was sad or sorry or worried, but because she was in New Hampshire, the land where yellow dogs wandered, husbands disappeared, and God had planted way too many trees.

CRASH INTO ME

Chapter 33

Barbara had never been a very good driver. In high school her teacher had said she suffered from road wander. Barbara, then Buffy, asked if that meant she'd do a lot of traveling in her life. She figured she only passed the driver's test because of the way her pale skin and red miniskirt had stood out against the black leather of her daddy's Cadillac.

There were some things beauty could still buy.

She hated that she might have passed that idea on to Chamonix, a girl who learned early that charm was not to be wasted on the Santa at the mall or a grandmother who was bound to love you regardless, but to be used on parents of friends who delivered hand-me-downs and birthday gifts, on teachers who graded papers and presented awards, on fathers who wanted all the best for their children all the time.

When Chamonix turned sixteen she went to find Barbara in her bedroom, closed the door, and said, "I need to get away for a little bit. Could you get me a hotel room for the night for my birthday?"

Barbara wondered where her daughter had picked up such a notion—that she needed to get away from her life and that you could do it at a local hotel, that that was even acceptable.

"Sarah's mom lets her," she said.

Sarah's mom was known to have a different man every month, a man who usually worked too little, drank too much, and always ended up making an ass of himself in public.

"You would if you loved me . . ." Chamonix said.

"Baby, why would you want to spend your birthday alone?"

One look at Chamonix gave away the answer. She wouldn't be alone. There would be the boyfriend. A smart-mouthed kid from a wealthy family that Chamonix had met at some school event, a long-haired kid in torn jeans and a blazer who showed up in his dad's Porsche one day but wouldn't let Chamonix ride in it until she changed her clothes.

"Mom, I'm on the pill, so don't worry about that."

"Oh. I feel better already . . ."

That was the beginning of the mother-daughter relationship change. From then on, Barbara felt like the kid, like she was the one getting a lesson. She listened, added information, and found herself wishing she had experienced a childhood like her daughter's, that she had been blessed with a cool and understanding mom, that she had understood the world around her as well as Chamonix did at such a young age.

Over time, she and Mick found it was easier to let Chamonix have her way, simpler to believe her, better to just go along. Mick assured her they had a good girl, a daughter wise beyond her years.

"We should consider ourselves lucky," he said. "Our little girl is so mature."

It was more than that for Barbara. She knew children were supposed to grow up. It was just that she felt the cord had been wrongly severed by the baby, leaving her floating around stemless.

When Chamonix went away to art school, Barbara joined every volunteer group she could find that involved children. She filled the gap with borrowed daughters, none of them white, none of them pretty, none of them as beautiful, bright, or hopeful as her own.

By the time Chamonix moved back to Syracuse, Barbara felt almost nothing for her; she'd become a stranger. The baby she'd raised was gone. In her place was a cynical woman with her daughter's eyes. She tried to renew the relationship by meeting Chamonix for lunch, helping her furnish her loft. But what her daughter needed couldn't be found at any store.

When she asked Chamonix to paint something for a girls' club, something sweet, something hopeful, Chamonix said she was sorry but she couldn't, that wasn't her vibe. Barbara knew then she'd lost her baby forever.

At a downtown community center, Barbara finished reading to the children. She said her good-byes, then left the building and crossed the street to reach a small café. She sat at a black iron bistro set in front of the window, wishing she still smoked. She had nothing to do with her hands. She glanced at the paper menu, pretended to have important business on her cell phone. She imagined herself in France, a place she had never been but knew she'd love. They'd watched taped episodes on the Travel Channel, so many in fact that sometimes she thought she really had walked the Champs-Élysées smoking a Gauloise and strolling in designer clothes with a white poodle on a thin gold chain.

She almost ordered an espresso when the waitress greeted her, but remembered her surroundings and her desire and ordered a glass of Beaujolais instead, thinking it still sounded French.

She thought of four-year-old Duane, the little boy she'd just left. His dimpled cheeks made him a shoo-in for those mommies looking for a little boy to love. Unfortunately his medical history and the large birthmark on his neck gave some of the "shoppers" pause.

It was hard to not think of people who came to the home in that way. Barbara wanted to believe that everyone was sincere, but there were a fair number of sleezebags swayed into fostering by government money.

In Barbara's mind, in every poor household, in every family being run down by an angry drunk or failing because of an inattentive parent, there was a child who wanted to succeed and make a new start. A kid with the kind of attitude that had founded this great country, and on the days Barbara felt like her work didn't matter, she chose to look for the Thomas Jeffersons and Benjamin Franklins, for the Einsteins, for the sad, misunderstood, left-behind youth that would save us from ourselves.

Barbara finished her fourth glass of wine, paid her bill, slipped on her coat, and made her way back to the parking lot of the foster facility. She may have been distracted more than inebriated, but one thing was certain. Her ability to discern right from wrong had dimmed. Later she would wish for this moment back, a single stolen second of time that would make a difference—where she could replace a you-should-have-known-better grimace with a smile born of the right decision, the one that sounded like this: *I am too drunk to drive and I have enough money in my purse, enough contacts on my phone that I don't have to.*

Barbara got into her car on the third try. She drove out of the lot, rolled through the first stop sign, and neglected the following traffic light entirely. A speeding sedan rammed into her front end, spinning her around and aiming her car into the path of two lanes of oncoming traffic. Barbara saw headlights as her slow brain formed one word: surreal. A word followed quickly by others: danger, fear, pain.

The man from the other car, an older-model Chevy, ran toward her, smashed his fist through the broken passenger-side window, flipped up the lock, and tore open the door.

"Lady, are you okay?"

He reached in, unbuckled Barbara, and pulled her out. In the process he banged her knees on the pavement, scraped her arms across the broken glass.

"Hey!" she yelled, slapping at him. "What the hell?"

But her voice sounded far away even to her own ears, and her objections senseless. The first of three skidding vehicles crashed into her car, pushing it into his. Windshields imploded, smashed bits of vehicle skittered across pavement as the sounds of crunching metal, blaring horns, and screaming people filled the night.

The stranger dragged her away from the road as both cars ignited. The last car in the line-up swerved to avoid the fiery heap, jumped the curb, and crashed into a pharmacy storefront. And Barbara, with blood dripping into her eyes from the cut on her forehead, slumped against the man who'd saved her. He smelled like pine and a little like her old dog, Samson, but that might have been the smells coming from where they were sitting and not the man, she thought. Barbara watched the flames grow in the car fire, felt the heat. She was confused, tired, so ready to say "You win, I give up. Can we go home now?"

The man mumbled, "That must have been how it was for my father. Only this time no one died. See? No one died. Right, lady?"

"That's right," Barbara said, as if he was one of the children she soothed all day long. "That's right." She reached for his hand.

She was too close to see all of him, only pieces. A strong chin, high cheekbones. He was an attractive, sandy-haired young man with the saddest, oldest eyes she'd ever seen.

He spoke quietly, staring off as if entranced. "He drove into somebody, just like I did to you. I never thought about how *he* felt, only me. He left me. He killed those little girls and never even knew. Didn't have to go around hearing about it, paying for it, or living through it again and again. He was dead and gone. Fucking guy had it easy. Me and Mom? Not so much."

Upon hearing the words "killed those girls," Barbara tried to pull her arm from his grip, her fingers from his, but the man was caught up in his story, lost in a past only he could see. As she struggled he held her tighter, but when she said, "I'm going to be sick. Please!" he released her and Barbara lurched forward to vomit.

When she finally sat up, wiping her mouth, he was gone.

The cops had questions. A lot of questions. All she could tell them was that the stranger had nice eyes. Sad eyes.

JIMBO/JAMES LIKED TO WATCH

Chapter 34

Jimbo rubbed his eyes and shook himself awake. He glanced at the computer monitor, checked that he was able to see both registers behind the bar and the front door. Not that he thought anyone was ripping him off, or that he even cared about the money. He just liked to follow the progress. In and out. Money and doors. Open and shut. Some days he hardly remembered this wasn't real. He almost forgot where he'd come from, who he truly was.

He let the chair drop into place, feet hitting the floor. It was getting louder downstairs, almost time for the bouncer to make a pass. Guy was beefy, bald, and mean-looking. As long as you didn't talk to him, he was damn intimidating. Poor bastard had a voice like Tyson, complete with a lisp. Jimbo knew it was better to have someone else to do the dirty work, someone who could control himself and who knew the limits of his job. Especially after that episode with the two drunk assholes.

If Chamonix hadn't shown up when she did, he wasn't sure how it would have ended. Those kids owed their lives to her. Thing was, most chicks would have been disgusted by the scene, by the brutality of an alley fight, by the blood and broken bones. But not her. In a weird way, it seemed to turn her on. Jimbo had no problem with that. As the boys limped off, one cradling his arm and the other blubbering about calling the police or telling his dad—some big swinging dick in local government—Jimbo had simply brushed off his shirt and pant legs, and said "Sorry about that" to Chamonix.

"Don't be," she said, approaching him. "They deserved it. Maybe more."

"You think so?" Jimbo said.

She reached out and touched his cheek. Even in the dim light of the alley, he could see the blood on her finger as she pulled it away. "Yeah," she said, then licked her finger and met his eyes. It was a first for him: sex, standing up, in an alley, the deep bass beat of a jukebox song rumbling through the wall, a vibration he felt in a hand braced against the brick as he slammed into his waitress, again and again.

Jimbo stood before the one-way glass wall of his loft office thinking about that night, wondering if it might happen again. He scanned the scene below. A girl in a blue dress snorting coke off her friend's watch, a geek beside the jukebox fixing his hair then adjusting his package—as much as possible—before he approached a girl standing near the exit. He watched two lesbian regulars at the end of the bar pretend they were bi, flirt with some jocks, probably trying to make each other jealous but ending up only more confused in the end.

Behind the bar, Chamonix pushed some bills into the communal tip jar. Roxie served a round of shots to a group of guys in biker jackets while Cress eyed them from the kitchen doorway.

The guys in the kitchen had it easy. The menu was bar food on the healthy side, if that was possible for an Irish pub. You needed to serve something salty so they'd order drinks to wash it down, and some carbs to soak up the booze, Jimbo knew. In his opinion, a bar should be about drinks, people, and ambience—not food.

Flannigan's had plenty of ambiance. The decor, the lighting, the music. It all led to one thing. People hooking up, or in the case of the geek, trying to. The music was right, just loud enough that you had to get close to the person you were talking to but not so loud that you confused their words and ending up making an ass of yourself because you thought they said, "I think you're hot," when they were asking about your drink: "What you got?"

It was Friday night. That meant more drinking and a bigger crowd. Most weeknights they filtered out by midnight, but on days when there was an option of sleeping in and the potential of having someone to wake up to, the girls usually had to escort stragglers to the door at last call and sometimes usher them into a cab. Jimbo was strict about that. No one left his place driving drunk. No one. He didn't care how much it cost him, or how many cabs he needed to place on retainer. Everyone that drank at Flannigan's got home safe.

Even if they reminded him of his wife, Angel, or any of his girlfriends pre- or post- marriage—those broads who had been quick to remind him of his inadequacies. It seemed everyone returned at some point, like they needed to ram home one more time how fucked up he was, how much he'd ruined their lives, and on occasion, to impress upon him how wonderful their life was now that he was no longer in it.

That was exactly what he needed to hear. Another affirmation that he was a total loser.

It was one thing to have failed as a man in the procreation department. It still felt strange, looking at all the bastard kids in the world—that he didn't have one out there somewhere, given all the unprotected sex he'd enjoyed. If he thought about it, he might start believing there was something else wrong with him, something more than bad mojo, more than a feeling of being cursed. He knew he'd risked a few diseases, taken a few shortcuts. At least forty-one times. Okay, exactly forty-one times.

Some days, Jimbo pretended there was a little Jimbo VI

out there and the cunt just hadn't told him, because that's how those bitches were when you told them the truth about their flabby ass, or they caught you porking their roommate in the bathroom at a party, or found out you'd been jerking off at work in the stockroom to pictures on your phone from some woman in Wisconsin you met on Facebook.

The shrink he'd seen when he was a kid told him he might grow up with alcohol issues. He couldn't remember her name, only that she'd been nice—a woman who smelled like fresh-cut grass. She always wore red and black, like she was part sexy hooker and part serious widow. Many nights he lay in bed with one hand down his pajama bottoms thinking of shiny black pantyhose, tight red skirts, and the space under the desk of Doctor Part Sexy Part Serious.

During one of their sessions, Jimbo fell asleep and dreamed of her wearing nothing but a strip of black electrical tape over her privates. She kept asking, "What do you think?" and "How does that make you feel?" as she jammed a screwdriver into a wall socket to send waves of electricity through her body.

Jimbo didn't think he had issues with alcohol. He had issues with loads of other things: sex, the size of his dick, women, the size of their tits, commitment, responsibility, money, planning, trust, guilt, religion, red meat, black people, honesty, porn.

Since he had arrived in Syracuse and slipped into his new life as James John Smith, reformed poker player and pub owner, he'd seen that most men his age were also struggling with their identities. It wasn't far-fetched to claim a midlife crisis as the reason behind their choices, but when you were legitimately two different people—but not psychotic—you had to be careful every step along the way.

There were nights where he just wanted to let his hair down, wanted to invite some people over and get high and play board games and listen to music and tell stories, but he was afraid he'd tell the wrong story, that he'd let something slip, that a piece of who he really was would be revealed.

Not that he was 100 percent sure that hadn't already happened. Quite a few nights, after they'd turned up the lights and kicked everyone out, Jimbo drank with the girls. The kitchen help was mostly Spanish-speaking and eager to get home, so after they closed the doors behind them, he'd dim the lights again, enter the special code on the jukebox that made the CDs play for free, and they'd drink whatever weird concoction Roxie came up with. Cress would dance for them in a way that both thrilled and frightened Jimbo. She reminded him of his wife when they first met, a tough broad in an angel's body, someone he'd never be good enough for.

Chamonix would be the first to go, leaving with a simple wave at the door. The others wanted hugs or cheek kisses. She never said she was going to the same place twice; Jimbo knew she was hiding something. It attracted him, that part of her, in the way a hunter stalks the lame animal lingering at the rear of the pack.

One night after they had closed he invited them to his apartment, or maybe it had been Roxie's idea.

"I'll bet James has some Hendrix upstairs, don't you?" she said.

They'd been discussing the most wrongly sung lyrics in the world and Hendrix had come up, along with Elton John and several metal bands.

"I'll bet he has more than just music up there," Cress said, holding a pinched thumb and forefinger to her lips and inhaling.

It was the first time they had included him in their party

talk and Jimbo, hungry for companionship, gave it up quickly by saying, "You wanna find out?"

Cress pranced past him, singing, "Purple haze was in my eyes, don't know if it was day or night . . ."

Roxie joined in, dragging Chamonix behind her as they chased Cress up the back stairs.

Jimbo laughed, then yelled, "Hey, what about me?"

"Nice place," Chamonix had said, turning in a slow circle in the living room. "I love the minimalist approach."

"See?" Cress said, sprawling on the couch. "I told you he wasn't gay."

"Thanks," Jimbo said, adding, "I think," then tossing a throw pillow at Cress.

"Material possessions are so overrated," Roxie added, heading to the fridge. She reached in, moved some stuff around, and then came up with a bottle of white wine. "Anyone?"

There was a chorus of yeses.

Jimbo scrolled through his phone, then docked it in the stereo and sat next to Cress on the couch. Hendrix filled the room and Chamonix surprised everyone with a wild air guitar solo, complete with tongue play. Jimbo fired up a small blue bowl and passed it around.

Roxie poured the wine into the only cups she could find—vintage burger-joint glasses that seemed too large. Interestingly, the more they smoked the more perfect they became.

"Let's play a game," Cress suggested.

"Like what?" Chamonix asked. "Charades?"

"Okay. What am I thinking?'

"That's not charades, Cress."

"No?"

"What is it?"

"Psycho," Chamonix said. They all busted up laughing as Jimbo poured the rest of the wine.

"I know. How about cards?" Roxie asked, digging through her purse.

Cress snorted. "You carry a deck of cards?

"Not usually, but last week—"

"Whatever. Deal," Chamonix said, crossing her legs and dropping to the floor in front of the coffee table.

"The game is five-card draw," Roxie said. "Nothing's wild."

"Except me," said Cress.

"Raarrrh," Jimbo said, fake-clawing the air, which made Cress giggle.

"Oh shit." Roxie looked at her cards, then slapped them down on the table. "I am a fucking idiot."

"And so . . ?" Chamonix said.

"No you're not," Cress said, leaning over Jimbo's lap to try and hug Roxie, who wriggled out of her reach.

"Yes, I am," she said. "Here I am suggesting we play cards with a shark. A real live pro! Doh."

Jimbo sang, "Oh when the shark bites with his teeth, dear . . ." He started laughing first. Then he realized Roxie was talking about him. He put on a serious face. "I'll play dumb. I promise."

It wasn't hard to do, as wasted as he was. Besides, he had never been into poker as much as the real James Smith. He held his cards in a tight fan, unsure what he was looking for. He hated games with rules, worse yet ones that had a time limit and people watching your every move. He switched the cards around in his hand, grouping them first by color, then by numerical order.

Chamonix said, "What are we playing for anyway?"

"Fun," said Cress.

"Money," said Roxie.

"But no one ante-ed up," Chamonix pointed out.

Clothes, Jimbo thought, chuckling to himself.

"What's so funny?" Cress asked. "Do you have a royal house or something?"

Chamonix laughed. "A royal *house*? What the hell is that?"

"I think the technical term would be *castle*," Roxie said, making them all laugh.

Jimbo said, "I don't have shit. I'm out." He got up to open another bottle of wine.

Later, Chamonix would be the one to point out that James hadn't seemed to know even the basic rules of the game. For starters, he'd claimed that two pair trumped three of a kind. The girls thought she was being picky about the whole thing and told her she shouldn't judge anyone too harshly after midnight. And after all, they had been pretty stoned. Chamonix knew she had made some really bad judgment calls herself after midnight, so she dropped the subject. But it never sat right with her.

She wasn't the only one with doubts about her boss. Roxie had been the one to say James didn't seem like the gambling type, and that she could have sworn he'd told her that he was married. So where was the wife? And what kind of guy doesn't own at least one vehicle?

When the three girls left that night, they closed the door on an apartment that was a lot like a hotel room—clean and presentable with all the amenities, but lacking warmth or true personality. Cress had once described the sober James John Smith the same way.

"On the outside, he seems put together, on top of things to do with money and business. But if you ask him something that veers off course, something personal, there's a hesitation, not like he's a private person and I'm intruding, more like he's fact-checking. I get the feeling if we were playing the telephone game, by the time his story got back to him all screwed up and wrong, it would be the one he'd start believing."

MAKING A SNOW ANGEL 101

Chapter 35

Angel had to admit there was something to that idea about everything happening for a reason. Hitting that dog had slowed her down, perfecting her timing, even giving her a prop/weapon she could use to her advantage.

She remembered reading some trite poem sent by a friend who'd recently gone through therapy after a suicide attempt. The woman had become the kind of person who thought she was being helpful with her unsolicited advice, the kind of person who believed you needed her to share her thoughts and feelings, the kind of person Angel began to wish had been bright enough to know exactly how many pills to swallow in the first place.

That said, parts of the poem had stuck with her. It said someone might come into your life at a certain time to serve a purpose—good or bad—but only temporarily. And how other people were only passing through during a particular season of your life: to share, to teach, to comfort, to change. And only *some* people, a very select few, would be with you for a lifetime, teaching you lessons in all areas of your life to make you a better person.

Angel also believed in karma, that what you put out there in the universe would come back at you. It could be in the form of a man, an awesome business deal, or perhaps a mangy mutt running away from home. At any rate, Angel was so far down the pike now, she figured she was totally fucked. So why not take it the rest of the way?

It was pure luck that she found the road that led to the big Victorian in the woods. She was lost, with no GPS signal and a map that she could barely read. She was about to say "screw it" and turn around when she saw a wood-paneled station wagon with chained tires delivering mail.

The music filtering out of the open window of the car sounded like "The Best of Elvis" on an 8-track player. The way the guy drove suggested he'd had so much to drink that even if he did talk to Angel, he wouldn't remember a damn thing. Still, she heard Marshall's voice in her head and remembered what he'd taught her. She dropped back and slowed to a crawl, following far enough behind to not look obvious.

It was easy enough to scoop the mail out of the box. A tire store offer was addressed "Mr. James Smith or Current Resident." She waited until the mailman was well out of sight, then backtracked down the road to find a place to hide her car. She returned to the driveway on foot and made a path around to the rear of the Smith house, walking under the eaves on compacted snow and ice, leaving no prints. She was pleasantly surprised to see that the fake stone house key holder looked exactly like a fake stone house key holder.

It was warm inside. Angel locked the door and stripped out of her coat and boots, transferring the gun to her waistband. She was tired and still hungry, but she was certainly not going to pull a Goldilocks.

"Hello? Anyone home?" she said.

No answer.

She took a circuitous route from the mudroom through the kitchen and into the living room, where the TV was on.

She reached for the remote and turned up the volume. It was another Jimbo-style film. All black-and-white, with somebody mad about some injustice, a broad crying about a guy, and some crap-ass music letting you know when the bad thing was going to happen.

She left it playing and started up the stairs.

The place was nice. Nothing like what she and Jimbo had in Virginia. Nothing like what she'd imagined her husband would run off to. It felt off. Too neat, too put-together for a man who rarely made the bed. She couldn't put her finger on why the idea of Jimbo living like *this* now bothered her, but maybe it was like when your boyfriend moves on and you meet again years later only to find out that he has fixed all his issues that bugged you so much, all the things you told him he should do he's done, and now he has the balls to stand there and give credit to the ditzy new girlfriend for helping him see the light.

"Assholes," Angel muttered as she made her way down the hall, pushing open doors to more perfect rooms, more clean and uncluttered spaces. She was pretty sure she hated the fucking little homemaker that Jimbo was shacking up with.

She crossed the room and stared out the window, at woods and snow and nothingness, trying to make sense of things. It might have been for a minute. It might have been an hour. The sight of three people walking up the driveway jarred her back to reality. Angel hurried down the stairs, taking them two at a time, grabbed her gear from the mudroom, and slipped out through the garage.

TEDESCO, WHO SHOULDA, COULDA, WOULDA

Chapter 36

It was supposed to be a fun road trip, the three of us singing songs, telling jokes, playing the car games of our youth. Problem was if you were the only one who hadn't been drinking—by default the designated driver—your passengers were only fun until the booze ran out and they fell asleep.

I was crossing the Massachusetts state line when Tommy woke up.

"Where are we?"

"Guess," I said, watching him rub his eyes, stretch, and yawn. It was obvious the guy was part cat. "And thanks for doing your part."

"What was my part, again?"

"Navigation," I said.

"Oh. Right." He sat up, shook all over, and smacked his lips. I wanted to smack *him.*

"Better?" I asked.

"Yeah, thanks." He looked at me looking at him in the rearview mirror. "What?"

"Nothing."

"Hey look, Tedesco." He pointed to the road sign that read: WELCOME TO NEW HAMPSHIRE. "Cool."

I glanced at the sleeping lump in the backseat, then pulled over. "Yeah. Cool."

Stepping out into the cold air, I took three deep breaths. As if I could clear my lungs of a decade of dying, industrialized Central New York by living with a few gulps of clean New Hampshire air. On the fourth breath, I started coughing and hacked up a thick wad of Syracuse that I spit in the road before I climbed in the back seat, switching places with Tommy.

I said, "Directions are on that yellow paper. Stop at all the stop signs, don't speed, and don't wake me until we're there."

"Okay, okay," Tommy said. "Sheesh, you're a Grumpy Gus."

I watched Tommy put on his seat belt and adjust the mirrors, then I laid my head on Barbara's soft ass and passed out.

It might have been the yelp of the dog that woke me, but probably it was the thump.

I sat up to see Tommy banging his hands on the steering wheel and praying or cursing or offering up some combination of the two. "Shit. Oh, Jesus. Oh, Sweet Jesus."

I said, "If that thump was what I think it was, Jesus isn't going to help you." I leaned over the seat. "Last I heard, He was real good at raising sinners, but not so much in the dog department, though I could be wrong. I pretty much stopped reading after the Old Testament. It seemed to all go downhill after Sodom and Gomorrah."

The removal of my face from Barbara's warm ass must have been what woke her. She pushed herself upright and looked around, blinking, as if she expected her surroundings to change. To find herself home in the suburbs under her down comforter with the "Today" show coming at her live from some small European village.

Tommy made a frenzied escape from the car after wrestling with the seat belt. He stood in the road, his hands in fists, eyes squinted as tight as a child making a wish on a birthday cake.

I couldn't stand it.

"Oh, for Pete's sake," I said, getting out of the car and zipping up my jacket. I walked around the front of the car and saw a yellow dog, kind of like a mini Old Yeller, but this scrawny mutt had nothing regal about him. No one was writing *him* a hero role, probably no sad boy was even home on the farm pining for him to return either.

"Is it bad?" Tommy asked.

"For him it is," I said.

"No, no, no," Tommy wailed.

"What's the matter?" Barbara asked, joining us.

Before I could say, "Don't. He might not be friendly," she ran to the dog, knelt by his side, and cradled his hairy little head.

"It's going to be okay," she said, running a thumb up the ridge between his glassy eyes.

I saw the blood on his mouth, his twisted lower half and thought, *No, it's not. Why are you lying to a dog?*

Tommy sat on the ground next to Barbara. He reached out and timidly stroked the dog's pinkish belly. "I'm so sorry. I didn't even see him lying there."

I watched, feeling like I should do something but having no idea what that something could be.

Barbara inspected the dog. "No collar, no tags. He's been abused, maybe even living outside for a long time from the looks of his coat and paws."

I almost took offense at her comments. I was supposed to be the observant one here. That was *my* job. I was close to wise-cracking a few comebacks. Like what was she, some kind of psychic tracker? Was she going to smell his breath and tell us what he ate for dinner or which side of the road he was headed for when Tommy changed his little doggie plans forever? But when I saw the tears welling up and heard her voice go thick, I knew that for Barbara this was more than a mangy dog dying in the middle of the road.

She wiped her eyes and stroked his bloody muzzle and his dirty, matted coat. She whispered to him, easing his pain as if she could make up for other times, other people, other mistakes.

Tommy laid his hands on the dog's head like an old-timey preacher.

Low and soft, I started to sing "We Are Going Down the Valley," the song the choir had sung at my father's funeral, a song that made my mother cry. I thought the dog would like that. As I got to the last verse, his little body went limp and as I held the last note, he closed his eyes. In one stuttering exhale, he was gone.

We buried him in a ditch off the road. Tommy added a forked branch that sort of looked like a cross if you used your imagination. Barbara cried more than you ought to for a dog no one knew, and we let her.

We drove away in silence without looking back. By the time we reached the dirt road with the mailbox stenciled "Smith," we were ready for a distraction.

Barbara said, "So tell me again how a part-time stripper and real estate agent found this house?"

Tommy said, "Candy, I mean Susan, was great. She input the Smith name, James, John in the database, then looked for a place in these mountains over a lake, or near one of the three lakes in New Hampshire that are home to the common loon, the bird—not duck—as identified on the tape. The rest was merely using a computer program to sort it all out."

"I see," she said.

I could tell she didn't, but also that she wasn't listening very hard. If all she understood was that this seemed too easy, then maybe she wouldn't think I was worth what I was charging her. Now that I had to cut Candy in for a piece of the action, I needed Barbara to see a little more.

"If only it was that easy," I said, turning the car onto the dirt road. "There were multiple hits. I mean, Smith, right? So we had to narrow each of those down, follow the lead on the gas receipt from the area, make calls and, well, I won't bore you with the details . . . but needless to say, it wasn't like some thirteen-year-old on his basement computer could have done what we did."

Tommy raised his hand. "Actually—"

I shushed him with a glare in the rearview mirror, then threw the car into park.

"Come on," I said. "The road doesn't look like it's been cut back in a while. I'd rather not scratch the Lincoln. Besides, we could all use some exercise, right?"

I walked around to Barbara's door and reached for her hand.

Tommy followed us, his corduroys rhythmically rubbing with the melody of private band pants. The swooshing sounds broke the silence—a silence that might have been soothing if we weren't up to what we were up to, if we didn't already have death on our minds.

Tall hemlocks bordering the road created a fake dark that hung heavy and thick, like the cloud over Eeyore's head. I could almost hear the whining of malnourished saplings in the ground below. The air smelled like decay, like a sharp tang of rust on old tin cans with a hint of mold—the green kind that some people think is good for you.

Above, gray fibrous clouds were doing their best to obscure what the hemlocks couldn't—a sliver of brilliant blue sky. The chill in the air turned into more of a stab as we pushed into the shadows.

"C'mon," I said, stepping up the pace, hoping to stave off both the cold and potential arguments. "I can see the house. It's not far."

If houses have genders, this one was most definitely female. Wide on the bottom with a broad, inviting porch and ample stairs, the structure narrowed and developed as it went up. Just like my favorite ladies. She was at least three stories tall, but from the lay of land I suspected a deep cellar beneath her.

"Wow. Nice place," Tommy said. "Are you sure this guy wasn't gay?"

Barbara snorted. It was the first happy sound that had come out of her since the dog, so I restrained myself from slapping Tommy on the back of the head.

Looking up at the house, you could only see sky and tips of trees beyond. It was framed perfectly in the landscape. I wondered how long someone had stood right where we were and imagined their dream house.

It was certainly pretty here, but remote. Hermit remote. Who lived like this? Someone angry at the world? Someone hiding from it, or someone who felt he no longer needed it? There was a certain utopian pleasure in the choosing of nothing over something, of wilderness over civilization, even if that wilderness came with electricity, telephone, and satellite TV.

The house appeared well-maintained. Her steps were sanded smooth and painted, rocking chairs on the wide porch suggested that at least one person would be welcome. The clean windows and white drapes beyond said "home." Someone loved this house.

Barbara put her arm around me. I felt like a newlywed showing his bride their forever home, a man offering hope as a gift.

She said, "Do you have the key?"

One word changed everything. "Nope."

Tommy started creeping up the stairs.

Barbara said, "Then how are we going to—"

"Shhh! I hear something." Tommy motioned for us to get down. Barbara dropped to a crouch behind me.

I shoved my hands deep in my pockets, wishing I had a hot cup of coffee, maybe even a donut. As Tommy motioned again for me to crouch down, take cover, do whatever it was he thought he was doing, my fingers closed on a strange key ring.

Tommy duckwalked across the porch, inched toward the front window, and held his ear to the glass. He cocked his head, his eyes wide.

I bent down and whispered to Barbara, "What does he think he's doing?"

She shrugged.

I shook my head and stomped up the stairs, jabbed the key from Smith's underwear drawer into the keyhole, and surprised everyone by swinging open the door as I called out in a pathetic Cuban accent, "Lucy! I'm home!" I walked straight to the bathroom.

THE WOODS ARE LOVELY, DARK AND DEEP

Chapter 37

When I came out drying my hands on my pants, Tommy and Barbara were in the front room. The TV we'd heard outside was playing an endless loop of old movie clips.

"The best of film noir," I said, reading the screen. "I loved the original version of *The Big Sleep*. Never thought Jimmy Stewart was the right guy for the role of General Sternwood in the remake. Hard to see him as a tough guy after *It's a Wonderful Life*, you know?"

Tommy fell into the leather chair. "Go on. Say it."

"What?" I feigned.

"You knew. The whole I was out there creeping around, the whole time I thought I heard voices, that I thought we were in trouble, you knew it was only a movie and you let me look like a fool."

I grinned.

Barbara stepped in. "Tommy, if it's any consolation, I thought someone was in here too. I mean, you really had me going out there, the way you snuck up those stairs. You were brave."

"Yeah?" he said.

"Yeah. I'm proud of you," she said, hugging him.

"All right, cut it out you two," I said stepping between them.

"Now that we're here, we've got work to do. Put these on."

I handed them both surgical gloves and tugged on a pair

of my own, then hit the TV remote. The house went still.

"Barbara, get started in the kitchen. Tommy, why don't you see if there's an office or den."

I took a quick look around before heading upstairs. The house was a blend of Victorian and something more practical. There were turret rooms and odd hallways that ended in more odd hallways, but the stairwells had been modernized to be wider and not as steep as they might have been back in the day.

I found the master suite. Apparently Mr. Smith liked white and pale blue. He had a penchant for toile and a love for the open sky, if his choice of artwork had anything to say about him. I sat on his bed and closed my eyes, waiting to see if he was going to talk to me and knowing how weird it was for me to admit that.

When I didn't hear anything, I got up and started opening drawers. Extra-large T-shirts, brown socks, size forty-two boxers. The guy was big and boring. There were few clues in the dresser, and when I came away empty-handed from the underwear drawer I began to suspect our pal James John Smith had a different secret hiding spot. I made a pass over the room, checking under the bed and behind framed art, then opened the door to a large, mostly empty walk-in closet.

I was knocking on the walls, listening for hollow spots when Tommy popped his head into the room.

"I got something you should see."

I followed him downstairs to Smith's office. It was a good-size room, done in yet another shade of blue. An L-shaped dark-wood desk unit held two computers, a fax machine, and two telephones. Across the room was a large flat-screen TV, some audio equipment, and a wall of books. A quick glance showed a diverse interest in reading material—from songbirds and waterfowl to science fiction titles with covers that suggested the reader might enjoy futuristic romps with armor-plated dudes who drove motorcycles adorned with demon heads and three-pronged tails.

"Okay," Tommy said, "I found the transaction for the game that won him Flannigan's. He played other games before that too, where winnings included a vintage Corvette, a house in Norway, and on one occasion even a pair of Malaysian twins. In each prior circumstance, Smith simply re-bid the win in another game."

"Interesting," I said.

"And then there's this," Tommy said, pulling up a page on the computer screen. He waited until I had moved beside him, then started scrolling. It took me a minute to figure out what I was reading. It was a saved messaged conversation written in a shortened version of regular English, the same I was used to seeing when I received a text.

"There are at least twenty-five files like this," Tommy said. "All conversations with young men—or people pretending to be young men."

I pointed to the thumb-size profile photos next to the words on the screen. "What do you mean, pretending? There's pictures."

Tommy shook his head. "You can fake that."

"Why would they?"

"Lots of reasons. Some people are just plain lonely. They go online, make a friend, and then they're afraid to tell the truth, afraid to say what they really feel. Maybe even who they really are."

I looked at Tommy. The kid was serious. It made me sad to think he might be one of those lonely guys pretending to be someone else.

I stared out the window at the trees and the space, at a sky so blue it looked like a kindergartener's art project. "All right, so we know our guy Smith went online and made friends. What we don't know is if they ever came here or if they ever met with unfortunate circumstances. We know he bets online and apparently wins. But he never took possession of any of the winnings before. What was different this time? What drew Smith down from these mountains all the way into Syracuse? I mean, who would want to leave this behind?"

Tommy grunted and kept scrolling.

I went over what we knew. The guy was into guys. He liked his privacy. He used to fly. He had money. Apparently he played a decent game of poker, and comparing the size of the boxers in the master to the size of the corpse in the Flannigan's crime-scene photos, the man had recently lost a significant amount of weight.

"You want to take this with us?" Tommy asked, motioning to the screen.

"Can we?"

"I can download everything to something more portable," he offered.

"That would be good," I said. "I'm going to have to make that call soon."

"Captain Seton?"

"Yep."

"Shit. There's no telling how badly those cops will screw up this hard drive. I'd better get what I can now." He pulled a zip-line cord from his pocket, inserted two devices into the front of the computer tower, pushed his hair back, and rolled his chair closer. "Give me fifteen."

I left him to it and went to find Barbara.

She was still in the kitchen, running her finger down a spice rack. "I've never heard of some of these," she said. "Mahaleb cherry, grains of paradise, mugwort?"

"Maybe our guy was a gourmet," I said.

"So what's he doing running an Irish pub?" she asked, opening the freezer drawer of the stainless refrigerator. "Look at this."

Neat rows of white butcher-paper-wrapped packages were stacked four high and eight across, lining the interior. Barbara pulled one out. It was labeled in neat, tiny cursive: Venison, Gray's Meadow, January 12, 2007, marinade: pinot noir, pepper, and garlic.

"Sounds good."

"They're all different," she said, handing me more packages.

I read them and handed them back, suddenly hungry for a venison stew or a cheesy rabbit rarebit. Barbara slid the drawer closed then leaned on the fridge, lost in thought.

I tapped her arm. "So, where do women hide their secret things?"

"I beg your pardon?"

"You do have secret things, don't you?" I stepped closer.

"I suppose," she said.

"So where do you hide them?" I ran my fingers up her arm to her shoulder. "Men generally use the underwear drawer or under the mattress. We've never been known for our creativity."

Barbara smiled. She cocked her head up at me the same way she used to in fifth-period science when we were lab partners. It was still cute.

"I could tell you," she said. "But then I'd have to kill you."

It should have been funny, the corny line from some corny cop show, but here in the kitchen of a potential murderer, it wasn't funny. Barbara felt that too.

I stood on the porch, wondering what had caught my eye in the tree line. Scanning the area again, I saw nothing. There didn't even seem to be a breeze to rustle the branches of the pines.

Tommy came out of the house, wrapped his arms around himself, and shivered. "It's freezing out here. Looks like it's going to snow."

"Deal with it, small man."

I scanned the yard again, moving my eyes across the spread of lawn to the bushes where I'd thought I'd seen something. A shadow, a bird, a mountain lion? Whatever it was, it was gone, or hidden in the woods, even more of afraid of me than I was of it.

"We should get going," I said.

"Yep," Tommy said.

And still we stood there.

Barbara stepped up behind me. "Why don't you guys finish up inside while I go down and get the car?"

"Pretty much done inside," Tommy said. "But I think I will use the bathroom."

"Yeah, you do that," I called after him. "And don't forget to wash your hands!"

Barbara poked me. "Be nice."

"I am."

"You know what I mean."

She poked me again, this time leaning into it. It almost hurt. I said, "Hey, easy now."

She giggled and tried for me again, but I backed out of reach, knowing how 95 percent of all tickle fights end. My cell phone rang, giving off one of those annoying blares like a broken birdcall. I put up a hand to ward off Barbara and worked the phone out of my pocket. She reached in my other pants pocket and jangled my car keys, then pointed to the road. I nodded as I put the phone to my ear.

"Tedesco," I said, watching her jog down the drive and

disappear around the corner. I tried to keep an eye on her, caught glimpses of color through the woods, but the sun was setting and blending all the colors into hues of gray.

"Tedesco? Captain Seton here. I got your message. You know we'd like to close this case. You're putting me in an awkward position by running off to New Hampshire, leaving these little teasers, like a game of Clue. Don't try to tell me it was Professor Plum in the library with the candlestick."

"Now why would I do that? You know I was always more partial to Miss Scarlet," I said, stepping back into the house to finish the conversation.

"Tedesco. Tick. Tock."

"All right, all right. I don't have any answers yet, but it looks like we were on the right track with the New Hampshire connection. A cursory check of the premises suggests there's more to our Mr. Smith than we thought. Something still doesn't feel right. I haven't followed up on the gas receipt yet either."

"Don't bother. I've got a team on the way. We can take it from here."

"Of course. I just wanted to—"

"I said we've got it, Tedesco. Pack it up and head home. I'm sure some broad needs you to catch her husband in bed with his secretary."

Seton could be such an asshole. I started to tell him just what I thought of his remark when I saw Tommy exiting the bathroom with a portable hard drive in hand.

I held the phone like a walkie-talkie and spit out the words, "Yes, sir. Over and out!" then slapped it shut and tucked it in my pocket.

"Always nice to hear from the captain, eh?" Tommy said.

"As nice as a visit from the gastroenteritis fairy."

"Okay? So, I shouldn't ask, right?"

I shook my head and led the way to the porch. "Let's get out of here. They're on the way."

"Where's Barbara?" Tommy asked, pulling the door closed behind us.

"She's pulling the car up," I said, checking my watch and staring down the driveway.

A few minutes later Tommy said, "You don't think she went to get gas, do you?" He stomped his feet and hugged himself. Dressed in one of Smith's coats, he looked like a kid in his dad's clothes.

"She wouldn't go without saying anything," I said as I stepped off the porch to try and see around the bend in the drive. "Right?" I called back, trying to ignore the twinge of fear slowly rising inside me.

I broke into a run.

The slap of boots on hard-packed snow confirmed Tommy wasn't far behind.

We rounded the bend at the same time, skidding to a stop. "Shit!"

The spot where the Lincoln had been parked was empty.

Tommy spun in circles, then cupped his hands and yelled to the sky, "Barbara? Barbara?"

"She's gone. What the hell?" I sat on the cold ground, partly to catch my breath and partly to still my body so my brain could sort this out.

Tommy ran toward the woods, then down the road and back up to the house like a fickle dog that had to pee.

I clenched my fists. It wasn't Barbara. She didn't have anything to do with this. She hadn't even known where we were going. It had to be someone else, someone who didn't want us here, didn't want us close to Smith. And the girls' killer was dead.

But what if I was wrong? What if we were all wrong? What if the real killer was here in New Hampshire? And now he had Barbara?

Tommy came back, panting, the big coat hanging off him, snot dripping from his nose. "Tedesco, I don't want to alarm you. But I've been thinking. What if someone took her?" He went white. "What if they're still here?"

I shushed him with a warning look, then said loud enough for the whole woods to hear, "Let's go back to the house. The cops are on the way. We'll wait for them there."

Pacing the porch felt like giving up. Barbara was out there. She was in trouble. She needed me. "Wait. Doesn't this place have a garage?"

Tommy grinned, "Follow me."

There were three vehicles: a 1970s Camaro that looked like it had never left the showroom, a beastly white pickup truck with tires guaranteed to conquer mountains, and an engine-less rusty sedan that had seen better days.

Whoever this guy Smith was, he wasn't into luxury vehicles. But he knew how to get around when he wanted to get something without letting anything stand in his way.

IT'S A CATFIGHT, BITCHES

Chapter 38

Angel wasn't a stranger to fighting for her man—or her honor, as fleetingly pure as it might have once been. She might be a rich chick who came from earned money, the kind of girl that wore designer labels, but get a few shots of tequila into her and she'd reduce herself to redneck trailer trash in a hot minute. Seeing those people coming up the driveway, coupled with the fact that her man had been hiding something from her, was all it took to flip the switch.

Angel waited under a low-hanging bough of evergreens as the broad approached the Lincoln, mumuring under her breath and jingling the keys.

Before the driver's door was even open, Angel jogged up, collar in hand, calling, "Spike? Spike?"

"What's the matter?" Barbara asked as the woman in the puffy coat crouched beside the Lincoln to peer underneath it.

She said, "Are you under there?" Spike!"

Barbara bent down to look under the car. "You lost your dog? I haven't seen him. I hope he's okay."

Angel slipped behind Barbara, choked her with the collar. They fought, scuffling and slapping until Angel yanked hard, smacking Barbara's head against the Lincoln and knocking her out.

Angel dragged her into the backseat, retrieved the keys from the door, and drove off, pleasantly surprised at her strength and resolve. Men weren't the only badasses in the world.

She'd found the clearing when looking for a place to

hide her own car. She figured some kids or hunters must have been here before her. It was nice of them to make a path back in the woods perfect for a big-ass luxury car from New York.

She glanced in the backseat. The broad was still out cold. She hoped she hadn't done any permanent damage. Nah, screw that. The bitch was going to get what she deserved. And Angel was going to get Jimbo back.

No one stole *her* husband and got away with it. Not after all they'd been through. Angel could still remember the day they met.

Jimbo had been in town for some sort of convention. Angel never nailed that down. It didn't matter in the end. It was just another job he'd lose. It was never his fault, nothing he'd done or didn't do. It was them. Always. When Jimbo was fired or laid off or downsized, he'd always say the same thing. They'd regret it. It was their loss. He didn't need them. One day he'd be his own boss, run his own company. Wait and see.

Angel wanted to believe him—every time. He was so sincere, his tears so real.

More than anything else, Jimbo was a charmer. He had a way of making you want to root for him. He could twist a tale around so much that if his story had been a person it would have been a bony, bendy ballerina spun like a top then hurled into a fouetté jeté with no one to catch her.

Angel and Jimbo were married less than a year after they met. Being an efficient man, Angel's father offered the newly engaged couple a nice fat check if they'd elope and forego a messy wedding day that would clutter his calendar. Jimbo and Angel worked an early withdrawal plan from the family trust into the negotiation and, like a sordid prenuptial agreement, a deal was struck.

They used to joke that they chose to stay in town because "Virginia Beach was for lovers." But you can only live a T-shirt-slogan life for so long. One morning you're going to wake up and realize the guy has been unfaithful, you're unhappy, and there are no kids and not even an overweight dog to keep you from splitting up.

Friends will convince you over drinks that this is a good thing. You'd be free.

"You're young," they say.

"You can find someone else."

"He's a jerk," they tell you, ordering another round.

You know they mean well, but mostly you just want to go home and call him and ask him why and please could we talk and what's wrong with me? Even though the truth would kill you, because you know it will be something you can't change. Something you love about yourself. Then you'll begin to wonder if he's right and that's why you've been so unhappy all these years.

Angel never thought that would happen with Jimbo. How could it? He loved her and she still loved him. Possibly even more now than in the beginning when she fell crazy in love, losing herself to a man, heart and soul, for the first time.

She was sent to France by her father less than two months after she and Jimbo met. It was first time they'd been separated for more than a day. Her father said he needed her to meet with French backers, to be there with his team. He said she was the only one he trusted. He had a staff of idiots and everyone knew you couldn't trust those "frogs."

Angel called Jimbo three times a day, telling him she missed him. She tried to overlook his insecurities, tried to see them as endearing, believing that he loved her so much that it only came off as needy, jealous, and paranoid. She promised that her heart belonged to him alone, that she was, even then, in her hotel room overlooking the Champs-Élysées, imagining the pillow beside her as Jimbo.

He told her to hug it close to her breasts, then blow him a kiss and send the picture on her phone.

They made plans to meet in their favorite bar on the night she returned. He said he'd be counting down the hours, even attempted to tell her in French that he loved her, that she was his beautiful girl. She forgave his improper use of *vous* and the poor pronunciation, because after all, he was trying, wasn't he?

Angel remembered how hopeful she'd felt. Now, as she parked the Lincoln parallel to the New Hampshire cliff, she felt that hope renewed.

Tall, thick trees acted as a windbreak for her spot in the clearing. It was quiet, still, almost serene. Snow and ice hung heavy from branches, birds flitted from berried bushes to treetops. For a minute, Angel almost forgot she was a criminal with an unconscious, kidnapped woman in the backseat. She turned off the car and checked on her victim—breathing, and apparently quite comfortable. A small purse in the woman's coat pocket revealed an ID and sixty dollars in cash.

"Hello, Barbara Leonard from Syracuse, New York. Come here often?"

Angel tied Barbara's hands and ankles, then slid back over the front seat to examine the contents of the purse and wait for Sleeping Beauty to wake up.

Barbara eventually began to stir in the backseat. Angel locked eyes with her in the rearview. As she pushed herself upright, Angel casually turned around, aiming a very large gun at Barbara.

"Good morning, princess. Did you sleep well? I think we have something to talk about."

Barbara wriggled, tugging at the rope bindings securing her hands behind her.

"I think we do too. Let's start with why you you've tied me up, and move on to the gun. How's that?"

Angel laughed. "I don't think so. Get out of the fucking car. Now!"

She tied Barbara's hands to the handle of the Lincoln's passenger door—the side of the car facing the cliff—then stepped back, still pointing the gun at Barbara, though it was getting heavy and she was fueled solely on adrenaline. She was fading fast.

"You don't look like his type," Angel said running her eyes over Barbara. "He usually likes them younger. At least that's what I was told. This is a first for me. You're my first cheating husband stealer."

"And your last," Barbara said under her breath.

"What's that, sweetheart? You have something to tell me? Feeling all guilty and ready to confess now, are you?"

"Confess what? I have no idea what you are talking about."

"Cut the shit! You stole my husband and I want him back."

"I didn't steal anybody's husband," Barbara said, pulling at the rope bindings. "Wait. Who did you say your husband was?"

"Cute. Real cute," Angel said, leveling the gun. She didn't look amused.

WHEN BEING BUFFY IS A GOOD THING

Chapter 39

"She's cute, but she's also smart, Tedesco," Tommy said.

"I know. She'll be fine. Now let's just find her."

Tommy attempted his best warrior gaze. "We'll leave no stone unturned."

"She's not a freaking earthworm," I said.

"Salamander."

"What?" I said.

"Salamanders live under rocks. Earthworms live in the soil. But there are beetles, and those fat white things." Tommy shivered. "Ew."

"Are you calling Barbara a fat white thing, Tommy?"

"What? No! I was just saying—"

"Enough," I said. "Quiet. I need to think."

It was almost dark. We were driving Smith's pickup in the direction we'd come, thinking no one would want to go in the other direction if escape was on their mind. We'd tried that way, but all we'd found were more woods, a downed tree with too many branches and a dead end with a wicked—that was New Hampshire speak for "gnarly"—drop-off into a very deep ravine, housing what I expected were a whole bunch of wild animals and maybe some of those fat white bug things that creeped Tommy out.

"Shit we missed it," I said braking hard and yanking the wheel left, fishtailing the truck, reversing our direction to the perfectly arranged fallen tree.

Tommy looked surprised, then he got it. "When in doubt do the unpredictable. Smart Criminal Rule Number 7."

Prowling through strange woods might seem like a cool thing if you are fourteen and playing paintball, with the whiz of colored bullets flying overhead midbattle, the sound of your breath coming back at you in the face mask, your heart beating, the adrenaline racing.

But in reality, it fucking sucked. I was too old to be crouching under tree limbs, crawling through brush, squatting in wait —and I knew it from the creaking of my knees to the ache in my lower back and the numbness in my flattened ass. I was cold. I was hungry. I wanted to find Barbara, beat someone up for making me so miserable, and get the hell out of there. Tommy, on the other hand, appeared to have found some long-lost masculinity that he was firmly embracing.

I was aware the kid might have played a few too many war video games, because he knew all the hand signals and pointing gestures and performed them as if I could see him in the fading light. Which sounds too poetic for the all-encompassing darkness that was falling fast.

The only thing that was keeping me there in the woods was the fact that Barbara must be in a worse place. Whatever I had to suffer through was deserved because I'd dragged her into this. She should be home with her husband. She should be safe. I swore I wasn't going to mess up her life again, not like last time.

I made my way into the clearing, felt Tommy behind me, and kept going, thinking whoever was out there with my Lincoln and Barbara was probably having as much trouble with the dark and the cold as we were.

I heard her before I saw her. Apparently my ex-sweetie had reached deep down and found herself a pair.

"Go to hell!"

The acid in Barbara's voice reminded me of times I'd failed her in the past and she had yelled at me about it. Once I'd left her behind and gone out with the guys on her birthday. Another time I'd neglected to answer her call, which resulted in a very long wait in a bus terminal over Christmas.

I whispered a promise to myself to do better.

Barbara yelled, "You dumbass! You're making a big mistake!" Two things no kidnapper wanted to hear.

As the clouds parted, allowing the moon to shine into the clearing, I saw Barbara tied up and wriggling against the car door, trying to free herself. She was shouting to a shadow beyond the bright circle made by the Lincoln's headlights.

"I don't know what you're talking about. I swear I don't know anyone named Jimbo. You need to let me go."

A woman stepped out of the dark wearing a puffy parka and matching red boots.

She scoffed. "You think it's that easy? Just keep saying the same thing over and over and suddenly I'm going to say, 'Oh, I'm sorry, miss. I must be mistaken. Apparently you're not fucking my husband in that fancy house of yours, not keeping him from coming home where he belongs. Here, let me untie you and let you go.' Is that what you think?"

She laughed, a harsh chortle that needed a *yeah right* after it, or something caustically British. "Sorry pretty, but that ain't happening. What *is* happening, is *you* are going to tell *me* exactly where my Jimbo is and *exactly* what you've been doing with him."

Barbara leaned back against the Lincoln. On the surface, it appeared an exercise in restraint, but it was more than that. She was using the door handle to work at the bindings on her wrists.

"Ok," Barbara said with a sigh. "You found us out. Me and *Jimbo.* We're in love. He said he'd take me away from it all. How was I to know he meant New Hampshire? All that time I was thinking Syracuse."

"Syracuse?" The woman laughed. "Who the hell goes there?"

"Jimbo," Barbara said.

"No way. He hates the cold almost as much as he hates clouds. God knows how he ended up here."

"Things happen," Barbara said, buying time.

"Yeah, things fucking *happen*. You get pissed off one day at your husband and speed away. Think you're the one holding all the cards. No. I don't believe you, I know Jimbo. *I. Know. Him.*"

The woman stepped closer to Barbara. It was the first clear look I'd gotten of her tear-stained face—or the gun. The broad might look like a puffy suburban housewife, but she was packing like a killer.

"Are you okay?" Barbara's voice turned soft.

"Yeah. Love hurts."

Tommy and I circled the area. The woman had dropped her gun arm to her side. She was crying, and Barbara was murmuring something as she continued to work on her wrists against the door handle. I started getting a whole different vibe from the situation. I was afraid if Barbara did get herself untied she'd run *to* the woman instead of trying to escape from her.

I stepped on a branch. The crack it made in the silence of the clearing was deafening. The woman swung toward me with the gun, drawing aim down her puffy arm, wiping her nose and eyes with her gloved hand.

"Who's there?" she called.

The way she was squinting in my direction made me think the headlights were bright enough that she'd have trouble adjusting her eyes. I made a decision that I knew I might later regret. I decided going in low and fast would be the best approach.

As I crashed through the woods I went somewhere else in my head, where it wasn't cold or damp or dangerous. I managed to block out snapping twigs, slapping branches, crunchy bugs, and lurking creatures. I must have also blocked out Tommy, because as I broke cover so did he. He came out the other side of the clearing and leaped onto the puffy lady from behind. It should have been enough to take her down—if Tommy had been me. As it was, the woman slapped and brushed at his grip like he was a spider that had dropped onto her shoulder while she was reading in her window seat.

Tommy yelled. Barbara screamed. The woman spun, waving the gun, slapping at Tommy. She stumbled backward into the woods, taking him with her.

I ran to Barbara who tried to give me an armless hug. "Oh my God, Bill! What happened? How did you find me? That lady's nuts!"

"I know," I said. "Here. Stand still. I'm trying to untie you." It took a few fumbled attempts and a pocketknife to release Barbara from the door handle. She wrapped her arms around me as soon as she was free. Part of me wanted to do the same to her, to stay like that until the good guys came and everything was fixed—but only a small part of me.

I opened the car door, started to push her inside. "It's gonna be okay, Barbara. Wait here. Lock the doors. I'm going to get Tommy. I love—"

She screamed before she fired, a banshee yell. I shoved Barbara in the car and turned in time to see the woman trip as the gun went off.

Barbara screamed my name, banged on the glass.

"Stay—"

The impact took the rest of my words.

The shot echoed up the ravine and off the cliff's sides. Birds took flight, screeching a warning. I saw in Barbara's face astonishment turning to disbelief and back again. She flattened her hand on the window, matching mine, as I sunk to the ground.

THIS IS THE PART WHERE TEDESCO DREAMS

Chapter 40

Every good story has a dream sequence. Though this one isn't full of rivers, bananas, naked ladies, or fast cars, there's still enough symbolism in it to keep me on the shrink's couch for a few more years.

I was the young me, with hair longer than I'd ever worn it in real life. The way it kept blowing in my eyes, tickling my cheeks, and irritating my neck made me wonder even in this pleasant dream place why any man grew his hair long.

There was a puddle of water, the sound of dripping. I knew if I looked down I would be barefoot, so I didn't look down. Someone was calling my name, but it wasn't really my name. I knew that if I wanted to, I could fly.

There was a hall with doors lining either side, and as I passed each one, it closed. Slowly. Quietly. At the end of the hall, I came to a river and dove in. As I floated along, I saw people from my past on the riverbank. My Uncle Buddy, who died of a heart attack on a roller coaster; a neighbor who'd been killed by a drunk driver; my first-grade teacher, who would have been a hundred if she was alive.

Someone yelled, "Watch out!"

But it was too late. I'd swum right into a crocodile and my arm was in his mouth. I wasn't afraid, just a little embarrassed. I told him I was sorry and he opened his jaws and swam off, splashing me in the face with a swish of his tail. My arm felt warm and slimy from being inside him, so I went to find a towel and found myself back in the hallway. A man with a fishbowl head walked past, shooting me with finger guns. I rose taller than everyone around me and felt the floor rumble as I walked. Forks and knives jangled against fine china as I strode past an elegant dinner table set for three pretty girls: a blonde, a brunette, and a redhead. When I raised my hand to wave they all mouthed in unison "We love you. Thank you."

A champagne bottle clinked against ice in a silver wine cooler, water in gold-rimmed glasses rippled. I was suddenly thirsty. So thirsty. When I reached for a glass, everything changed.

Afterward they told me I hadn't moved for three days. They said I was lucky to have missed the ricocheting bullet, and the chances of getting punctured in the back of my neck the way I had—at that depth and angle—by a chunk of flying metal "National Forest" sign was next to impossible.

One nurse had prayed over me, telling me there must be something I was put on earth to do, because there was no way I should have survived. Had the shard penetrated a little deeper, it would have struck a major artery and I would have bled out. Had the metal entered my skin a millimeter to the left, it would have embedded itself in my spinal column and paralyzed me.

Barbara never left my side. The nurses called her "Bulldog." She was my Buffy after all. Even though she had a husband and a recently deceased daughter on her mind, I was still important to her. That meant a lot to me, even if I was in an induced coma and couldn't tell her.

* * *

Maybe when you think you're dying you dream differently than when you know the whole world's out there for you—just like it was there yesterday, and you assume it will be tomorrow. Maybe a part of your sick brain unlocks when that assumption's taken away, when schedules, chores, and responsibility don't exist.

Maybe that was the reason I didn't open my eyes right away. There's a certain peace in nothingness.

I could feel my body. Pain in most parts, heaviness in others. I heard someone crying, someone complaining about cafeteria choices, another asking for the truth, saying, "C'mon doc, don't blue-sky me."

I thought about opening my eyes, about setting them all straight, telling them I was fine, really. But then something took me deeper, and I liked that floaty, uncomplicated feeling. I wasn't ready to give it up. Lying there, I started to question everything I once thought was real and right, every judgment call I'd ever made. I could relate to schizophrenics, to people leading double lives—like the ghost I'd been chasing, James John Smith. Guy was one person up there in New Hampshire, living a hermit's life in a cozy house full of knickknacks with a fully stocked, labeled freezer. But he was a totally different dude in Syracuse, living on a busy downtown street in a sterile apartment over an Irish pub. Something really bothered me about that.

When I woke to the buzzing of the TV, it was dark and late according to the clock. Someone had left it on with the sound muted, but the picture was clear enough. It was one of the movies that had been playing in Smith's mountain house, *The Big Sleep*. The irony wasn't lost on me.

Jimmy Stewart had started his career as James Stewart, cast in his first movie, *Murder Man*, with a very minor role. That bit part was the start of his career. He played the nice guy, genuine, innocent, and vulnerable. Audiences loved him. Women wished their husbands were more like him: friendly, kind, outwardly generous, and likable.

But the war interfered, and when Jimmy/James Stewart returned from his bomber pilot missions, he wasn't a movie star anymore. No one wanted a nice guy. No one wanted a mushy-mouthed, vulnerable man. They wanted a tough guy. A savior. By the time the *Big Sleep* remake came around in 1978, Stewart was too old for leading man roles, but cast as the bad guy retired general, he was finally believable. He'd learned to adapt, how to be what was needed to get on in the world, and that got me thinking about another James. Our dead guy, James Smith.

It was all so confusing. I was zoning in and out, partly from morphine and partly from all those memories bumping around. When the nurse came in to check on me, I thought *I* was Jimmy Stewart. Not the man, but the actor. I was Jimmy as George Bailey. And the nurse? She was my Mary. A movie camera rolled down the street in front of us, a director yelled through a megaphone, "Be happy." The nurse stumbled and I grabbed her arm. I smiled and sang "Buffalo gals, won't you come out tonight . . ." and she smiled back at me.

The next thing I know, I'm me. The old me. Bill Tedesco, a boy with a future. I'm holding Buffy's hand and swinging it between us, and we're singing that song together, but when I look at her again, she's turned into Michelle, my almost ex-wife, and she's got her sad face on, like the dog ran away or I've let her down again.

Michelle says, "I'll tell you what I want. I want to be loved. I want someone who will love me and never leave. Is that too much to ask?" And I think she's talking about a dog.

But that can't be right.

I know I am missing something important, because Michelle morphs back into Barbara-as-Buffy. She's wearing her cheerleading uniform and crying. She's saying, "Bi-ill. You know what I need. Don't leave me." And when I step closer to her, she pushes the hood off her red parka and it's the woman in the woods, pointing a gun in my face.

"You never should have left me, Jimbo."

I see her finger tighten on the trigger, I watch the bullet discharge like I am some sort of superhero with really great vision, except I must be a stupid superhero because I don't duck or do a *Matrix* backbend. I don't even hold up a Superman hand to stop it. I just stand there like an idiot, thinking, *What do you want? What do you need?*

ANSWERS FROM THE GHOST OF JIMBO PAST

Chapter 41

Out of all of them, Chamonix should have figured it out. She was the most like him, after all. She was the kind of girl who had the answers, even if you didn't ask the questions—but on that day, the day she died, it was as if she'd been left holding the game show buzzer while chubby Tracie from Tallahassee squeaked, "What is Athena?" and took home the ten-thousand-dollar prize Chamonix had already spent.

And now the only question left was: Why did he do it?

Jimbo had no answer. He just got to a place where he couldn't turn back. A male *Thelma and Louise* moment. He was sorry now that it had come to that, because he'd never really thought of himself as a *killer*, not the original Jimbo. But this new guy? Yep. That guy could have done all those horrible things and then some.

He supposed the first time he knew his alter ego was a bad man was right before he pushed the original dude off the cliff in New Hampshire, not long after the sad shmuck had experienced his first truly pleasurable and consensual sexual act.

Unlike some of the girls Jimbo had been with, James slipped into place eagerly. It was like training a puppy to follow you—you simply had to be a more interesting option than sleeping or eating. Jimbo was. They watched movies that Jimbo chose and listened to *his* music. They read books and took long walks at the edge of the woods.

James never knew what hit him.

Jimbo had learned the art of manipulation at an early age. *Thanks, Mom.*

During his formative years he had read self-help books, watched late-night makeover programs, and dated self-evolved chicks—all things that helped him become a better crazy person. His likability and charm were eclipsed only by his good looks, which gave him an instant "in" with both genders. His extensive knowledge of popular song lyrics, added to well-rehearsed lines from romantic comedies and famous poems, didn't hurt. He could appear exceptionally vulnerable and in touch with his feelings, while never speaking an honest word. It was a talent. The kind of talent that usually led to a life in prison.

If Jimbo had spent any time on the therapist's couch he would have been diagnosed a borderline sociopath with checkmarks next to every symptom on the list—and for some, he'd be given stars.

He learned to admit up front that he wasn't perfect. *Hook.* That he was working through some issues. *Line.* That he might need a bit of fixing. Most women bought it, especially when his eyes welled up. Then he'd say the one thing they all wanted to hear: You make me want to be a better man. *Sinker.*

You can pull a pig out of a mud hole, you can wash him off and even spray cologne on his hairy little pink body, but in the end? He will always find his way back to the mud hole.

So even though for the last five years Jimbo had been trying to be good, had been living the life of a pretty loyal married man in the suburbs who went to work every day and came home every night and basically did all the things a good man was supposed to, he had only been burying the old Jimbo. Hiding him from prying eyes.

He'd been lying to himself. Reinvented as the new James John Smith, bar owner, Syracuse resident, Jimbo was finally able to release that part of him. He could be the man he'd been destined to become. A man made complete by the three women who had walked into his bar and chosen him.

Or so he thought. Until each one rejected him, leaving him with nothing.

He'd gone to Cress first, thinking a woman who'd reinvented herself would be the perfect match for him. He'd just forgotten her polyamorous tendencies. He had pulled her onto his lap, painting a picture of their future: moonlight strolls, dinners served picnic-style in front of a roaring fire, neighborhood gatherings, Saturdays at the theater. He continued by talking about the perfect baby, who slept through the night, and family vacations to amusement parks where they'd breakfast with cartoon characters. He spoke of a wedding in a castle, a honeymoon in the South of France. They would keep each other beautiful. Money would never be a concern.

"Oh, baby," she'd said, cradling his face in her hands. "I can't. I promised the other boys they were first. Which makes you fourth. I have be to true to the system. Otherwise, what do I have?"

Jimbo acted on his connection to Roxie, the feeling that it was more than physical, that it might possibly touch his heart, if he wanted to admit he had a heart. He admired her vitality, her crooked sense of humor, the way she used both of those to hide her pain and loss. He understood her confusion in starting over after the death of Daniel, after uprooting and moving across country from Paradise to Not-So-Much.

He knew people that filled broken, empty, sad parts of

themselves with the kindness and generosity of strangers, surrounding themselves with the kind of big-eyed people who always look startled, like life just threw them a curve ball and they weren't sure whether they should swing or duck. Roxie wasn't like that. She was smart and good. She was better than that.

He found her in the stockroom on a slow afternoon and stepped in close, smelling her soap-and-water freshness. Roxie was a cottage by the shore. She was puppies and suckling infants. She was church groups and minivans. She was the hand on his shoulder, calming his anger. She was the warm back he spooned into at night. He saw it all so clearly.

But when he dropped his walls and told her he was falling for her, she laughed, slapped his arm and said, "James, you crack me up!" She had walked away, laughing.

Chamonix came to him. She knew he was hurting. She was attuned to his pain. His desires. His need. Jimbo enjoyed their secret connection. He spoke to her differently than the others, played her little games—both the mental and physical ones. He enjoyed being with her, was constantly entertained. She was the most interesting woman he had ever known. Exciting and scary at the same time. She was a roller coaster at midnight. She was a tattoo on a tender spot, a bruise you didn't remembering getting. She was screaming heavy metal concerts and shots of whiskey. Hate her. Love her. She didn't care. She had no filter, no soft spots. She was one big hard edge. She was city living and three-day parties. She was a trip to Burning Man. A hike in a rain forest without bug spray. She was a soul mate who scared the shit out of him. He loved those parts of her, but hesitated at the idea that she might prove to be more evil, more conniving, perhaps even smarter than he was, which might make him feel stupid. He could never abide that. No one did Jimbo that way.

It might have been that combination of emotions coursing through his blood—love, loss, dismissal, abandonment, anger, despair, misery, ruin, finality—added to the effects of booze and Blue Cali weed that made Jimbo-James load the gun, leave his apartment, and go into the bar.

TEDESCO HEARS ALL ABOUT WHEN THOSE FAKE MOVIE CLIFF-SIDE BRANCHES ARE REAL AND FUCKING SAVE YOUR BONY ASS

Chapter 42

For the three women who had walked into that bar, peace would be theirs now. Captain Seton and his men had picked up where we left off.

I wish I'd seen it. I really wish someone had videotaped the whole thing from some treetop locale, because that was probably the most fucked-up thing ever. I mean, even days later, as the story broke and people in Syracuse were talking about it, it still seemed like a publicity stunt or something from that TV show where all the guys get their balls wrecked in extreme sports—except for guys like Tommy, whose only extreme sport was cooking in the nude, which could be dangerous if you were using a lot of hot oil.

Then again, I'm not sure how much fun a video would be, since I would have been well on my way out by the time Tommy realized the squirrelly situation he was in.

Barbara told me later that the kidnapper lady hadn't been *so* bad. She went by the name Angel, short for Kara Angelina Di Sarranno Smith, and had opened up enough to Barbara out there in the woods that she had actually started feeling compassion for the crazy broad. My Buffy had always suffered from a large heart.

While all that was happening, Tommy and I were dashing through the woods, only we didn't have a sleigh. And instead of going to grandmother's house, Tommy tackled the Puffy Coat Lady and I ended up getting to play hero by rescuing my ex-sweetie. Which lasted all of like, oh, a minute, because Puffy Coat tossed Tommy off the cliff and then turned her gun on me.

She might have killed me.

If she hadn't tripped and hit that tree with the sign first. It was a weird combination of timing and circumstance, cheap bullets and bad aim. Still, it scared the hell out of Barbara and put me out of commission for a good long while.

I know. Things could have been worse. Much worse.

As it was, I had to hear the rest of the story second- and third-hand, because if there was one thing I'd gotten good at as I grew older, it was passing out.

Tommy said when he went over the cliff he thought he was a goner. He did all the things they say to do when you think your time is up. He offered up frantic prayers of forgiveness, brought a few happy images to mind, and instantly regretted the things he had not had time to do in his short life. And then he realized he wasn't falling anymore, had all his body parts, and actually felt fine. Even though he'd tumbled down a snowy cliff before landing with a dull thud on a very well-padded and somewhat brightly dressed corpse.

"I tell you, Tedesco. It makes you wonder," Tommy said weeks later in the hospital.

He was wearing a pinstriped suit with a purple shirt and a geometric tie. His hair looked more normal than it ever had, groomed like a TV anchorman.

"Are you wearing eyeliner?" I asked.

"In the business, we call it *guy liner.*"

"And what business would that be?"

"You know, show business. Entertainment. The social media network."

I looked across the room to Barbara for some help. "How long have I been asleep, again?"

She laughed. "Tommy is quite the wanted property now, Bill. Ever since the shooting, he's had major television appearances, been asked to consult for some news networks and—"

Tommy jumped in. "Appear in a famous boy-band music video!"

I raised a brow.

"I know. It's amazing, right?" he said.

"Oh. It's amazing, all right," I said.

Tommy's pocket vibrated and he slipped out a shiny new cell phone. He slid and tapped his fingers while grinning. "I'd better take this," he said. "It's Ellen's assistant to her assistant."

As the door closed behind Tommy, I caught Barbara's eye. She sat on a corner of the bed, reaching for my hand. "He'll be okay," she said. "It's just his fifteen minutes."

"I guess so. But you know Tommy once he latches onto something. It's going to be hard to let it go."

"And *you* know Tommy," she said. "He is bright enough to get out before the bottom drops out, and he knows better than anyone how fickle the universe can be."

"Fickle. I like that," I said, smiling, trailing my fingers across my bandaged wound and then to her hand and up her arm.

"Better than 'fucked-up'?"

"Why, Barbara Leonard!" I said. "The words coming out of your mouth!"

"I'm only quoting you, Bill Tedesco."

"Me? When did I say that?"

"Only about a hundred times since you've been laying in this bed. Don't you remember that?"

"No. What else did I say?"

"You don't remember anything?" she asked.

I shook my head. "Lots of doctor babble, people poking me, but nothing else, really."

She slid her hand from under mine and turned away, but not before I saw the tears. "It's not important."

Which made me think it probably was. And got me curious about what the hell else I'd said before waking from my fairy-tale sleep. I was about to ask her to refresh my memory when Tommy pushed his way back in the room—and the conversation.

"So," he said. "Things have been a little crazy around here."

"I can only imagine," I said, looking to Barbara for help. She was digging in her purse. I was on my own.

Tommy shifted his weight like a toddler who had to pee. I let him suffer a few seconds, then gave him the opening. "So, what did I miss? The last time I saw you, you came screaming out of the woods and made a running dive onto a broad in a puffy coat."

"Yeah," he said. "I know. Messed up, right? But here's the thing. I know that jacket, used to have one. Once you're zipped in, there's no way you can do anything fast, including raise your arms. Thank God for retail training."

He crossed himself—backward and with the wrong hand, but the altar boy in me still felt his sincerity.

"Right. So then what?" I asked.

"All right." Tommy took off his suit coat, laid it across the back of the chair, rolled up his sleeves, and cleared his throat. "Here's how it went down. She was a fighter, our kidnapping Angel. She slapped, kicked, punched, and somehow hit me in the head with the gun. But not the business end, mind you." He added a wink and finger guns before continuing. "Though it was enough to make me stumble backward. Yes, I'm embarrassed to admit it, but the villain did not throw me off the cliff." Big pause and sincere eyes. "I simply lost my footing and fell."

"The 'villain'?" I looked at Barbara. "Is he serious?"

She shushed me with her eyes as Tommy continued his story, acting out the scene like a game of charades, complete with wide eyes and flailing arms. "I grabbed for branches or something to stop my deadly decline, but alas—"

"Alas? Did you just say 'alas'? Barbara, help me out here." I said, patting the empty space on the bed she'd recently vacated. She hesitated, but I saw her shoulders drop an inch and she smiled, then sat with me, laying her hand on mine.

"Okay?" Tommy asked, as if he had been asked to pause a movie for someone to take a piss or get another beer.

"Yes," I said, pressing the painkiller pump beside my bed. "Please continue."

"So there I am, falling to my certain death, when I hear a gun go off. The shot is followed by a girly scream—"

"Wait. Did you say 'girly' scream? He's not talking about me, is he Barbara? Tell me he is *not* talking about me."

"No dear. Of course not," she said, patting my hand like my mother did the first time I got the crap kicked out of me in grade school.

"Soooo . . ." Tommy continued, "I land on this wide ledge, at least I think it's a ledge. I pat myself to see if all my parts are there and I really am a little surprised that nothing's broken. I'm just about to climb back up that steep, slippery slope to rescue you and Barbara—"

I had to stifle a laugh at that one, but Tommy continued.

"When the snow slides off the face of the ledge I'm laying on. And yes, I mean *face*." Tommy paused for a dramatic eye roll and a hand-flutter-over-the-heart moment. "I was saved by a fat, frozen dead guy. I *know*, right?"

Without waiting for us to agree, Tommy continued. "The dead man who saved my fall was later identified as James John Smith, *the* James John Smith, whose residence we had recently plundered."

"Is he talking like a pirate?" I asked Barbara.

"Ah-ah," Tommy said, stopping me with a waggle of his finger in my direction. "No interruptions. Do you know how many James John Smiths there are? Over forty-six thousand in the United States alone, according to the name search I ran . . ."

He said some more about Smiths and men and computer programs, but I was watching Barbara shred a tissue in her lap. I reached out and stroked her arm as Tommy began to pace.

"At any rate," Tommy continued in his best Perry Mason—though I was thinking more of a *Perrier Masonic* manner. "There were a few missing pieces to be assembled before Captain Seton arrived."

"That lazy asshole finally showed up?"

Tommy nodded. "With his help and the help of his team, we were able to—"

"We?" I asked.

"Yes, *we*." Tommy said. "We were able to positively identify the deceased on the cliff as one James John Smith, originally of Rindge, New Hampshire."

"Ring?" I asked.

"No. *Rindge*."

"Ridge?"

"No. R*in*dge," he said.

"Whatever."

"Tedesco. Please," Tommy said.

I waved for him to continue.

"All right, so the dead guy on the ledge was James John

Smith and the guy who came to Syracuse, now also dead, was only *pretending* to be James John Smith. What's his name?"

"James John Smith."

I was getting confused. I couldn't imagine how anyone else might be feeling at this point.

"Allow me to clarify," Tommy said. "Thanks to my infinite knowledge and extensive connection via social media networks—"

"There's those words again," I said.

"I know." Barbara smiled.

"Because of that," Tommy said, "I was able to access and download a private video shot in Flannigan's one month before the murders. You see, Tedesco, with a little effort and technological expertise, the world of investigative . . ."

TEDESCO'S GOT A POCKETFUL OF SUNSHINE, ANGEL'S GOT A POCKETFUL OF SHIVS

Chapter 43

It was a funny thing. Learning that I had been asleep for days, but finding that my job was done when I woke up, all the loose ends wrapped up tighter than the back of a hospital gown. It was as if I'd been working even in my dream state, or had visiting elves. I was ready to admit it wasn't really me doing the job, but I wasn't sure. As the doctors kept telling me, part of my brain hadn't been asleep. I may have been operating on a higher level. My very thoughts might have incited change.

If that was truly the situation, I should have done more than solve a single murder case. I should have cured cancer or perfected space travel or put a new president in office, right? I mean, if I was going be using my thoughts for good, shouldn't I have been dreaming a bit bigger?

And if I could do that? If I could really change the world around me, just by thinking? It made me wish for that ability on other days, like when I had to work a boring surveillance job, or deliver bad news, or run sixteen miles or complete a juice fast.

When I was more awake and a little more clear-headed, everything was reexplained to me.

Tommy and some *friends*—who really weren't friends, but called one another that, in a cyberspace way on something called "Book Face" or "Face Hooker" or something—had found a video posted by some SU fraternity guys who were out partying on the hill, the neighborhood of bars and eateries located three hundred feet above downtown, near the college campus.

The guys were only out doing what college boys do—meeting college girls in a bar. But being college boys of today, someone had caught them in the act. From girl-on-girl navel shots to thong-and-bra-revealing flashes to dancing that looked more like something you'd see in a certain kind of movie, this video had it all, including a clear shot of the then-alive, now-deceased owner of Flannigan's.

From that frozen video image, enlarged and de-pixilated, Barbara's almost-kidnapper and my almost-killer, Mrs. Angel Smith, was able to positively identify her husband, one James "Jimbo" John Smith V, of Virginia Beach, Virginia. This assisted the detectives at the Syracuse Police Department with filling in the blanks on their case paperwork and helped her with her own situation, at least a little bit.

Barbara explained it all to me, speaking slowly, carefully, patting my bandages, fussing over me. I could see the strain in her face, the new lines around her eyes. She still wore her wedding band, though she told me she and Mick were "on a break." It sounded so high school. I felt even worse for hearing it.

"You should go," I told her.

"What do you mean?" she asked.

"You should go home."

"It's okay, I'm not tired. What can I get you? Are you hungry?"

"No, Barbara. Go home."

She met my eyes and I saw the hurt. I felt like a shit for being the one to make her look like that, but I *was* a shit.

"Find Tommy before you leave. He has something for you. Something I want you to see."

"Bill? What's this about?"

"You should go. Good-bye, Buffy."

She leaned over and kissed my forehead, then wiped her eyes and headed for the door. I waited, but she didn't look back.

Later, Tommy came in shaking his head. "Nice one, slick. So the Tin Man does have a heart after all."

"Shut the hell up, Tommy."

He made an "oooh" face and stepped back with his hands up.

I said, "I want to see her."

"What? You just sent her away!"

"Not *her*," I said.

"Who? Michelle? Hate to tell you, pal, but she's gone too. You signed the divorce papers the *first* time you woke up. You were pretty broken up about it, made all the nurses cry when you told Michelle, 'Follow your dreams. Make a new life with a better man.'"

"I guess that wasn't a dream, then."

"Afraid not."

"Shit. Well, I still want to see her."

"Her. Well the only *her* left would be . . . your *killer*?"

"I'm not dead, Tommy."

"She's in jail, Tedesco. And you're in the hospital."

"Not for long," I said, swinging my legs over the side of the bed and instantly regretting the rapidity of my movements. I took a few deep breaths and felt my stomach recede to its original location.

"Hand me my pants," I said. "And make the call. Tell them we'll be there in an hour. I want her in a room waiting for me."

* * *

When I was in junior high school, we took a personality test that told us what careers we'd be best suited for. No one ever thought to question the answers. It was as if the test paper was a late-night psychic we'd called and paid for. No matter what we felt in our hearts or what we desired, our choices were presented to us as predetermined, limited by the selections a thirteen-year-old test offered.

There was always someone in the class designated to be teacher-perfect, another was aligned for government service, and the sloppiest kid always got janitor or sanitation management. The jock, the one who seemed so cool and surrounded by girls all the time, the one who never looked into the camera, who always looked like he was hiding something? The test might say he'd be a great manager, a born leader. But you knew he'd grow up to be a wife beater or an emotional abuser, a man who'd never be happy because his daddy didn't love *him*.

When I took the test, I thought it was a joke. Until five years later, when I was doing exactly what it had pegged me for—entertainment, theater, and performing arts.

Stepping into the county jail, I wondered about the people who worked there, what *their* tests results had been. Especially the female guards. How is that a normal job for anyone, much less an attractive woman? I imagined them going home at night and putting on old pairs of sweats, pulling their hair back, making dinner, helping kids with homework, and then retreating to their bedrooms. I imagined them booting up internationally connected laptops, logging in as a dominatrix for the masses, unleashing all the brutality they had witnessed during the day on an unsuspecting public, using such names as Mas Pain, Miss Whippett, or The Dungeon Mistress. But maybe that was just my twisted brain.

When they led Angel Smith into the room, she was

wearing shackles. She wasn't as thick as I remembered her, but then again, she wasn't wearing the puffy parka and I wasn't dodging bullets.

I'd read the transcripts of her interviews, skimmed the court documents, and after getting the wrap-up from Tommy, I was pretty sure what I was about to hear. What I wasn't prepared for was Angel's intelligence—or her utter purity.

I'm not saying she was pure as in perfect. No one is. But she chose strong, smart words. She had an honesty in her eyes and very, very full lips that made me *want* to believe her. She sat so straight and determined in that plastic chair that if I had been the one pointing a finger at her for the bad things she'd done, I might have wanted to take whatever I said back. I was pretty sure she could convince a jury that sometimes bad things are done for good reasons. I didn't want to like her, but I did.

She'd been an open book during the taped interrogation, even suggesting that maybe she'd driven her husband to do the things he'd done because she wasn't there for him, because she hadn't supported him as much as she could have.

It scared me a bit to see someone give so willingly, confess so fully, be so racked with sorrow. She was honestly believable, and had an inherent goodness about her like a halo over her head. She was *that* good. Not in a psycho way, not in the way of the truly deranged, but like a pregnant nun no man has ever touched and yet who no one believes is a virgin.

We might go around saying we have faith, saying we understand and accept and even desire miracles, but really we're cynical, pessimistic, mistrusting sons of bitches.

Faith. It was fucking with my head.

My mother had dragged me to church after church when I was young. We never really found one that stuck, but I felt in every building a different kind of glory, a charm and a lightness of heart that lasted for days, a peace that wasn't bound to the material.

I still believed in God, in the idea of heaven and hell, in all the things my mother wanted me to learn in those churches. But I had a problem with the business end of things, the passing of the basket, the placing the needs of third-world strangers over the needs of our own. As a result, my current church attendance was limited to Sunday morning radio programs.

So as Angel talked—and yes, even her name was messing with me—even as she spoke about loving Jimbo and failing him and feeling responsible, even then, I knew she'd be all right. She'd get through this and move on.

"I'm glad you came," she said. "I want to apologize. I never meant to hurt you. I—"

I held up my hand. "Let's just talk about your husband, and not any of this." I motioned to her in her jumpsuit and shackles and me with my bandages, my wound.

She nodded.

"There's been a lot of press around this story," I said, watching for her reaction.

She shrugged and looked toward the window. "People are curious by nature."

"And James, was he?"

"James," she said, scoffing. "I can't get used to hearing that name. He was always Jimbo to me. Sure, I guess he was as curious as the next guy."

"How?"

"What do you mean? How was he curious?"

"Yes."

"Well, about women. About people's interactions. Who we really are . . ." She shrugged. "He was curious about a lot of stuff, like how things were made, said his dad had been good at building things." She smiled, "Jimbo knew more about those old black-and-white films than anyone I ever knew."

She seemed proud of him even though the guy had so obviously been a loser, a borderline sociopath. Maybe there really was someone for everyone.

"Did he ever talk about starting anew? About wishing he was someone else?" I asked.

"No. He seemed happy. I thought *we* were happy. I asked him once, you know, if he could do anything, have anything, what would he want?"

"What did he say?"

"He said he'd want a quiet place in the Caribbean. A hut on the sand, with a beach bar." She laughed. "It was probably something he'd seen in a movie. Jimbo wasn't much of a planner. I mean, if someone handed him money and a plane ticket, maybe he'd do something then, but if he actually had to come up with an idea on his own? No. Not seeing it."

I pushed a bit. "So, this whole taking over someone else's life thing was quite the surprise?"

"Yeah. You could say that."

"Even with your father's connections?"

It was her turn to redirect the conversation. "Let's leave him out of this," she said, trying to hold up a shackled hand. The chain stopped her short.

"Fair enough," I said. "Did you know that before your husband left he'd been running an Internet scam, had three girlfriends in two states, and was holding the money he collected every Christmas for orphans in a private savings account—"

"Stop." Her eyes welled up. "Please. They've already told me all of that."

She raised her face to the ceiling as tears ran in rivulets down her cheeks. She looked me in the eye. "'A person doesn't change just because you find out more.'"

I knew that line. "That's from—"

"*The Third Man.* One of Jimbo's favorites." She smiled.

"They don't make films like that anymore." I said, smiling back.

She stared at the walls and the ceiling, then said, "The only thing he liked more than movies were dogs. He used to volunteer at the SPCA. He wasn't *all* bad, like they're saying."

"The SPCA? What did he do there?"

"He was the Goodnight Man."

"What does that mean?" I asked.

"He held the euthanized dogs as they died."

"He killed them?"

"No." She shook her head. "He couldn't. Someone else did the injecting. Jimbo just held them and talked to them. He always said, 'No one should die alone.'"

Something happened in the next few moments that I wasn't sure I really understood, or needed to. On the job I watched people, I analyzed data, I made judgment calls and decisions based on prior experience. I usually felt good at the end of the day, if not a little empty.

But in that concrete room, behind that locked door, sitting across from a woman I hardly knew, I felt something fill me that I hadn't felt before.

I stood and walked to the door, knocked on the glass panel, and nodded to the cop outside. As he unlocked the door, I turned around.

"Be okay if I came back sometime?" I asked.

"Sure," she said, and threw me a smile. "I'm not going anywhere."

EXPECT THE WORST, YOU'LL NEVER BE DISAPPOINTED

Chapter 44

Saying good-bye isn't easy for anyone. When you're in love, when someone's dying, when you're moving on, and they aren't. When you've found someone new, or you've found out they have. A piece of you has to die to allow a new piece to grow. Saying good-bye to a part of yourself may be the toughest farewell of all.

Grandma Tedesco called it "pruning," losing a bit of yourself now to be a better person later. As if people were plants. She'd tell me how even though, right now, the rose bush in the front garden was beautiful and blooming and as perfect as could be, she was going to go out there and cut it back. Make it ugly. She'd find the bend in the branch where the new growth would sprout, where next season more roses would bloom. Cutting off beauty and promise meant a stronger, better-rooted plant with more flowers, healthier limbs. A plant that was not only more attractive, but sturdier, better able to withstand anything the world might throw at it.

Barbara tapped the envelope Tommy had given her at the hospital. Thinking it was something to do with Chamonix, she'd sent a text to Mick asking him to meet her at the house, said it was important. She poured a glass of wine and waited for her husband.

Mick tore open the envelope and slid out the DVD. An old movie. He set it up, then took a seat beside his wife on the couch. They sipped their wine without saying a word as the opening credits to *Leave Her to Heaven* rolled. Sometimes even husbands know when to be quiet.

At one point, Barbara reached out and took Mick's hand in hers.

In the film, when Richard Harland said to Ellen, "When I looked at you, exotic words drifted across the mirror of my mind like clouds across the summer sky," Mick spoke the words with him.

And when Ellen said, "'I'll never let you go. Never, never, never.'" Barbara spoke them to Mick.

Sometimes good-byes are also hellos, and sometimes you figure out the piece of you that was missing has been sitting beside you on the couch the whole time.

Barbara reached for Mick, and before they knocked the remote to the floor, before the TV clicked off, they heard, "There's nothing wrong with Ellen. It's just that she loves too much."

In the aftermath of your death, many people will touch your body and your things. If you're a person who believes in the spiritual realm, you may want to find something else to do, someplace else to hover, in the seventy-two hours after your passing.

Sometimes, people are lucky enough to die quietly at home in their beds, lying next to a loved one, someone who will make sure that even in death you'll fool the whole world into thinking you were perfectly wonderful, with no secrets or devious habits. If you aren't lucky enough to die that way, you need to be prepared.

In the case of murder, preparation goes out the door. No one knows when it's coming, even if they say later they had a "feeling." Roxie, Cress, and Chamonix? When James told then to stand there and close their eyes, that he had a surprise for them? There was no way they could have known what was coming, that the surprise was an automatic handgun, fully loaded and recently imported from Germany.

The invasion of their homes, their closets, drawers, and computer files—that all came later. Their right to privacy was ceded with their last breath. And for those girls, lying on the floor of Flannigan's, the first interaction with their lifeless bodies came not from a gentle hand or an intelligent mind, but from a simple janitor.

He'd worked for Flannigan, but stayed on for Smith. This was his last stop before the sun rose. He lived alone, hated the cat that slept under his porch, and if you asked his mother, he also drank too much. But that wasn't the point. The point was, he found the bodies first. Being a curious guy, he took a few minutes to probe pockets, poke breasts, and in one case, slip a hand up a tiny red skirt to see if she really did have *that tattoo.*

It was a powerful thing to own, a quiet moment surrounded by death. The feeling that it could have been you—but it wasn't. As you pick up the phone and make the call, it hits you. You have to bite back panic and swallow your fear. Hopefully, you're able to take away from all of that a sense of entitlement, a new appreciation for life.

Soon more hands would touch those bodies. All with a different purpose. The cops to the medical examiner to the people from the morgue. Parents and loved ones would want to view the bodies when they claim them. They might remove a ring or a necklace. The funeral director, his staff, and even some guests at the wake, they'd all lay a finger on cool skin, stroke a perfectly shaped cheek, kiss lips that had been stitched together.

In the homes of the deceased, things would be thrown away, donated, stored, and mulled over. Questions would be asked about one's choices, desires, secret dreams. No one would be there to answer. Answers come from perceptions. Most are wrong.

The coffee table is more than a table. It's a tableau of misery punctuated by wine glass rings, full ashtrays, unopened bills, and travel magazines addressed to the neighbor. The nightstand drawer, the back of a closet, or a bathroom cabinet might tell your story with depilatory creams or Viagra, with extra-strength mouthwash to dandruff shampoo. It speaks of hidden imperfections.

When you die, your door is opened to strangers. Your money, possessions, the secrets you thought no one would ever know all become public. Alive, you might excuse away the extraneous bits that make up a life. Dead, there's nothing you can do about it.

Across town in a half-empty office at a half-empty newspaper in a half-empty building that had seen better days, Sam Cheever finished proofing the day's shoot from the dog park. There was something equally sweet and pathetic about the photos he captured. The redheaded girl with the toppled ice cream cone, the spotted puppy licking the remains. The crying black boy whose ball had been stolen by the yellow lab and the dorky guy with the bug-eyed Chihuahua who looked like he only read the first part of the dating guide: Get a puppy, you'll be a chick magnet!

Sam pushed his chair back and stretched. The job was wearing on him.

What the fuck had he been thinking? As if Seattle hadn't been gloomy enough. He ended up in Syracuse? What a dumb ass.

Sure he'd come for the girl, but if she hadn't noticed him in high school, what the hell made him think she'd give a shit twenty years later? And seriously, why had he believed that she was even available? Of course she wasn't. That was the problem with virtual romance. You only had to be semitruthful, and you got to pick which side of "semi" you wanted to embrace.

Fuck it. He was done with this. All of it.

Last night, he'd watched one of those survivor-man episodes, where they drop a dude out of an airplane with a knife and maybe a flint and tell him they'll pick him up in a week. That kind of shit looked pretty good right about now.

The computer behind him dinged, announcing another e-mail, another interruption. Somebody else needing something he wasn't willing or able to give.

He spun his chair around and rolled up to his desk. One hand on the mouse woke the monitor. It was a request from his boss to add a photograph to the follow-up story on the three dead girls in the bar. He'd read the article they'd run on Chamonix, Roxie, Cress, and the two James John Smiths. It was front-page news. He remembered how pretty they'd been, even dead, and how he'd mentioned to the detective that the scene sounded like a joke, like a bad headline for a fake newspaper.

He sat drumming his fingertips on the desk, listening to the noises of an empty building. Then he clicked on the browser, opened a new window, and typed "Samuel Michael Cheever," then hit Return.

ACKNOWLEDGMENTS

Thank you to the many people who made this book possible. To the crazy people who seem to be drawn to me, I told your stories well. To the members of my old writing group: Don, Jackie and Barbara, we did this together. To my agent, Josh Getzler who was one of my first readers, thank you for continuing to believe in me and the voices in my head. To the Kindle Scouts who voted for *3 Women Walk into a Bar*, without you none of this would be possible. I truly hope you like the rest of the book as much as you liked the opening pages. Huge thanks go to my editor Stacee who axed my commas with vigor and got most of my jokes. Of course endless thanks to my family (M, C, P) for their love and support, but more than that for putting up with me all these years, especially when I put words and paper before people.

ABOUT THE AUTHOR

Linda Sands is the author of the Southern Gothic novel and Kirkus Star recipient *Not Waving, Drowning*, the internationally published legal thriller *Simple Intent*, and a multitude of award-winning short stories and essays published in magazines, newspapers and anthologies around the globe. Linda is represented by HSG Agency and lives in the suburbs of Atlanta with her husband, two kids, fast cars, and furry things. Follow her at lindasands.com, on Facebook as LindaSandsAuthor or @lindasands on Twitter.

OTHER TITLES FROM DOWN AND OUT BOOKS

See www.DownAndOutBooks.com for complete list

By Anonymous-9
Bite Hard

By J.L. Abramo
Catching Water in a Net
Clutching at Straws
Counting to Infinity
Gravesend
Chasing Charlie Chan
Circling the Runway

By Trey R. Barker
2,000 Miles to Open Road
Road Gig: A Novella
Exit Blood
Death is Not Forever

By Richard Barre
The Innocents
Bearing Secrets
Christmas Stories
The Ghosts of Morning
Blackheart Highway
Burning Moon
Echo Bay
Lost

By Eric Beetner and JB Kohl
Over Their Heads

By Eric Beetner and Frank Scalise
The Backlist (*)

By Rob Brunet
Stinking Rich

By Dana Cameron (editor)
Murder at the Beach: Bouchercon Anthology 2014

By Stacey Cochran
Eddie & Sunny

By Mark Coggins
No Hard Feelings (*)

By Tom Crowley
Vipers Tail
Murder in the Slaughterhouse

By Frank De Blase
Pine Box for a Pin-Up
Busted Valentines and Other Dark Delights
A Cougar's Kiss (*)

By Les Edgerton
The Genuine, Imitation, Plastic Kidnapping

By A.C. Frieden
Tranquility Denied
The Serpent's Game
The Pyongyang Option (*)

By Jack Getze
Big Numbers
Big Money
Big Mojo
Big Shoes (*)

By Keith Gilman
Bad Habits

(*)—Coming Soon

OTHER TITLES FROM DOWN AND OUT BOOKS

See www.DownAndOutBooks.com for complete list

By Richard Godwin
Wrong Crowd (*)

By William Hastings (editor)
Stray Dogs: Writing from the Other America

By Matt Hilton
No Going Back
Rules of Honor
The Lawless Kind (*)

By Terry Holland
An Ice Cold Paradise
Chicago Shiver

By Darrel James, Linda O. Johnston & Tammy Kaehler (editors)
Last Exit to Murder

By David Housewright & Renée Valois
The Devil and the Diva

By David Housewright
Finders Keepers
Full House

By Jon & Ruth Jordan (editors)
Murder and Mayhem in Muskego
Cooking with Crimespree

By Andrew McAleer & Paul D. Marks (editors)
Coast to Coast (*)

By Bill Moody
Czechmate
The Man in Red Square
Solo Hand
The Death of a Tenor Man
The Sound of the Trumpet
Bird Lives!

By Gary Phillips
The Perpetrators
Scoundrels (Editor)
Treacherous

By Robert J. Randisi
Upon My Soul
Souls of the Dead
Envy the Dead (*)

By Ryan Sayles
The Subtle Art of Brutality
Warpath (*)

By Anthony Neil Smith
Worm

By Liam Sweeny
Welcome Back, Jack (*)

By Lono Waiwaiole
Wiley's Lament
Wiley's Shuffle
Wiley's Refrain
Dark Paradise

By Vincent Zandri
Moonlight Weeps

(*)—Coming Soon